THIS I KNOW

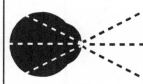

This Large Print Book carries the
Seal of Approval of N.A.V.H.

THIS I KNOW

ELDONNA EDWARDS

THORNDIKE PRESS
A part of Gale, a Cengage Company

Farmington Hills, Mich • San Francisco • New York • Waterville, Maine
Meriden, Conn • Mason, Ohio • Chicago

Copyright © 2018 by Eldonna Edwards.
Thorndike Press, a part of Gale, a Cengage Company.

ALL RIGHTS RESERVED
Thorndike Press® Large Print Basic.
The text of this Large Print edition is unabridged.
Other aspects of the book may vary from the original edition.
Set in 16 pt. Plantin.

LIBRARY OF CONGRESS CIP DATA ON FILE.
CATALOGUING IN PUBLICATION FOR THIS BOOK
IS AVAILABLE FROM THE LIBRARY OF CONGRESS

ISBN-13: 978-1-4328-5134-7 (hardcover)

Published in 2018 by arrangement with Kensington Books, an imprint
of Kensington Publishing Corp.

Printed in Mexico
1 2 3 4 5 6 7 22 21 20 19 18

For Queenie, LuLu, Izzy, Ree, and Gus; and in loving memory of Nete.

ACKNOWLEDGMENTS

One day I woke up and realized I'm one of the luckiest writers ever, ever, ever. Writing is a mostly solitary effort, but mid-wifing a story into a published book requires an amazing team of extraordinary individuals. How fortunate am I to have found Claire Anderson-Wheeler, the most enthusiastic agent an author could ever hope to have on her side? She rooted for my little cast of characters as if they were her own family, and I consider her part of mine.

Many thanks to my amazing editor, John Scognamiglio, whose name I can finally pronounce, and who fell in love with Grace on his first date with this book. Your editorial support combined with your trust in my instincts provided a perfect balance of guidance and empowerment. From answering all my newbie questions, to creating a stunning cover, to getting the word out ahead of release, the entire Kensington staff

7

has been absolutely incredible.

Thank you to all the seasoned authors who held my hand on the debut path, offering advice and shadowing me through the various benchmarks between first draft and publication. A special shout-out to Donna Everhart, who generously shepherded me throughout this process. Thanks also to WFWA, hands down one of the best writers' groups on the Internet. It's so refreshing to see writers champion each other within such a competitive arena.

I'm forever grateful to my early readers — especially my siblings, who cheered me every step of the way. You can move a girl away from her family but you can't move the family out of the girl. Thank you, Anna Banana Unkovich, for your happy faces, sticky notes, and constructive remarks in the margins of my tattered manuscript, but mostly, for your unwavering friendship. I love you.

Thank you to my loving parents, Rev. Lew and VaLoyce Edwards, without whom this story never would have been born. I miss you every day.

My deepest gratitude goes to my beloved partner Brer (William Braddock), who pored over these pages through many months, more times than I can count. His brilliant, kind, and valuable suggestions helped make THIS I KNOW the best book it could possibly be. You had me at "I'm not crying, you're crying!"

AUTHOR NOTES

Given that I'm a preacher's kid from the Midwest who grew up in the 1960s and 70s, people are bound to ask if this story is autobiographical. The answer is yes and no. Aside from Aunt Pearl, who I based upon my beloved Aunt Ruth, and Joy Carter, a darn close replica of my older sister, Anita, the characters are a collage of every person I've ever met, read about, seen in film or just dreamed up in this overactive brain. Every story begins with "What if . . . ?" and here's where truth and fiction part ways. What if my dad had been a bit of a tyrant rather than the loving, compassionate, imperfect man that he was? What if instead of a rebellious teen with a wild imagination, one of his children was born with something that challenged his deeply held convictions? What if his beautiful wife fell into a deep depression after birthing all those kids? (I'm number five of seven children.) What if I

11

swapped some of the characteristics of my family members, my townspeople, and our many congregations and molded them into fictional characters who remind us that despite our differences, we all just want to belong? THIS I KNOW is an homage to all of you, all of us, who grew up with a profound assuredness in divine order and yet sometimes wondered, what if . . . ?

■ ■ ■ ■

PART ONE

■ ■ ■ ■

Jesus loves me, this I know
For the Bible tells me so.
  — Children's hymn by Anna B. Warner

Part One

March 13, 1958

I'm spooning my Other, my belly to his back. I love the way his body feels against mine. Although we've changed positions many times, we always come back to this. Over the last month our warm-water pool has slowly transformed into a room with soft walls shaped like us. Now we're squeezed so snugly together I sometimes forget where I leave off and he begins.

From the time we joined each other in the darkness we've felt as one, exchanging thoughts merely by thinking them. If a question forms in my mind, he answers. We know each other as well as we know ourselves.

I am to go first. A few days ago my Other slipped away from the entrance to the world and waited while I settled into the soft floor of this now nearly waterless ocean. I'd always assumed he would lead the way.

15

Our mother sang to us this morning. Sometimes she reads to us or occasionally she just talks, as if she knows we can hear her voice above the thundering of her heart. I wish she could hear my thoughts as clearly as I hear her laugh. I'd tell her how wonderful it's been, this liquid home where she's nourished us with her rich blood. And I'd assure her we're healthy and anxious to be in her arms.

I'm afraid, I think to him.

It'll be okay, he thinks back.

I don't want to leave you.

I'm right behind you.

What if the door closes?

It won't.

The walls are closing in. The pressure against my body is nearly unbearable as our mother pushes me out of the safety of our home. She's crying, begging us to come to her. I close my eyes and allow myself to be funneled into the snug passageway.

He's right behind me. He's right behind me. He's right behind me. . . .

1

I make people nervous, even Daddy. Especially Daddy. I know this by how they look away, as if their darkest secrets will be exposed like tea leaves scattered in the snow. The truth is, I can't know another's thoughts without their permission. I have to be invited. It's one of the rules that goes along with having what I sometimes think is a curse but what Aunt Pearl calls a gift. I'd give anything to be normal like the rest of my sisters.

If you asked when I first realized I had the Knowing, I wouldn't be able to say. It started like a seed and then grew bit by bit, just slow enough not to notice. I guess I was born with it. Maybe it was just supposed to be a regular amount of intuition. Maybe when Isaac died I ended up with a double dose, like dots sliding off dominoes placed end to end on a crooked table.

17

Even Billy Wolf — the meanest kid in Cherry Hill — won't give me the full Evil Eye. He aims it at my shoes or my chest or lately at my crotch, yet he still looks away sooner than he does with other kids. It's hard to imagine out-creeping Billy.

I know things, such as when the telephone's going to ring. Sometimes I hear and see things, too. Like the red bulge inside the back of Hope's head that no one else sees or the lilies under the snow that I can smell long before they bloom. And that I really do hear my brother's voice. We talk to each other all the time.

I don't remember when I started hearing Isaac's voice separate from my own. To me they were always just thoughts, my thoughts, from a different side of me that was still part of me. According to my family, from the moment I was able to make sounds I talked aloud to myself, babbling on and on in a language nobody but me understood. When I was about three years old I saw a photograph of Mama when she was pregnant with us. I was filled with wanting something I couldn't name. When I pointed to Mama's belly in the picture, she said, "That's you in there with your brother, Isaac."

I tried to grab the photo. She wouldn't let

me have it. I searched the house for days, but she must have hidden it away. I kept crying, "Isik! Isik!" They thought I was saying "I sick" and kept taking my temperature and feeding me soda crackers. Mama asked me where it hurt, but I couldn't describe the pain. I was screaming in my head that I wanted *him,* that Other I couldn't name before she showed me the photo. Nothing soothed me until I heard the voice in my head and realized for the first time that it wasn't my voice, it was his. Ours.

I'm right here.

And just like that, I stopped crying. From then on I carried on full conversations with my brother. Up until this year my parents ignored it, calling Isaac my imaginary friend. "Isn't that sweet," they'd whisper, "how little Grace talks to her dead twin?" Then they'd sigh like it was so sad.

Since I'm now eleven I guess I've outgrown cute. The last time I got caught talking to Isaac was on my birthday. I'd saved a piece of cake and a candle and brought it up to my bedroom closet. I was singing "Happy Birthday" to Isaac when the door flew open and Daddy stood glaring down at me. My sisters snickered behind him until Daddy stomped his foot and yelled, "Stop it!"

I was so startled by his booming voice I dropped the piece of cake and the candle landed in my lap, catching my dress on fire. Daddy grabbed me and furiously patted away the flames.

"No more, Grace! You could have set the house on fire, do you realize that? Burned us all down."

Mama came up later and tried to comfort me. She lay on my bed and curled herself around me.

"Why can't I talk to him?" I said through sobs.

"Because he's gone and talking doesn't bring him back."

"But he's not gone, Mama. He's here."

Then she started crying and it was me comforting her instead of the other way around. She begged me not to talk to Isaac because it upset Daddy and made her sad. I don't like when Mama's sad. I promised her I'd stop. I didn't stop. I just hide it better. I'm good at hiding things, especially my feelings.

I love my Daddy so much, but it doesn't feel like he loves me the same way back. Like he loves me because he owes his devotion, not because I've earned it. I don't think anyone in this family knows how lonely I feel sometimes. Just once I wish

Daddy would look at me with the same gleam in his eyes he does with Joy and Chastity or even poor Hope.

Mama says how I was born is how I live, my thoughts racing faster than what I know what to do with them. She claims I came hurtling into the world screaming bloody murder as if I were trying to raise the dead. Then she gets a faraway look that feels as if someone has pulled the scenery from the room and you're left standing in the dark with no walls and no ceiling. I know she's thinking about Isaac and that if I'd been born second they'd have their boy, the wish God never granted them and the thing I believe she's never forgiven Him for.

I got the rest of the story from Aunt Pearl. She told me our family was in Mississippi visiting Daddy's relatives when Mama's labor started early. The doctors were confused because normally boy-girl twins don't share the same sac. "It was quite unusual," she'd said. "Probably why Isaac got strangled by the cord and died before the doctor could save him."

Mamma was distraught. We stayed with Aunt Pearl until after the funeral; then Daddy drove straight through the night back to Michigan. He couldn't wait to take Mama away from the place that housed all that sadness. What he doesn't understand is that she brought the memory of that dead baby with her, packed her grief into every last bag before we drove out of Rankin County. Of course I brought Isaac with *me*, too. We might no longer share a womb but we share most everything else.

There's something else I carried with me from Mississippi. Even though I learned to speak in the North just like my sisters, people say I sound a bit like my Aunt Pearl. I guess when I was born part of me got planted in the South. A twang rides on my words and I can't do anything about it. To tell you the truth, I don't want to. When Aunt Pearl visits us I know why. Her voice is like honey, slow and dripping. She calls me Sweet Pea, but it comes out all at once missing the *t*. "SweePea," she'll say. "Come here, shoog, and sit on Aunt Pearl's lap." Not only do my knees wobble when she talks to me like that, but Aunt Pearl has about the best sittin' lap I've ever been in. Her big bosoms like to wrap around each side of my face and hold me tight just like when Isaac and I were in Mama's belly.

Folks don't believe me when I tell them I remember being in the womb. They think it's my wild imagination. "There goes Grace in her fantasy world," they say. But I know what I know. The thing is, they could remember, too, if they wanted. Maybe they don't because they'd be sorry they were ever born if they recalled the sweetest place they've ever been and how they had to leave it.

I don't remember being born so much as I remember being unborn, when it was just the two of us wrapped around each other, waiting for everything and nothing at the same time. I remember those moments right before we separated and then all that light blinding me, a sudden sorrow, my lungs filling with air. As soon as I was out, a door closed behind me and I forgot him until much later when I saw that picture of Mama pregnant with us. When the images and thoughts came back, they were like a movie playing on the walls of my brain.

That's why I love the closet in my bedroom. It's the closest I can get to being back where we started. I like to sit on the rickety board over the heating duct that runs between my room and Hope's. If I'm real quiet I can imagine the thrum of the furnace is Mama's heartbeat. And this is where Isaac sometimes comes to visit me. Not in his body, but in a place that is both inside and outside of me. I hear his voice and I feel his presence just like I know my cat, Pippy, is at the end of my bed even when we're not touching. I only have to call my brother inside my mind and just like Pippy he shows up.

After breakfast I sneak upstairs and close the closet door behind me. I'm not afraid of the dark.

"Isaac?"

Yes?

"I was just thinking. What if I killed myself so I could be with you?"

But you are with me.

"No, I mean *with* you. Out *there*."

Oh, Grace. No. That wouldn't be a good thing.

"Why not?"

Because then we'd have to start over.

"What do you mean? Start what over?"

Well, we're like parts of a story. If you died the story would end too abruptly and without completion. We'd have to start the story all over again.

Isaac uses big words because he's not a baby anymore. But the way he says them I almost always get the meaning.

"Maybe you could remember not to get tangled in the cord and we could be together."

That's not how this story goes, Grace.

24

I lean back against the wall, hoping the dresses hanging on the rod will muffle the cry in my voice. "Why does our story have to be such a sad one?"

He's quiet for a minute.

Grace, do you love me?

"Of course I do. More than anyone in the whole wide world."

And I love you. This isn't a sad story. It's a love story.

The back door slams downstairs, lifting me off the board. Mama's already started taking laundry baskets outside.

"Isaac?"

Yes?

"How come nobody else can hear you?"

Because they're not connected to me like you are.

"Not even Mama?"

Not even Mama.

"I don't feel like I'm connected to anyone in this family besides you."

Oh, but you are. You're very important to them.

The door slams a third time. Three baskets. We've got a lot of hanging to do this morning.

"I better go."

Yes. She needs your help.

"Bye, Isaac."

25

Goodbye, Grace.

And just like that I feel him go. Not like something leaving the world. More like just leaving the room.

Saturday is when we change the bedding. Mama says nobody has whiter sheets than she does. I can tell by the way she says it she's real proud of this even though Daddy preaches that pride is a sin. Mama hands me a pillowcase from the basket and takes one for herself. She snaps it out straight like she's done a thousand times before. I try to do the same but it flaps back in my face. Mama laughs. It's the kind of laugh that makes you feel loved, not teased. She peels it off my face and kisses my damp forehead.

My younger sister, Chastity, hands us clothespins to fasten the linens against the wind. The three of us make a pretty good team and it only takes half an hour to empty all the baskets. Mama clips the last corner of the last pillowcase, then props the rope up high with a board cut into a V at the end. She stacks the empty baskets one inside the other and turns them upside down to keep any bugs out. When she heads back into the house I close my eyes and lean into a billowing sheet. Hiding behind the smell of bleach is a tiny promise of spring.

Mama pushes through the back door holding a brown coffee cup in one hand and a plateful of powdered donut holes in the other. She sits on the back stoop and pulls her flowered housedress over her bare knees. Chastity and I plop down on either side and wait for her to say it's okay to take a treat. We may have a bit of a wait because Mama has a way of staring off into space when she drinks coffee. She doesn't even look down to dunk her donut, does it by feel, as if she doesn't care about the soggy clumps floating in her mug. I know what that's like. Not the soggy donut part, just the staring into space. My teachers call me a daydreamer, but I'm not dreaming. The me who goes places in my head is a lot more awake than the bored me sitting at my desk.

My sister and I stare at the donut holes, little snowballs with skin-colored patches showing through. Chastity touches Mama lightly on the arm to remind her we're here. She nods for us to go ahead and we each take two. I make a face when Mama tilts the mug back and drinks the last swallow of thick coffee. Chastity nods, holding her powdered fingers out in front of her so as not to get any on her dress. Mama stands and wipes her hands on her apron. I do the same, leaving white handprints on my green corduroy pants. Chastity is a bit of a fuss-budget and runs inside to wash up before our walk to the post office.

Mama pulls my head to her hip and smooths my kinky, red hair. "Grace, have I ever told you your hair reminds me of a sunset?"

"No, Mama."

"Well, it does."

She eyes the brown grass along the edge of the sidewalk leading to the front yard as we wait for Chastity. "Almost time to plant flowers," she says. "What do you think?"

It doesn't matter what I think because Mama plants her favorites every year, but I play along. "How about roses? Big, fat, white ones that you can smell a mile away."

"Maybe," she says, smiling. But we both know that come summer the sidewalks will be lined with red and pink petunias, and bluebells and daffodils will fill the spaces next to the house.

The back door slams and Chastity bounces down the back steps wearing her red plaid jacket and patent leather shoes. Mama pulls a light blue scarf out of her pocket and ties it under her chin before taking our hands.

"Let's go," she says.

"Let's go," Chastity mimics, pulling on

Mama as we head down the driveway.

We turn right toward the post office, five blocks away. As we round the corner at Montmorency Street I catch sight of the blind girl swinging high on a board hanging from the branch of a dead elm tree. Tangles of brown hair flap in front of dark eyes that look off in different directions. She's singing a song of nonsense words. I smile even though she can't see me. Funny thing, she smiles too, almost as if she's smiling back at me. I start to wave at her. Mama grabs my hand before it's all the way up and pulls me forward.

"Come on, Grace," she says. "Don't bother that poor child."

The sound of a hammer slamming against a nail startles all three of us. Mr. Weaver, our church janitor, is repairing the roof on the dilapidated house next to the tree swing. He does handyman work part-time, mostly for church members. The blind girl and her grandma don't come to our church, but everybody knows Mr. Weaver. He used to be a drunk before Daddy converted him during his chaplain visits to the county jail. Daddy not only saved him from h-e-l-l but probably from falling off a roof as well. Couldn't save his marriage, though. Mrs. Weaver left town with their two daughters the last time he was in jail and nobody has heard from her since.

Mr. Weaver waves to us from the peak of the Andersons' roof. Mama nods but keeps moving forward. The three of us walk the last block to the post office hand in hand. I love the soft flesh of Mama's warm palm against my own even though sometimes I feel a deep sorrow through her skin. Mama usually does a good job of hiding behind her preacher's wife smile, but sometimes her crinkled forehead gives her away. I wish I could draw her worries into my hand and shake them off like donut powder.

When we reach the post office, Dean VanderPol waves from behind the counter. He's the only person who works here besides Louise, who delivers mail to the rural routes. I wave back but Mama heads straight for our postal box. She lets me dial the combination. As soon as I open the tiny compartment the papery smell of mail crawls up my nose. Mama pulls the envelopes out and shoves them into her apron pocket without looking at who they're from. I'm not sure if this is because she doesn't care or she can tell by the smell who sent them.

Dean waves again on our way out. "Have a good day, Missus Carter."

"Thank you," Mama says back, but not until it's too late and he's out of earshot.

Lately it's as if Mama's one step behind the rest of the world. On Sundays she sometimes waits until the second sentence of a song to open her mouth, and her last note dangles in the air after the rest of us have closed our hymnals. I wonder if it has to do with the extra heartbeat thump-thumping inside her that nobody else can hear. I won't ask because Daddy gives me The Look when I mention things I'm not supposed to know without someone telling me.

The first time it happened I was five. We were all at the breakfast table and I said, "Somebody should get that boy out of the lake."

Daddy said, "What boy?" and I just shrugged.

We went on eating our pancakes. When I looked at the bottle of syrup on the table I saw a boy struggling, then slowly sink to the bottom.

"Too late," I said.

Mama dropped her fork and pushed away from the table. She ran to the front window just as the ambulance flew by with sirens blaring. When she came back, her hands were shaking as she leaned over my shoulder and whispered, "How did you know?"

"I saw him in the syrup," I said.

My sisters laughed at me. Not Mama and Daddy. They looked at each other for a moment like they'd seen a ghost before Daddy raced out the front door toward the lake.

Later that day Daddy took me into his study and told me I should ignore it when I think I know what's going to happen. Then he prayed and prayed over me for what seemed like hours. I don't remember his exact words but I got the idea. He pretty much said that the devil had planted something bad in me, and he asked God to take it out. Ever since then he's treated me different, almost like he's afraid of me. His fear has built a wall between us that I can never seem to break through, no matter how much good stuff I do to try to tear it down.

I started to feel ashamed after that day but Isaac assured me I was special. He reminded me of the words to the Sunday school song "This Little Light of Mine," and that God doesn't want us to hide our light under a bushel. The truth is, I don't think there's a bushel big enough to hide the Knowing. It keeps getting bigger and stronger, like a storm cloud before it grows into a tornado. I've spent most of my life holding it by the tail.

On our way home from the post office Sheriff Conner's police cruiser races by, which is unusual. He usually creeps along slower than I can walk. With the car window rolled down, he'll pause to chat with people as he circles the lake several times a day. Everyone knows one of his sons went missing in Vietnam, but you'd never know it to look at him. He's always so pleasant. It's been harder on Mrs. Conner. The Conners used to have an American flag raised on a tall pole in front of their house. Mrs. Conner took it down when their boy went MIA. Some people say she burned it.

Back at the house, Mama tells Chastity and me to sit on the front steps. My sister and I huddle against the chill. Mama doesn't seem to notice the cold even though she's only wearing a light sweater over her housedress.

"I have some news for you girls." She wipes a stray blond hair from in front of her blue eyes and tucks it back into the scarf. She's not wearing makeup but her cheeks are blushed. She opens her mouth and closes it again.

Chastity claps her hands in front of her. "Tell us, Mama!"

Mama looks toward the church across the street then back to us. "Pretty soon you're going to get a new baby brother or sister."

Chastity glares at Mama as though somebody has just grabbed a candy bar out of her hand and eaten it. In the next instant she leaps from the step and runs toward the backyard. By the time I catch up to her she's climbed halfway up the tree. I can hardly believe what I'm seeing since Chastity is usually such a little priss.

"You better come down from there, Chas."

"Leave me alone!"

"You can't climb a tree in those shoes."

"Can too. Go away!"

Up she goes higher. If it weren't for the sight of her fancy underpants I wouldn't believe it was my own little sister. I glance toward the house. Either Mama is still trying to figure out what just happened or she's given up and gone inside. I spit on my hands and swing a leg over the first branch. As awkward as I feel on the ground there's something about trees, especially this one, that gives me monkey feet and no fear.

I close in on Chastity near the top, where the branches start to get spindlier and more doubtful about holding someone up, even a child. She looks down and freezes, staring at the ground below. I pull up behind my sister and gently snuggle against her back, letting my arms circle the tree trunk along with her small body. Her legs are trembling.

"Don't worry," I whisper. "I'm right behind you."

I'm right behind you.

Her blond ponytail beats against her chubby cheek. "I want Mama!" she whines.

"It's okay, Chas, we'll go down a step at a time. On the count of three put your foot on the next branch under this one."

Chastity clutches the tree like it's her mother, at least the one she had before Mama got pregnant, meaning Chastity will no longer be the baby of the family. I figured that out just as soon as I looked at her face during Mama's telling of it.

"I can't," she says.

"Sure you can. I'll help you."

I slip my shoe between her leg and the tree and push gently.

"Stop it, Grace! You'll make us fall."

"No I won't. You have to trust me. Now lower yourself with me to the next branch."

She keeps whimpering, but her body relaxes a bit and we slowly move downward along the trunk until her red-checkered jacket snags on a nub. I give it a yank.

Chastity screams so loud it hurts my eardrums. "You're ripping my coat!"

"Don't worry. Mama will sew it back up."

This is the wrong thing to say.

When Chastity cries she does it with her whole body. It's all I can do to hold on as she flails her arms and stomps her feet.

"Stop it, Chas. You're going to make us . . ."

I know it a half second before it happens. The next few moments play out in slow motion: Chastity throwing a fit, Mama rounding the corner of the house just as my sister pushes backward with her head, ramming hard into my chin and knocking me off balance. The two of us start down in a free fall, smacking into branches along the way. I cling desperately to my sister.

Help!

Suddenly the air feels thick and spongy. In my mind I clearly see a path through the rest of the branches. We stop tumbling and weave our way dreamlike through the tree. The next thing I know my feet find a firm landing on the bottom limb. Chastity steadies herself against the branch in front of her. I don't understand what just happened.

"Isaac?" I accidentally say his name out loud.

Mama clasps her hands over her mouth as she drops into a heap on the lawn. Chastity pries herself from my grip and leaps to the ground, her dramatic protest suddenly forgotten as she runs to Mama's side.

When Daddy gets home from his church office, Chastity practically attacks him to share our exciting morning. She already told Joy and Hope, and each telling gets a little more exaggerated. By her third report you'd think I was wearing a cape and a shirt with a big S on the front of it.

Daddy spends a long time in the bedroom with Mama before supper. I picture him sitting on the bed, the way it sinks when he lowers himself onto it. Daddy tends to leave a dent in soft things. Not just because he's big, but because he means to. Everything about him is heavy, from his voice to the way his foot lands on the floor. Sometimes just in the way he looks at you.

After a while the door opens and he calls me inside. Mama is sitting on the opposite side of the bed with her back to me, gazing out the window. Daddy stands near the doorway, his tie loosened and the top button of his white shirt undone. Sweat stains circle his underarms. He's not exactly smiling, but he seems pleased just the same. I figure for once I've done something right and he's going to thank me for protecting Chastity.

"Grace, you know that was an Angel of

the Lord that helped you and your little sister down from that tree today."

"No, Daddy," I say. "I think it was Isaac!"

The sting as the flat of his hand burns across my cheek sends my frizzy hair flying along with my thoughts. All three of my sisters gasp from where they're eavesdropping in the next room. Daddy has swatted us on the behind but never in the head. Mama starts to stand, but Daddy holds his hand in the air and she sits back down.

"Your brother is dead, Grace!" His face flushes as red as Jesus's words in my New Testament. A Southern drawl creeps into his voice, the one he works hard to hide but always comes back when he's sad or angry. The one that sounds a little like me.

"But Isaac *is* an angel," I say, bracing for another swat.

Daddy looks back and forth from one of my eyes to the other, green, same as his. "That's it! Don't you ever mention his name in this house again." A hunk of cinnamon-blond hair has fallen down over his forehead and it hops up and down with his words. "Do you hear me, Grace Marie?"

I look away from his face and straight into his round belly, not knowing whether to lie to him or to God.

"I said, do you hear me, Grace?"

38

"Yes, Daddy. I hear you."

He waves me away and pulls the door closed. Hope walks up from behind and rests her hand on my shoulder, but I shrug it off. I run past Joy and a smirking Chastity before slamming the bathroom door behind me. The cool water feels good on my face. I look in the mirror and place my hand over the red marks, fitting my own hand to the memory of his. When my brother's name crawls up my throat I swallow it before it reaches my tongue.

Mama and Daddy kneel beside Chastity and me for bedtime prayers. Chastity mumbles a few words about keeping everybody safe, then crawls under the covers. Daddy looks at me and waits. I know what he expects, so I say what he wants to hear.

"Dear Lord. Thank you for saving Chastity and me today. In Jesus's name, amen."

Daddy opens his mouth to say something, but Mama rests her hand on his freckled arm and he keeps quiet.

"Good night, Grace," she says. When I climb in bed she pulls the covers to my chin, then pats Chastity's cheek. "Good night, Chastity."

Chastity turns toward the wall. "Night, Mama. Night, Daddy."

When they move on to Joy's room my sister yawns from the pillow next to me.

"Grace?"

"What?"

"Do you really talk to Isaac?"

"Not supposed to speak about it," I say to her back. "Go to sleep."

"Does he have wings?"

"How should I know? I've never seen him."

"Grace?"

"What?"

"If it was Isaac that saved us, will you thank him for me?"

"I suppose. Now go to sleep I said."

When I'm sure she's no longer awake I tiptoe to the closet. I wait in the dark for my brother, but he doesn't come.

2

We live in a town called Cherry Hill on account of all the cherry orchards. The hill is just a big dune above Cherry Lake where most of the houses look like they were trying to get as close to the water as possible without getting wet. The rich folks from Blue Rapids come for the summer to live in cottages on the beach across from our side of the lake. Up the hill from them are the nicer year-round houses with real lawns instead of beach sand and a view of gorgeous sunsets over the lake.

Less than a thousand people live in and around Cherry Hill full time and they're separated by two things: which side of the lake they live on and what church they attend. Daddy comes from a long line of Southern Baptists, but our church, The Church of the Word, is nondenominational. That's supposed to mean anyone can come, but I bet if a Catholic walked in they wouldn't feel too comfortable. Daddy thinks the Catholics got it all wrong. We believe in dunking, not sprinkling. If you're saved you get to go to heaven instead of hell. And you don't need a priest to forgive you when you can go straight to the Lord Himself. There aren't any Catholic churches in Cherry Hill, but there's one in Little Dune up the road about ten miles.

Since our church is the oldest, the town cemetery sits behind it. I like our church best because it looks like it belongs on a jigsaw puzzle. It's boxy and white with stained-glass windows on three sides. The roof has a steeple pointing to God. The other two churches are on the opposite side of the lake. Both are built out of tan bricks and look too new to be sacred. I don't know what the difference is between Reformed and Christian Reformed, but I guess one doesn't think the other is Christian.

We go to services three or four times a week. I sometimes feel like the church is as much my home as the one we live in. Our two-story house sits across the street from the church and Cherry Lake is two blocks away. The house is white, same as the church, with a glassed-in front porch. There's only one bathroom, but the claw-foot tub is big enough for two kids at a time.

We moved into this place when I was five years old. The first day we visited, Daddy carried me while a deacon showed us around the parsonage. With my head over Daddy's shoulder, I saw the rooms as we were leaving them.

The bedroom I ended up sharing with Chastity is light green with an entire wall of glass bookcases. Of course Daddy went and filled them all full of books about the Bible, which was too bad since it would have been the perfect place to show off our Barbie dolls. When the new baby arrives she'll sleep in the room that used to be Daddy's study. He's already moved his desk into a corner of the dining room. Not that he studies there much anyway. Mostly he uses an office in the church, and the rest of the time he does his studying in the bathroom. Half of his books have toilet paper hanging out of their tops because he uses the squares as bookmarks when one of us comes banging on the bathroom door.

Hope and Joy have been helping to paint the new nursery. We already have a crib left over from the four of us girls, so it's just about set. One of the ladies from the sewing guild called to tell us they're making a framed needlepoint for the wall. They can't finish it until they know the name and birth weight of the new baby. She wanted to know what colors we're making the room before they buy fabric. Daddy chose blue. I'm not about to tell him God is giving them another girl. I wasn't trying to find out. A few weeks ago I sat in front of the sofa while Mama combed tangles out of my wet hair. When I leaned back so she could get to the front, my head rested against her belly and I just knew this one's coming as a girl.

I don't know her name because that's up to Daddy. Mama tells us that after each baby was born Daddy held his fat, black Bible over our tiny bodies and the Lord bestowed upon him a name for his children. To tell you the truth, I don't think Daddy was listening very well. Or maybe God changed His plans, because none of us fit our given names except for maybe Hope, who is the oldest. When Mama was barely pregnant with Isaac and me she had a premonition about Hope, who was three at the time. Mama was standing at the sink washing up the lunch dishes when she "saw" an accident in her head. She raced to the front yard barefoot, still carrying the wet dishrag, just as the ice-cream truck backed over Hope. Mama fell in the ditch and rolled in the pricker bushes before she reached her little girl lying in the road. I imagine that's where I got my prickliness.

Daddy doesn't like Mama to talk about the premonition. He says it's normal for a mother to worry about her children. He also claims the only reason Hope survived her head injuries is because all the ladies started a prayer chain at Community Bible Church, where he preached before we moved here. The ladies took turns kneeling in the sanctuary in shifts throughout the night.

"By morning, the blood was pouring out of your sister's ear," he said. "If it weren't for the Lord God Almighty the pressure on Hope's brain would have killed her, but He saw fit to let her live."

Hope recovered, but her brain didn't. She goes to a special school on account of her learning disabilities caused by the accident. I can't really tell anything is wrong with her except that she's small for her age and kind of clumsy. One thing I do know is that since the day all those ladies prayed for her she got a huge dose of religion and it stuck. She might be brain damaged, but she can memorize Bible verses like nobody's business. Sometimes right out of the blue she'll spring some of God's Word on you. Like the entire twenty-third Psalm, for instance, which is her favorite.

Next down the line is Joy Ann, one year

younger than Hope and two years older than me. Unlike her name she's one of the most serious people I know. The only thing that seems to bring her any joy is putting another dollar in her passbook account. She's been saving for college ever since she was seven, which seems like a pretty dumb way for a kid to spend her allowance. Even though she gets all As, Joy bites her fingernails until they bleed and paces in circles around the kitchen table when she's studying. I've learned not to interrupt her when she's doing that. Or when she's counting her money.

Chastity just turned eight years old. Her name might be the biggest joke of all. I wouldn't be surprised if she ends up starring as a saloon girl in the movies by the way she insists on wearing dresses every single day of the week and makes sure everybody sees her flowered underpants. Last year she begged until Mama gave in and bought her play high heels with elastic straps to hold them on. They're silver and sparkle like crystals. She sleeps with them just so nobody else can play with them, but one time I tried them on when she wasn't home. I fell down five times before I finally gave up.

This is because, although Daddy named

me Grace, I'm about as agile as a three-sided rock. I've always wished I could take tap and ballet, but it would probably be a waste of money on someone as klutzy as me. Not to mention the fact that good Christians aren't supposed to dance or listen to certain kinds of music. Daddy says dancing and rock and roll lead to fornication, which means sex. Seems like it would be hard to make a baby when you're dancing.

The other thing about me is I don't look like my sisters one iota. They're all blond and blue-eyed like Mama, which makes my red hair and green eyes look like a sourball accidentally mixed in with a bowl of butterscotch candies. But the thing that separates us most isn't on the outside. My way of knowing things stands out even more than my fiery hair. If it weren't for my connection to Isaac, I'd surely believe I was adopted.

Daddy named my twin brother after a story from the Old Testament. He says his son was sacrificed as a way for him to prove his love and devotion to the Lord, just like Abraham. I once asked Isaac if that was true. He told me that what's true for one person isn't always true for another, but that doesn't make it a lie. It's another one of those fuzzy replies that doesn't really answer my question. I have a lot of unanswered questions.

Mama stands at her dresser and tears pink tape off her spit curls, then teases her blond hair into a flip. She sprays so much Aqua Net she sneezes. We girls scramble around the house looking for a clean dress and shoes while Mama and Daddy prepare the fixings that will slowly cook while we're at church. Breakfast is a find-what-you-can kind of deal because we have such a big meal after Sunday services. Joy made scrambled eggs for herself and Chastity. They always eat early because Joy likes having the bathroom to herself. Hope and I are slow-pokes. I help take soft rollers out of the back of her head while she spreads jelly on our slices of toast.

Daddy slides our pot roast into the oven, then clips a striped maroon tie on his white shirt. He scoops up his big, black Bible that has papers sticking out every which way and calls for us to hurry up. Mama joins Daddy at the front door, where he hands us coins for the offering plate and checks to make sure we all have our Bibles. Chastity has a pink one, which I tried to trade her for mine, but she wouldn't do it. Pink is my favorite color.

I got my Bible from Mrs. Franks when I was six. She was praying at the end of Sunday school and asked who wanted to take Jesus into their heart. I peeked around to see if anybody was looking before sticking my hand in the air. I knew I didn't want to go to h-e-l-l. I saw a picture on one of Daddy's religious tracts that show how demons float around so they can rat you out if they catch you trying to sneak out of the lake of fire. Mrs. Franks told me that heaven is a glorious place where people spend all day worshipping Jesus. It sounded to me like going to church every day, a pretty boring way to spend eternity in my opinion, but better than going down inside the ground where the devil lives.

After Sunday school that day Mrs. Franks took me into one of the little side rooms where the deacons count the tithes. She asked me if I knew I was a sinner. Truthfully I'd wanted to grab a fistful of those dollars sitting right there in the offering plate, so I told her yes. She nodded like she already knew that and it was exactly what she wanted me to say. Then she told me to bow my head and ask Jesus into my heart.

I closed my eyes. "Dear Jesus," I whispered. "Will you come into my heart and forgive me for being a sinner?" I waited, but nothing happened. So I just said amen.

Mrs. Franks hugged me. "Now you're a child of God. Remember, Grace, He sees everything you do and hears every word you say. And if you're ever in trouble, all you have to do is ask for His help because He's right there." She patted my jacket over my heart.

Mrs. Franks handed me a little, white Bible and told me I should read from it every single day. I promised her I would, but knew I wouldn't. I don't even read my Richie Rich comic books every day.

When I got home from church that day I announced over Sunday dinner that I had been saved. Daddy said, "Praise the Lord!" But he'd just taken a bite of potatoes so it came out "Pwaise da Load." Joy rolled her big, blue eyes at me because she thought I was just trying to get attention, which in a way I was. Around here it takes a lot to be noticed unless you do something really good or really bad. In my case it's usually the second of those things.

Later that night as I lay in bed I rested my hand over my heart to see if it felt any different. I knew there were supposed to be three guys in there: God, Jesus, and the Holy Ghost. The third one scared me, so I pictured him like Casper the Friendly Ghost. Casper reminds me of myself, wanting to be friends but scaring people away. Anyway, it didn't feel one bit different. I thought I'd feel like a new person, but I just felt like plain old Grace. I still don't feel any different today. I don't tell Daddy that. I talk to God sometimes, but mostly I talk to Isaac.

Daddy holds hands with Mama as we cross the street. People are gathered around the sidewalk in front of the church, talking. It's started to sprinkle. When they see Daddy, they say things like "Morning, Pastor. Morning, Mrs. Carter. How are you today?" And he answers, "Morning, Brother" or "Morning, Sister," even though we aren't related.

I find a place at the table in my Sunday school classroom. Our teacher, Mrs. Lankfurt, sits at the end of the table squeezed into a little wooden chair not meant for grown-ups. Mrs. Lankfurt is about 100 years old. The kids call her Mrs. Stankfart behind her back. Her long chin has a single hair sticking out of a mole that almost touches the brooch on her blouse. I always stare at her chin when she talks. It's rude, but I can't help it.

Today Mrs. Lankfurt is telling the story of Zacchaeus, who climbed a sycamore tree to see Jesus because he was too short to see over the other people's heads. I've heard this story in every grade of Sunday school so I know it by heart. Jesus was so pleased that he honored Zacchaeus by having dinner at his house, which made the other people mad because he was a tax collector. I think the point Jesus was trying to make is that He loves everybody, even tax collectors. Even bullies like Billy Wolf.

After the story Mrs. Lankfurt hands out papers so we can cut out pictures of Zacchaeus and paste them onto the picture of a tree. It seems like such an immature project for ten- and eleven-year-olds, but I don't care. She's old so we probably seem like babies to her and besides, the Sunday school activities are the least boring thing about church.

I ask the girl next to me to pass the mucilage. Donna Sue hands me the brown bottle with a pink rubbery top and a slit in it. I smear a bit of what looks like snot on Zacchaeus's back. Just as I'm about to perch him in the crook of the tree a little voice inside me says, *Put him on Jesus's shoulders.* Not Isaac's voice. Just a silly voice like everybody has inside of them.

Apparently everybody but Donna Sue.

She looks over and yells, "Mrs. Lankfurt! Grace put Zacchaeus on top of Jesus!" When I glare at her she looks at me smugly and folds her pudgy hands in her lap. Mrs. Lankfurt walks over and peers at my picture. Her breath coming over my shoulder smells like fish.

"Grace, I'm going to have to tell your father about this."

I can't stand Donna Sue. She's gloating like she just won the county-wide spelling bee. But there's something I know about her that makes up for it. Someday Donna Sue is going to marry a preacher and be stuck going to church nearly every single day. Serves her right for being such a snitch.

The bell rings outside our door and we all head upstairs for the morning service. I lag behind the rest of the group so nobody can see my angry tears. When I kick the wall with the toe of my shoe a pair of hands slip over my eyes from behind me. I try to wheel around, but the hands grip tighter on the sides of my head.

"Guess who?"

I know the janitor's voice. "It's Mr. Weaver," I say.

He lets go, then gently cups my shoulders and turns me to face him. He squats down so we're eye to eye, then wipes my tear with his hankie. "What's wrong, honey?"

"Nothing," I say. I look down at my shoes. Partly because I'm ashamed and partly because Mr. Weaver has a funny-looking face and if I stare at it too hard I might start laughing. His face is shaped like the doll whose head Joy squished and it stuck that way. His head is small, but his forehead and chin bulge out.

"Well, in that case, why would you put a mark on the wall for Mr. Weaver to have to wash off later?"

I look up, but focus on the door handle over his right shoulder. "I'm sorry. I was mad at Donna Sue."

He smiles. "We all let our emotions get out of hand sometimes. I forgive you."

Mr. Weaver pulls a bag of pink peppermints out of his pocket and holds it toward me. I take one and immediately pop it into my mouth. "Thank you," I say. "You won't tell my daddy, will you?"

He pets my hair, then squeezes my arm. "It'll be our little secret, Miss Grace. Now get along upstairs, but be nice to the walls on your way or next time I might have to put you over my knee."

When he stands I scoot toward the front of the church. As I climb the steps to the auditorium I'm already feeling nervous about how mad Daddy will be when he hears what I've done. He's always saying how we have to set an example for the other children. Hopefully old Mrs. Lankfurt will forget to tell him.

I scooch past Mama and sit next to her in our pew with Joy to my left and Chastity to the left of her. Hope helps in the nursery, a room that smells like spoiled milk and poopy diapers, so she's not here. Mama digs into her big, black pocketbook and fishes out a breath mint. All three of us lean forward and watch her slip it between her glossed pink lips. She gives in, peeling three more wintergreen Life Savers from the roll, and hands them to us.

"No biting," she whispers, just as I crunch mine into a hundred pieces.

Loretta Smith starts playing the processional hymn on the organ, which is Daddy's cue. He walks up the left aisle stopping to pat Mama's hand as he passes. Daddy clutches his Bible, nodding and smiling at his congregation all the way to the podium. Burt Lohman, the deacon who gave us the first tour of our house, walks up the right aisle at the same time. Burt has a round face with rosy cheeks and ears that stick straight out from his head. I like Burt. Joy gets to have him for her Sunday school teacher this year.

Daddy stands at the podium and smiles as he scans the crowd. And then he says the same thing he says every single Sunday.

"This is the day the Lord hath made. Let us be glad and rejoice in it!"

Loretta bangs louder on the keys, the signal for all of us to stand and sing "Praise God, from Whom All Blessings Flow." Mama always sings the harmony part. She's an alto. Then Daddy prays in his up-and-down voice and we all sit down again. I'm supposed to keep my eyes closed during prayer, but I know Daddy's are never closed because he's looking around for stuff on the pulpit at the same time he's saying the prayer. I do my fair share of peeking, too.

We sing a few more songs while Burt waves his hands around like he's swinging an invisible jump rope. When Daddy starts preaching I find things to use up the minutes. I start by counting the organ pipes, all lined up like broken matchsticks from short to tall in the front of the church. I'm only about two thirds of the way through when they start to blur and I lose my place. Joy pokes me in the side and points to a song in the hymnbook. The song is titled "Hold the Fort," but she has her finger over the second *o* and I know she wants me to fill in the blank. This is one of Joy's best finds so far and I can't help but giggle. Mama reaches over and twists a hunk of skin on my upper arm. I turn my head away from Joy, who is trying to get me to look at another song title, and concentrate on the back of Earl Felt's head.

Earl is a farmer who spends a lot of time in the sun. The back of his neck has criss-cross crinkles that make me want to stick cloves in it like an Easter ham. He raises sheep way out in the boondocks. I think he and Mrs. Felt have about ten kids. Their family takes up two whole pews. He sits at the end with his wooden leg stuck straight out in the aisle. I can't believe nobody has ever tripped over that big, old, crusty shoe of his.

Daddy's talking about idols and graven images, but all I hear is blah, blah, blah. I stare at the patterns in the stained-glass window above our pew, the way all the colors swirl into a design that looks different every time I study it. If I look hard enough I can see a face with eyes, nose, and a brow. When I close my eyes and open them again the shapes remind me of rippled water after you throw a stone in it. The different ways of seeing the designs is kind of like my thoughts when I know something. Sometimes the message is clear like a drawing and other times my thoughts are more blurred, like a watercolor painting.

Somewhere on the edges of my eardrums Daddy's preaching breaks through the blahs and hits my brain like a smack on the side of the head. "One who hears what God has to say, who knows what the Most High knows, who saw the vision that the Almighty revealed, who keeps stumbling with open eyes . . ." When he pauses I glance up to see if he's looking at me. He's not. I grab my bulletin from the hymnal pocket on the back of the pew in front of us and open it to look for the Scripture reference before realizing I left my Bible downstairs in the Sunday school classroom again. I lean over Mama, trying to find the words in the open Bible on her lap. He's preaching from the book of Numbers. Mama sees me eyeballing the page and points to the verse. I read it again. And again, the words are like a drumbeat in my chest. That's me! This Balaam guy is talking about the Knowing, how I see things like dreaming with my eyes open, awake.

I'm bent so far over Mama's Bible that she just hands it to me. She's never seen any of us besides Hope take such a deep interest in one of Daddy's sermons. I catch her following my finger over the words of that verse, over and over. I want to scream at her, at Daddy, at all of them. *This! This is what I've been trying to explain! The Knowing comes from a good place. A God place.* I feel Mama shudder next to me like when you get a chill but it's not cold. When I look up at her she looks away. I close the Bible and go back to counting organ pipes. The big clock on the wall hits five after twelve and people start fidgeting, worrying about burnt pot roasts and such. Finally Daddy says, "Let us pray," and I can almost hear the walls let out a sigh.

After Sunday dinner, since it isn't my turn to do the dishes, I spread out the funny papers on the living room floor. Just as I prop my chin in my hands, Daddy walks by and swats me on the hind end with his rolled-up newspaper.

"Ought to be ashamed of yourself, Grace." I know better than to say anything back. "Blasphemy," he mumbles as he walks off on his way to the bedroom for his afternoon nap.

Guess I was wrong about Mrs. Lankfurt forgetting.

Joy and Chastity have run off to catch frogs in the creek together. I walk to the lake alone with the candy I hid from my sisters yesterday. Spending my allowance is always a hard decision. Every week, if Joy doesn't cheat me out of my dime first, I stand in front of the candy counter so long my spit gets to be too much for my mouth and I have to keep swallowing. I love Hershey bars, but it makes more sense to buy three smaller things. Yesterday I decided on a Tootsie Roll, a three-pack of wax bottles filled with Kool-Aid, and a candy bracelet.

We're not allowed to swim on Sundays, so I stop at the playground next to the beach and sit on a bench that looks out over the lake to eat my candy. A little girl sits directly in front of me on the beach, away from all the other children. Her brown curls remind me of ribbons on a Christmas package, as though somebody swiped the blade of a nail file down the length of each lock. Her mother is sitting farther down the beach with her curlered head deep in a book. I can tell it's her mama by the way she glances over this way every so often to check on her daughter.

The girl was digging in the sand with a pail and shovel when I got here, but now she has her eye on me, creeping closer bit by bit. By the time I finish my Tootsie Roll she's made her way to the edge of the bench and climbs up. I suck the juice out of a wax bottle before turning to look at her. She's staring at my wrist.

Candy? She says it in her head, not out loud. Just like Isaac speaks to me. Then, *Me have one?*

My heart does a somersault inside my chest. I look down at my wrist, then back to her and nod.

Okay. Just one.

She leans over and nibbles a pink pearl of candy off the elastic string before I have a chance to take the bracelet off my arm. I stare at her as she chews. She smiles up at me.

More?

I nod again. This time she pulls the bracelet away from my arm and chomps through the whole caboodle, like cleaning an ear of corn of its kernels. When all that's left is colored spit drying on my arm, she sits up and leans her head against the back of the bench. The way she stares out at the lake looks like an old lady in a three-year-old body.

You have talk in head like me, she says without speaking.

Yes, I have talk in head, too.

Her mama looks around and spies her daughter sitting with me. "Carolyn! Come

61

to Mommy!"

The girl squints up at my face before scampering off the bench. When she reaches her mama she glances back in my direction. It's too far away for me to see her face, but I hear her thoughts just fine.

Thank you.

I half skip, half run back to the house. I want to shout about what just happened, to finally convince my family I'm not crazy. But by the time I reach our front sidewalk I've already changed my mind about telling anyone. I keep walking toward the backyard. I know they won't believe me. They never believe me. They don't want to believe me. Every time I know a name before it's given or turn to the right page in the hymnal before it's announced or even when I gave details of the day I was born, they just make up silly explanations. Even when I knew that boy had drowned in Cherry Lake they wrote it off as a daydreaming coincidence.

Last summer I got tired of being teased and started saying, "Answer the phone!" as a joke before it rang, until Hope cried because it scared her. Daddy threatened to ground me for a month if I did it again. For all the times Isaac tries to convince me I'm special, there are another ten times when my family has hurt my feelings either by denying the Knowing or making me feel dirty because of it. Most of the time I feel crooked, like the old walnut tree in our backyard where Daddy strung a clothesline between the trunk and the barn. The branches poke at the air like a plump ballerina. That unruly tree seems to enjoy its uniqueness but not me.

I climb up to my favorite branch to think about what just happened at the beach. It's just like Isaac said. I'm not the only one. Little Carolyn has the Knowing too. I'll probably never see her again, but it doesn't matter because even if nobody else does, I know I'm not an oddball or a devil child like I've overheard Daddy say to Mama when he thinks I can't hear him. That little girl was as close to God as you can get. Maybe even closer than Daddy.

"Hey, Grace!" Joy stands under the tree and hollers up at me. "Come explore the loft with us."

I don't move.

"Grace, I know you're up there. I can see your foot."

I peer down at her between the leaves. "Daddy says we're not supposed to go up there."

"They're taking a nap. We're bored. C'mon."

Joy gives me her *I dare you* face, which she must've given Chastity or she'd never get Miss Priss near the loft.

"You going, Chas?"

Chastity nods while looking at Joy, probably hoping our older sister will change her mind as quickly as she thought up this stupid idea. Unfortunately for both of us she doesn't.

"Okay," I say. "But if we get caught I'm telling them it was your idea."

"We won't get caught. They're already snoring."

Joy waits for me to jump down before the three of us head toward the barn. It sets back from the house about five car lengths, although we don't put our car in it. The barn used to be red but most of the paint has peeled off. The inside is full of rusty pipes, Daddy's tools, and the lawn mower and such. Plus a bunch of boxes we still haven't unpacked even though we've lived here almost seven years since Daddy's last church.

Joy and I roll back the heavy wooden door. The three of us make our way to the row of old boards nailed against the wall at the back of the barn. Joy tells me to go first. This is not a surprise. Joy often comes up with bad ideas she wants other people to try before she'll give it a go.

"Why me?"

"Because you're the middle sister of us," she says, as if this makes perfect sense.

I don't feel like arguing with her so I head up, batting away cobwebs as I climb. When I get to the top rung I push up on a door that's set into the ceiling and slide it to the side.

"What do you see?" Joy yells from beneath me.

"I can't see anything until my eyes adjust. And I'm getting dust in my nose."

"Keep going!"

"All right, all right!" I say. But I purposely scrape the bottom of my shoe on the top step to make dirt fall in her hair for being so pushy.

I hoist my rear end onto the ledge of the loft floor, and leap to my feet. Several bales of straw lay scattered across the back of the loft. A heavy rope hangs from the rafters between rows of old wooden pews and a stack of hymnals piled up against one wall. A podium leans against a pile of broken pews, some on three legs. I wonder if they collapsed from sheer boredom after listening to all those sermons year after year.

Joy bounds up behind me. "What a perfect place for a fort!"

She stands with her hands on boyish hips and already I can see her taking over this space. She'll figure out some way of making neighbor kids pay to see an ugly old loft.

"I can't believe we're stupid enough to come up here," I say. "If Daddy finds out we're toast."

Joy calls down to our youngest sister who's still lingering near the bottom step. "Hey, Chas, climb on up."

Chastity inches up the ladder at a worm's pace before finally poking her head through the hole in the floor. Her pink barrettes twinkle in the one ray of sun coming through the back window. Joy reaches down and pulls her the rest of the way up. Chastity immediately starts dusting her dress with her hands. "It stinks up here."

"It's not bad," Joy says, sniffing. "Not *that* bad." She marches over to the split double doors at the front end of the loft and pushes the top half open wide. The view from the loft overlooks rows of neighboring houses in the distance all the way to the lake, the fruit processing plant, the railroad tracks, and the cherry orchards beyond. It's a long way down to the ground, where our rusty swing set sits, its sharp edges like an openmouthed crocodile waiting for its next meal.

I sense something behind us. Without

thinking I wheel around, but nobody's there.

"Let's get out of here," I say, taking a step toward the ladder.

Joy flutters her nail-bitten fingers in my face, mocking my fear. "What's the matter, Grace? You worried about tripping over your big feet and falling out the window?"

I'm not about to tell them that I don't think we're alone up here. "I just don't want to get in trouble," I say.

"Scaredy-cat! You go on down to Mama and we'll be in later, right, Chas?" She nudges our little sister, who sticks her adorable nose in the air, although it's obvious she's as nervous as she is disgusted with the filth.

"Jo-oy! Gra-ace! Chastiteee!" Mama calls from the back door of the house.

All three of us scramble for the ladder, but to prove my bravery I make sure to go last. While waiting my turn on the top step the rope swings gently as if waving to me, its frayed edges glimmering in a dusty sunbeam.

3

Joy and I dragged the screens out from the barn and sprayed them down with the hose. Daddy doesn't want Mama on the ladder, but she's stubborn like me. Joy left to babysit for a neighbor. As soon as Daddy left to study for tomorrow's sermon Mama propped a tall, wooden ladder under the first window and up she went. She won't let me climb past the second step so I just steady the legs while she snaps the screens into place and twists bent nails over the edges.

Mama never wears slacks, but I'm thinking it might be a good idea since if anyone came by they'd be able to see up her dress. Maybe that's another reason Daddy didn't want her up there. When I crane my head back to watch Mama, a bird flies past and lands on the barn. As usual I forget what I'm supposed to be doing and my mind wanders back to the loft and who or what might be up there.

I wonder if it's a ghost, a real one, not the holy kind. Every time I look toward the barn, I get that same uneasy feeling as when we were up there after church last Sunday. It feels a little like when you walk into a room after someone just left and you can still smell their breath. Or how a chair slowly finds its old shape again after someone gets out of it. It scares me a little and yet not. Maybe it's not a ghost. Maybe it's nothing.

"Grace, hold it tighter," Mama calls from above me.

"Sorry, Mama."

When she asks what I keep staring at I tell her my "eye is on the sparrow" and this makes her laugh. It's one of her favorite hymns. She immediately starts singing the chorus and I join in. *"I sing because I'm happy, I sing because I'm free, for His eye is on the sparrow, and I know He watches me."*

The last line gets me thinking about Isaac and I wonder how often he watches us. Was that him I felt in the loft? It didn't feel like him. When Isaac is with me it feels like a giant, warm light that I can't see with my eyes but makes me feel lit up on the inside. This other thing in the loft felt more like a dim flashlight under the covers.

69

Mama clears her throat and I realize I've been staring off toward the barn again.

"Sorry, Mama," I say again.

When we've finished putting everything away, Mama goes inside the house for a nap. Hope is holed up in her bedroom reading the Bible as usual. I make a peanut butter and jelly sandwich and bring it outside to eat on the back steps. I've only taken two bites when a figure flashes past the loft window fast as a blink before it's gone. I cock my head to one side and look up toward the empty barn window, concentrating. I feel the pull and hear the chatter of unfamiliar thoughts, but only one gets through. *Hungry.*

I glance down at my half-eaten sandwich. I can't go up there alone. What if it's that creepy man I heard Joy telling about? She said a bum lives in an abandoned school bus down by the railroad tracks and he got caught pulling his pants down in front of a bunch of kids. Plus it turns out the reason Sheriff Conner flew by Mama and Chastity and me on our walk home from the post office was because some girl had been molested. I'd be stupid to go up there by myself.

My head says no, but my heart is noisier. I wrap a napkin around the sandwich and slip an apple into my pants pocket. Even as I climb the ladder I can't believe these are my hands traveling up the ragged boards in front of my face. When I get to the top I poke my head up into the loft and look around. My voice comes out like a whisper.

"Hello?"

Nothing. I say it a little louder.

"Hello?"

"Hello yourself."

I follow the voice to the back pew, where he's sitting with his hands folded between his legs. I'm not sure if he's shy or embarrassed. I stay put.

"I won't hurt you," he says.

Isaac is always telling me to trust my instincts. I close my eyes and let my other sense take charge over what I can see and not what I've heard. I instantly feel safe instead of scared. I walk over and hand him my sandwich.

"I know you won't," I say.

He takes a bite, closes his eyes, and chews for a long time. He must be really hungry. I sit on a bale of straw, facing him. He's older than Daddy but not quite as old as my grandpa. Stains cover his wrinkled pants. One of his shoes is black and the other is brown. His eyes slant down just a bit at the edges and the corners of his mouth bend

71

slightly upward, almost like they're trying to meet each other. It's a kind face.

"Do you live up here?"

He sighs out of his long nose and opens his eyes. "Sometimes."

"Isn't it cold in the winter?"

"Sometimes."

He finishes the sandwich and wipes his hands on his knees just like I always do.

"Oh, wait, here's an apple," I say, remembering the treat in my pocket.

He takes it in his bony hand and rolls it around. "Looks mighty good."

But he doesn't take a bite. Instead he looks at me and grins really wide, showing the spaces where teeth used to be. I take the apple from his hand and bite off a piece, being as careful as possible not to get spit on it. I pluck it from my lips and hand it to him.

We sit there for a long time, me chomping off little pieces and him mostly gumming them while I talk.

"We're not supposed to come up here. Mama's worried about lockjaw if we step on a rusty nail or something. She said there was a story in the *Chronicle* — that's our newspaper — about a boy whose mouth rusted up in the middle of a sentence. My sisters probably wish it would happen to

72

me. Especially Chastity. She says she hates when I sing in bed, but I happen to know it helps her fall asleep."

I look at the old man, who, unlike my sisters, actually seems to be listening.

"I know things," I blurt out. "I know things other people don't, like the fact that you were up here. And you were hungry."

I wait for him to laugh at me but he doesn't, just nods as if that were a perfectly normal thing to say.

"You got a name, mister?"

"Lyle."

"Mine's Grace."

"Nice to meet you, Grace."

I walk to the front window and toss the apple core into the backyard, wiping my hands on the seat of my pants. "Well, I guess I better go."

"Thank you for sharing your lunch, young lady."

"Sure thing." I start down the ladder but stop when my head is even with the floor because I feel a question form in his mouth.

"Grace?"

"Yes?"

"You won't tell nobody 'bout me stayin' up here in the pastor's barn sometimes, will ya?"

"No, Mr. . . ."

"Lyle," he fills in.

"Lyle," I say.

I'm making another sandwich when Daddy tells me to get in the car so we can go buy groceries. I like when he chooses me and I get time with just us and no sisters. Sometimes when we're at the store I pretend I'm an only child and my daddy takes me everywhere because I'm his special girl. I make up stories about Mama and Daddy driving to Mackinac Island on vacation, where we eat homemade fudge and stay in the Grand Hotel, which Daddy can afford with only one kid to feed. I picture us walking hand in hand down the street with me, their precious child, smack dab in the middle.

Daddy pulls our rusty station wagon into a spot right in front of Norberg's grocery store. He hands me the list and pats his suit jacket to make sure he has his wad of coupons. He does. The pocket is so fat it looks like he's got an extra Bible stuffed in there. All his pockets already bulge with religious tracts that he keeps on hand for giving out to people. Sometimes he embarrasses Mama. I can tell because she looks around like he isn't really there when he's "witnessing" to the public.

"Let's go," he says.

I'm out of the car and in the store before he's even got his door open. My job is to cross things off the list as Daddy puts them in the cart. When our basket is nearly full, Daddy stops in the middle of the aisle and thumbs through his stack of coupons looking for ten cents off Charmin. When he finds it, he pulls three packages off the shelf and dumps them in the cart. He doesn't squeeze them even a little bit. I glance over the list and draw a line through ~~TP.~~ Daddy never spells it out. Maybe he worries about dropping the list and somebody finding out Pastor Carter wipes his behind just like everybody else. Which is kind of funny since he spends more time in the bathroom than anyone else I know.

At the checkout I help load the groceries onto the moving black belt. Daddy looks over our haul and pulls out matching coupons one by one. He hands them to me to give to Mrs. Norberg. When the cart is empty he looks up from his fistful of coupons and frowns.

"Grace, do you have the five-loaves-for-a-dollar bread coupon?"

I shake my head. "It's in your . . ." I swallow and start over. "I think I saw you put it

75

in your wallet after you cut it out of the paper."

Daddy pulls the black wallet out of his pants pocket. Coupons and little pieces of paper bulge from every compartment. Mrs. Norberg winks at me and I roll my eyes. I like Mrs. Norberg. She and her husband have owned the store for over thirty years. Whenever I come along with Daddy, I guess how much he'll save with coupons and she gives me a sucker if I'm close. Close pretty much means anything because she gives me a sucker every time, even when I'm way off.

It's not something I can use the Knowing on. Another rule that comes with the gift is I can't use it to make a profit. It's only for helping people and to learn things that'll make me a better person. I once asked Isaac if I could go to the horse races and know what horse would win so Mama and Daddy could have more money to raise us kids. He told me it doesn't work that way.

What do you think would happen if your mama and daddy got rich, Grace? he'd asked.

Isaac often answers my questions with one of his own.

"*Our* mama and daddy," I corrected him. "We'd probably move into a fancy house and Daddy could buy nicer suits to preach in and Mama could get her hair done at the beauty shop instead of having to do it herself. Us kids would all have new bikes and no hand-me-downs and —"

And that's what would make all of you happy?

Another question. I nearly chewed through my lip trying to come up with the right answer.

"No, what would make us happy is for Mama to be like her old self. That would please Daddy and we'd be a happy family like before you died."

There are lots of unhappy rich people, Grace.

I thought about Mr. and Mrs. Cole, who own the car lot and live in the fanciest house in town, way up on the hill overlooking the lake and all the other houses. I don't believe I've ever seen either of them smile. Mrs. Cole always looks like she smells something nasty with her lips all pinched and nostrils flared. Mr. Cole walks with his head down and his shoulders bent, as if he has one of those shiny new cars resting on top of him. Daddy doesn't make much money for his preaching, but at least he loves his job.

"I don't think I want to be rich," I'd finally said.

A tiny photograph slips out of Daddy's wallet and lands on the sticky carousel as he searches for another coupon. When it reaches the end I grab it before it gets swallowed up under the lip of the counter. The picture is of a sleeping baby lying in what looks like a dresser drawer lined with blue satin, surrounded by flowers in glass vases. He's wearing a white gown with a matching bonnet. A heart-shaped birthmark dots the side of his neck. I run my fingers over the picture and as I do, my heart swells up into my throat. I slowly turn the photograph over and read the inscription.

My beloved son,
in whom I am well pleased.
Isaac Henry Carter
March 13, 1958

"Daddy, you . . ."

I glance up at him. He's still searching through his pockets. I know I shouldn't, but I can't help myself. I bend over and tuck my brother's picture into my sock. When I stand back up Mrs. Norberg is looking at me and I know she saw what I did. She looks at Daddy and I brace for her to rat on me. All she says is, "There it is, Reverend," and pulls the coupon clipping from his breast pocket. When she turns to ring up the coupons I feel my breath come back into my chest.

"What do you think, Grace?"

My face flushes hot. What I think is that I stole Daddy's picture of Isaac and it's burning a hole in my ankle.

"How much did we save today?" Mrs. Norberg asks.

"Oh." Without thinking, I blurt out, "Three dollars and ten cents."

Mrs. Norberg cranks the lever on the side of the cash register to total the coupons. All three of us watch as the numbers spin and then $3.10 slides into the windows.

"Bull's-eye!" she says, and hands me two suckers.

Daddy gives me that look of his, but he doesn't say anything.

As soon as the groceries are put away I run upstairs and carefully unroll my sock. I take a flashlight into the closet with me.

"Is this really you, Isaac?"

It's what I looked like in human form.

"You don't have red hair like me."

We weren't identical twins, Grace.

"I know. Joy explained it to me. We came from two eggs, not one."

That's right. We were fraternal twins.

"*Are*," I correct him. I get the feeling he's

79

about to say something but changes his mind.

"Isaac?"

Yes?

"Do you think Daddy loves you even though he never got to see you alive?"

I know he does.

"What does beloved mean?"

It means dearly loved.

"Do you think Daddy loves me dearly?"

Of course he does, Grace. Very dearly. He would die for you.

"He would?"

He absolutely would.

"I should probably give him his picture back."

I think you should.

"Isaac?"

Yes?

"What color are your eyes?"

They were blue.

"Oh."

Grace . . .

"It's okay. I know we aren't exactly alike."

No two people are. He pauses. *But, Grace?*

"Yeah?"

We're more alike than you think.

I wait for Daddy to start snoring before tiptoeing into their bedroom. I stand quietly until my eyes adjust to the dark. His wallet is open on the dresser. I slide the photo in the slot under his driver's license, being careful not to make any noise. On my way out I dare myself to look back at my parents. The light from the moon shining through the window throws a glow on Mama and Daddy's bed. Daddy lays on his side, his mouth shaped like an O. Mama's eyes are open, staring toward the window. She turns her head toward me.

"Good night, Grace," she whispers.

"Night, Mama."

4

As if Mama doesn't have enough to worry about with another baby coming, Chastity is claiming to have the flu again. She's splayed out on the sofa, moaning into the cushion. Her pale complexion definitely helps make the act look convincing. I give her a look that says *I know your tricks* but take it back when I see her bloodshot eyes. The dark circles under them make her look like a sad puppy.

Joy stands next to the sofa and studies Chastity's face. "You're faking."

"Am not. My stomach hurts."

"Leave her alone, Joy," I say. "Maybe she really is sick this time."

Chastity turns her back to us, holding her belly. Mama leans over the sofa. She kisses Chastity's forehead and pets her chubby arm. She's not wearing stockings and the tiny blue veins behind her knees look like a cluster of rivers on a weathered map.

"Let her rest," she says to us.

I grab a banana off the kitchen table on my way to the loft, where I find Lyle napping on the back pew. I've started bringing softer things for him to eat. I set the fruit next to his feet and watch him sleep. Sometimes old people look like babies. Maybe time goes backward as people age. Maybe I'll get to see Isaac again someday after all.

Lyle makes a smacking noise with his mouth, waking himself up. He opens his eyes and nearly falls off the bench when he sees me.

"I'm sorry I surprised you," I say.

"It's okay." He rubs his stubbly chin and sits upright. "Force of habit."

"What do you mean?"

"When you've been kicked out of as many places as I have you learn to be ready to run. Even in your sleep." He eyes the banana. "That for me?"

"My sister's sick," I say, as he starts peeling.

"Well, that's a darn shame. Which one?"

"Chastity. She's the youngest."

"The one in the blue dress."

So he *was* watching us that day we came up here. Maybe he watches us all the time.

"Yup," I say. "That one."

"Kids are resilient. She'll be fine."

"You sure know lots of big words for a bum."

He laughs at this. "I used to be smart," he says. "Gettin' dumber by the day."

"How come you don't have a house?"

"Same reason I don't have a job."

"I bet Mrs. Norberg would hire you. Then you wouldn't . . ."

"Don't you worry 'bout me. I like it this way."

"You do?"

"Beats the hell out of being at work all day just to sleep in a real bed. I have enough to get by."

I've never heard anyone say the H-word except having to do with sinners. Daddy says that's where you'll go for swearing. I whisper a silent prayer for Lyle so he won't end up in h-e-l-l for naming it out loud.

"Pardon my French," he says, checking his pocket before resting both hands in his lap. I put both of mine on top of one of his to help make the trembling stop. Water rises up in the corner of his eyes, then quickly disappears as he pulls his thoughts inside himself and his hands from under my palms.

"You best go back to the house before someone worries," he says.

"Okay. Are you sure you don't need anything?"

"Not anything you can give me, Gracie. But thanks for asking. Now git."

I wake in the middle of the night to the sounds of Chastity whimpering in her sleep. When I put my arm around her, a sickly sludge moves under my hand, deep beneath her skin. Something inside my sister is foul. I'm just about to wake her when she sits up and pukes all over the bed.

"Stay here!" I say.

Chastity howls behind me as I run to the first floor, skipping every other step. I shake Daddy's arm real hard to wake him.

"Chastity threw up," I say.

Mama moves in slow motion, but Daddy throws back the covers and pulls on his flannel robe. By the time we reach my bedroom Hope is on her knees at the foot of the bed in her white nightgown, praying. Joy wanders in behind Daddy and me.

"Pee-yew!" she says, holding her nose, which makes Chastity wail even more pitifully. Hope prays louder.

Daddy tells us to hush. "Settle down, all of you. It's just the flu. Grace, change the bedding. Hope, go back to bed. Joy, get a bucket in case she does it again." He reaches across the pillow and rests the back of his big hand against Chastity's flushed cheek.

"You've got a little fever. I'll go get some aspirin."

I'm scared to say it, but I can't help myself. "She's real sick, Daddy."

He smooths his hair over his head and it falls back over his brow. "The flu's going around. She'll be okay."

Chastity clutches herself, knees drawn to her chest, moaning.

"Daddy, please believe me," I say. "Something inside her has gone bad. I felt it."

He jerks his head toward me. "What do you mean you *felt* it?"

Mama appears in the doorway wearing a thin nightgown. A small bulge pushes against the fabric below her belly button. She glances back and forth between Daddy and me. She takes a step forward, then pulls back again.

"Here," I say, putting my hand where Chastity is holding her stomach. "There's where I felt it."

Daddy looks at me real hard, then back at Chastity. He tries to touch her belly, but she fights him. When he finally manages to get her hand out of the way and pokes his finger on the spot, I swear Chastity's scream could wake the neighborhood. Daddy's forehead crinkles into a row of uneven furrows and his mouth changes to a flat line.

He scoops Chastity out of bed and whirls around, nearly knocking Mama over as he runs down the hall.

The last I see of the three of them is my sister's legs dangling over the side of Daddy's big arms as he carries her out to the car. Mama lowers herself into the front seat, her face like a tired ghost in the moon's light as they back out of the driveway.

Joy shoves her hands into her furry robe pockets and leans against the kitchen wall, one foot crossed over the other, while I make my breakfast the following morning.

"How'd you know she had appendicitis?"

"I didn't. I just knew her insides were sick, that's all."

I pluck a slice of bread from the toaster and drop it onto a chipped plate.

"What are you, a witch or something?"

I stop buttering and stare at her.

"You act like a witch." She spits the words from her mouth. "Falling down a tree without getting hurt. Talking to dead people. Seeing people's insides like an X-ray machine or something. And look at your hair. You've even got witch hair."

"I'm not a witch!" I say, stomping my foot.

Joy flinches. She tries to disguise her fear of me with a frown, but I know better. Hope walks into the kitchen carrying the little Bible that she takes everywhere. She holds it in front of her when she passes by as if to protect herself from me.

"Hope, don't be silly," I say. "Joy's just mad because I knew Chastity was sick."

"The Word of God says seers are evil," she says. "Now, son of man, set your face against the daughters of your people who prophesy out of their own imagination. Prophesy against them."

"Be quiet, Hope." I turn back toward Joy. "What have you been telling her?"

"Ezekiel thirteen, verse seventeen," Hope finishes, as if I plan to look it up later.

"I didn't tell her anything. Except that our sister is a witch." She grins and sticks a finger in my face. "Hey, wait, Grace, what's that on your nose?"

"Stop it, Joy."

"Yup, pretty sure that's a wart."

"That's it. I'm telling Mama."

"Go ahead, but she hasn't slept all night. She was up until dawn after they operated on Chastity." She crosses her wiry arms back over her chest.

"Operated?"

"Yeah, her appendix burst. I thought you knew."

Hope drops to her knees. "Our Father in

88

Heaven . . ."

I don't say anything more, just walk back upstairs and into my bedroom closet. I shut the door and sit on the board that runs over the ductwork.

"Isaac?"

Yes?

"Was it you? Did you tell me about Chastity's sickness?"

Of course not, Grace.

"Then who did?"

You did.

"What do you mean, I did? I don't tell myself things."

In a way you do.

"That doesn't make sense."

Remember how your mama knew when Hope was going to get run over by the ice-cream truck? She has the Knowing, too.

"Mama does?"

Yes, but she's blocked it. She's afraid of what she might hear if she quiets her mind.

"Quiets her mind? My head is noisy all the time, like there's a whole choir in there. Not just you, Isaac, but a whole chorus of messages all coming in at once."

That's because you're still young. As you get older you'll be able to filter the Knowing better.

"Is that why I have this . . . this extra

89

intuition? Because Mama gave it up and I had to take it over?"

Everyone is offered this gift, but most people turn away from it at a very young age. Truth frightens people. You're one of the brave ones.

"Sometimes *I'm* frightened, Isaac. Daddy doesn't like me knowing things. He thinks it's of the devil. I can see it in his eyes when he looks at me. Even my red hair, like the devil." I hold out a thick wad of hair in case he hasn't noticed before.

He doesn't understand it. He's afraid of what he doesn't know.

"Grace! You're going to be late for church!" Joy hollers up from the bottom of the stairs.

"Coming!" I yell back.

"Isaac, are you still there?"

I'm always here, Grace.

"I wish you could be *here,* like a real brother."

I am.

"Grace, we're leaving without you!"

The front door bangs. I jump up without saying goodbye to my brother but by the time I get downstairs, they're all gone. I grab my Bible off the dining room table and run across the street just in time to make Sunday school before the singing starts. Joy is sitting in the back row with her friend

90

Mari-Beth. When I walk in they both set a pointy paper cup from the drinking fountain dispenser on their heads. Their whispered word bounces around the room like a perfect skipping stone.

Witch.

5

Chastity came home from the hospital the same day as Apollo 11 landed on the moon. Daddy wouldn't let us watch the landing because he says if the Lord wanted us to be on the moon he'd have put us there in the first place. But it's all they've been showing on TV. Even though we didn't get to view it in real time we've seen it play over and over again on the news. At night I like to go to the window and wave. I know the astronauts can't see me, but I figure they need us all rooting for them up there. Plus they still have to find their way back down.

By Saturday Chastity is good as normal, playing with all the coloring books and paper dolls the church families bought her for being sick. Mama says the fever made Chastity delirious so she doesn't remember much about the night she went to the hospital. Daddy remembers. He hasn't spoken more than two words to me since

Chas got sick. I catch him staring at me from time to time. Sometimes he looks away, other times he stares me down until I look away. In my mind I try to will him to smile, but it never works. His thin lips run across his jaw straight as the ironed crease in Joy's blue jeans. He thinks I'm afraid of him. I'm more afraid of the not-him, that person he becomes when he's around me.

Daddy isn't the only one being weird. Ever since she got back, Chastity and Joy have been acting all buddy-buddy. This is just fine by me. We don't like the same things, anyway. Take, for instance, peanut butter. I never get tired of it but Joy and Chastity can't stand it. The two of them wrinkle their noses when they walk into the kitchen just as I stuff the last bite of a PJ sandwich into my mouth.

"Bet you wish you hadn't spent your allowance already," Joy says, licking a Slo Poke sucker.

When I ignore her remark she leans forward with her elbows on the table and her skinny hind end pointing up in the air. "Hey, Grace, what if you were able to get money for more candy?"

"I'm not doing your chores, Joy."

"You don't have to do anything. Well . . . not *much.*" She turns toward Chastity and they make big eyes at each other. I don't like the looks of this at all.

Chastity takes a delicate lick of her sucker, then smacks her perfect lips. "We got an idea. A really good one."

"Yeah," adds Joy. "You've got something people need, Grace. You're special."

Chastity perches on her knees across the table from me. *"Special,"* she echoes.

I'm not about to fall for their tricks.

"What are you talking about? You mean because I'm a . . ." I pause just the right amount of time, then leap out of my chair and plunge my head toward them. *"Witch!"*

They both yelp. Chastity's Slo Poke slides across her cheek, leaving a trail of caramel from her mouth to her ear. I burst out laughing. She opens her mouth to holler, but Joy puts her hand over Chastity's face and stares back at me.

"Yeah, Grace," she says. "Because you're a witch. But not a bad witch. A *good* witch, right?" She tilts her head to one side, her right hand still cupped over our sister's mouth. Maybe it's stuck there. "One who can help people," she adds.

"What are you getting at, Joy? I don't trust you."

I swipe a dab of peanut butter off my plate with my finger and stick it in my mouth, just to bug them.

"We could set up a booth. Kids come to you with questions and you give them the answers in exchange for a quarter. It'd be fun. And it would help people, Grace."

Joy slowly removes her hand from Chastity's mouth and gives her a *stay quiet or else* look. Chastity pads over to the sink and cleans her face with a dishcloth before sitting back down and smiling sweetly at me. I don't trust them. The two of them being so nice, it doesn't feel right. Not one bit.

"I can't. It's not right to make money like that. Besides, Daddy would blow a fuse. You know how he feels about . . ."

"He wouldn't have to know, Grace. This is your chance to prove you have a good thing — what is it you call it?" She pauses to glance at Chastity, then looks back at me. "The *Knowing,* right? You know things that can help people. Like how you helped Chastity." She drapes her arm around Chastity's shoulder and pulls her close. They are downright pathetic.

"You know it's not something I would do for money," I say.

"The money is to sort out the people who really need you. Otherwise we'd have to help everybody. Remember how tired Jesus got when people found out he could heal

95

others? It'll be a secret club. I'll set up everything. All you have to do is, well, whatever it is you do."

I want to believe her, and the way she puts it I feel myself start to bend a little. "I don't know, Joy. It still doesn't sound right."

She moves to my side of the table and rests her hands on my shoulders, turning me toward her. "I'm sorry I called you a witch. I didn't realize how special you are."

I look over at Chastity, who is nodding like a dashboard bobblehead.

Joy squeezes my shoulders. "You don't have to do anything but show up when we're ready for the first club meeting. We'll hold it in the loft."

"No!" I say. "Not there."

"All right, all right. Not there. Whatever you say. We'll find another place. Okay?"

I don't answer.

"Okay, Grace?"

"Okay," I hear myself say. But even as I say it, it's like someone else is speaking the words.

I finish up the dishes, then follow the sound of the piano to the living room. Mama is practicing a song called "My God Is Real" for church tomorrow. I've heard it before on her Mahalia Jackson record. This is the first time Mama's tried it out for church. She sings the song a bit different than the record, but just like the hi-fi version it gives me goose bumps. When she gets to the part about his love being like pure gold I nearly start crying.

Mama stops and frowns at me. "That bad?"

"Oh no, Mama. It's that good!"

She closes the lid on our old upright piano. "It'll sound better with the proper accompanist."

Mama seems more like her old self today. Her cheeks are flushed and her shoulders are back, like she's about to open wings behind her. Singing seems to make Mama remember herself.

"You sound great, Mama. You always do. Better than the radio."

She stacks the sheet music into a neat pile on her lap and smiles. "I sang on the radio once."

"You did?"

"I did. It was the college radio station where your daddy and I met. They ran a singing contest and I won."

She gets a faraway look and I worry I'll lose her to that place she goes when she drinks her morning coffee, but she shakes her head and smiles. "That was another life.

97

This is a better one."

"Really?"

Mama holds her arm out and I sit next to her on the bench. She wraps herself around me and kisses the top of my head. "Really," she says.

I hold still as a statue, not wanting to move, not ever. I suddenly understand why that song makes me want to cry. Mama's love feels like pure gold.

The back door slams. "Izzy?" That's what Daddy calls Mama when he's in a good mood.

She tucks her sheet music into the piano bench and I follow her into the kitchen.

"There you are," he says. He kisses her on the cheek. "Grace, go round up your sisters. I've got a surprise for all of you."

Uh-oh. His last surprise, the one where he decided to use ketchup instead of tomato sauce on spaghetti, didn't go over too well. But it's the longest sentence he's spoken to me in weeks, which leaves me speechless and a bit dazed. Maybe he's finally forgiven me for knowing what I shouldn't have known about Chastity being so sick.

"Get going," he says to me, then whispers into Mama's ear and she smiles.

I find Chas and Joy in the driveway racing grasshoppers. Chastity flings her bug in the air just as I reach them.

"Ew, it spit on me!" She wipes her hands on Joy's pedal pushers.

"Hey!" Joy says.

"Daddy wants you both in the kitchen right now," I say.

Joy slips our little sister's dime into her own pocket. "I win!"

I run upstairs and stand in Hope's doorway. She's working on a Popsicle stick replica of Noah's ark. I wait for her to gently glue a stick to the roof so I don't startle her. "You need to get downstairs." She knows by the way I say it she'd better come.

Mama is waiting by herself in the kitchen when we get there. "Your daddy went to get something. He'll be right back."

"Somebody get the door!" he yells from the front porch.

I run to help and can't believe what I find. Daddy's arms are full, right up to his face, with toys and games. When I open the door he rushes to the kitchen and drops the whole pile on the table. None of us is brave enough to make the first move in case these are for a church family or missionaries. Daddy grabs a noisy round tin of Chinese checkers and holds it up. He waits until the marbles stop rattling.

"These are all to share," he says. "No

99

fighting, you hear?" He pulls a Bible trivia game from the pile and hands it to Hope. She clutches it to her chest.

Joy slides a Parcheesi game from the bottom. "What's the occasion?"

"Why do I need an occasion to treat my girls?" He slips a box from his pocket into Mama's hands. "Especially my best girl."

Mama flips open the lid and grins like a little kid. Daddy pulls a sparkly blue necklace from the box and drapes it around her slender neck, latching the clasp in the back. She fingers it with one hand, smiling. "We can't really afford this," she says.

"We got our tax refund. Apparently I overpaid last year. I wanted to do something nice for my family," he says.

I pluck a deck of Old Maid cards from the top of the stack. "Who wants to play?"

Before anyone can answer Daddy butts in. "Wait. There's one more thing." He holds up a set of keys. "I bought us a new set of wheels."

We all race to the window to find a green Volkswagen bus in the driveway. It's not new, but it's new to us. And way better than our rusty old station wagon. When Mama raises her eyebrows he pats her protruding belly.

"We're going to need more room," he

says. "It's only got thirty thousand miles on it and I got a clergy discount from the dealer. He said these things go and go forever."

Mama shakes her head. "I don't know, Henry."

"Who wants to go for a spin?" he says, leading Mama by the hand.

"I do, I do!" we all say at once.

When all six of us are finally settled into the bus, Daddy backs out of the driveway. The engine reminds me of our lawn mower. Daddy honks at Harold Weaver when we pass our church. The horn sounds more like the roadrunner cartoon than a car and we all giggle. Mr. Weaver waves from his ladder, where he's painting the window trim, but I don't think he recognizes us. To tell you the truth I hardly recognize us either, this happy family all together, nobody quarreling, our parents giddy as ducks in water.

6

Joy appears at the end of my bed the following Saturday while I'm working on my math homework. Her white Keds have grass stains on them, and one of the laces has broken off so the bow is tinier than the other. Her arms are stained with Magic Marker.

"We're ready for you, Grace," she says.

I add another set of teeth marks to my pencil before answering. "I decided I don't want to do it. It doesn't feel right."

"What? You can't let all those kids down now. They're counting on you. Besides, some of them already paid their money."

"How much?"

"Twenty-five cents each."

"How many kids?"

"Eight so far."

"Two bucks already?" Maybe this isn't such a bad idea. After all, it *is* to help people.

"Well, I get half for being your agent," she says. "You and Chastity split the rest."

"That's not fair! I'm doing all the work!"

Joy sits on the edge of the bed and gently takes the math book out of my hand. "Grace, we're not doing this for the money, remember? We're doing it to help people."

"It seems like you're the one getting the most help."

I reach for my book, but she sets it on the floor and kicks it under the bed.

I sigh. "Why does Chastity get so much?"

"To keep her quiet. If she tells we can't help anybody, can we?"

"What about Hope?"

"She rode along with Daddy to call on people at the nursing home."

When I don't move Joy taps her foot impatiently. "Look, Grace. You already agreed to it. Besides, I think you're going to like what we have in store for you." She grabs my arm and pulls me off the bed.

"All right, I'm coming!" I say.

As we round the corner behind the barn I can hardly believe my eyes. Joy has outdone herself this time. She and Chastity must have dragged a refrigerator box home from the hardware store. They painted it all swirly with markers and cut a square out for a window. A hand-lettered cardboard sign hangs above the opening:

AMAZING GRACE!
Fortunes Told: Twenty-Five Cents

Joy hands me Daddy's paisley bathrobe and a blue bath towel.

"What am I supposed to do with these?"

"Wrap the towel around your head. You know, like a gypsy fortune-teller. The robe will make you look more authentic. Here, I'll help you."

I stick my arms into the sleeves and Joy ties the belt at my waist. There's a foot of leftover robe puddled on the ground. She wraps my hair in the towel and clips it with a brooch from Mama's jewelry box, then snaps two earrings with silver balls dangling from them onto my ears.

"Ow!"

"Sorry, Grace." She takes a step back. "You look great!"

"I feel stupid."

Chastity runs toward us from around the side of the barn, wearing a yellow jumper and white sandals. "Wow! You look like a real gypsy," she says.

Joy shoves a kitchen stool under my rear end, then picks up the refrigerator box and drops it over my head so the window is in front of my face. She claps her hands together and squeals.

"Perfect!"

"I feel ridiculous." The words echo against the cardboard walls of my tall, dark room.

"You'll get used to it, *Amazing* Grace."

I have to admit I like the way that sounds.

Chastity bounces up and down, her blond pigtails flouncing behind her. "Here come the first two kids!"

Joy leans in close to my face. "Okay, Grace. Just be yourself. Except with, you know, a little flair, okay?" She winks at me and straightens my turban. "You really do look good," she adds.

Doug Lewis is first in line. Joy takes his quarter and tells him he can ask one question. He strolls up to the window, looking corny as all get-out with ears that stick straight out from a head that's too big for his body. Sort of like if Charlie Brown had a homely brother.

"Hi, Grace," he says.

"Hi, Doug."

"You look neato."

"Thanks."

"So is it true you can tell the future?"

"Sometimes. If you really want me to, that is. What do you want to know?"

Doug kicks at the dirt. "Well" — he drops his voice to a whisper — "I want to know if I'm going to marry Sheila Metzloff."

I swallow hard. Sheila Metzloff is fourteen, two years older than Doug, and a long ways out of his range in the looks department. He's smarter, but nowhere near smart enough to convince Sheila to marry him.

"You sure that's what you wanna know?"

He lowers his head and kicks some more. "Yeah, that's it. That's what I paid my money for. And you don't get to tell anybody what I asked, either. Joy promised."

"Okay," I say.

I close my eyes and think about Doug. I picture him as a man in an office with wood paneling. On his desk sits a photograph of a woman and two little girls. I squinch my eyes tighter to see the woman's face. It's not Sheila but amazingly, she's even prettier. She's looking up at grown-up Doug, smiling. Her face is glowing.

I open my eyes. "Doug?"

"Yeah?" he says. "Wait. You don't have to tell me. Better not to ruin my day." He starts to turn away.

"Hang on, Doug. Look, you're not going to marry Sheila."

His long face drops about a mile longer.

"But you *are* going to get married to a

pretty lady and have two beautiful children. And guess what?"

"What?" he asks, like he's not sure he wants to hear the answer.

I crook my finger for him to come closer. When he's right in front of me, I cup my hand around his donkey ear and whisper, "They got her ears, Doug. They're beautiful girls."

He backs away slowly, his freckled face flushed and grinning. "Really? You're not just saying that to make me feel better?"

I shake my head.

He smiles and walks off with his hands in his front pockets, his feet practically floating a foot off the ground.

Joy rushes up to me, laughing. "What'd you tell him?"

"Can't say. It's part of the deal."

"Oh, come on. You can tell me, Grace."

"No, I can't. Won't. I promised."

She glances at Doug walking up the street. "Well, whatever it was it sure is good advertising. Ready for another?"

I nod.

"C'mon, Shirley." Joy waves her hand and Shirley Newhouse walks up to the window. Shirley's in Joy's class but looks a lot older. All the boys stare at her because she has the right shape.

"You look silly, Grace," she says when she reaches me.

"I know. Joy's idea."

"Well, it's kind of like getting to play dress-up, I guess."

"Kinda."

"One question," Joy says.

Shirley glares at Joy until she walks away.

"Okay. Here's my question. How big are my boobs going to get before they stop growing?"

I stifle a laugh. I know mine will never grow as big as hers are already.

"And don't you dare —"

"Tell anybody. I know. Don't worry, I won't. I promise."

I look at Shirley's chest, from one pointy side to the other. She doesn't seem to mind. She just looks up at the clouds, snapping her gum. I suppose she's used to it.

"Size thirty-eight double D," I say.

"Shit! Really?"

"Really. And don't say s-h-i-t. It's not nice."

"Well, this is just for fun anyway, isn't it? You can't really tell the future." She pauses, snaps a double bubble.

"You got on a locket," I say. Shirley clasps her hand over the jewelry tucked inside her blue sweater. "And in it," I add, "is a picture of Elvis Presley."

Shirley gasps. "You of the devil, Grace?" Her jaw is going a mile a minute on that stick of Juicy Fruit. "That's what people say."

I slide off the stool and stick my face through the hole in the box. "Whoever says that is a liar! My gift is from God! Just like your bosoms."

She stops chewing. "I believe you, Grace," she says. "I'm sorry. . . ."

"Time's up!" Joy yells. She sure does love being in charge.

Shirley winks at me and strolls off, her full hips swaying like a cradle on greased hinges.

Next is Carol Anne Curtis. She asks about a lost ring, one her grandma gave her, and I tell her it's in her sister's top drawer. She stole it. Carol Anne marches off like a soldier to battle. "I knew it!"

My head is starting to hurt. I feel like I could fall asleep sitting up.

"Joy?"

My sister pokes her head in front of me. "What?"

"I want to quit now. I don't feel very good."

"Just a couple more, Grace. Donny Workman is here and Shari Parker. Then you can take a break, okay?"

"But —"

"It'll only take a minute. C'mon."

She shoves Donny up to the window and tells him to make it snappy. Donny Workman is small for his age — one year under me. I've seen him walking his little sisters to school. His family just moved here last year.

"What do you want to ask, Donny?"

He glances behind him, then peers back at me. "Can I just ask it in my head? I mean, if you're for real, you should know what I'm asking without my saying it, right? Nothing personal, but I don't want your nosy sister to hear."

"I guess so. I can try."

He closes his eyes and holds on to the ragged edge of the cardboard window with his hands. Dirt lines his fingernails. He squints hard, as if this will make it easier for me to get his question, but I'm not hearing it. I reach out and put my hand over his. At first he jerks it away, but then he puts it back, real gentle-like.

Does my daddy love me?

I squeeze Donny's hand to let him know I got it. He opens his eyes and looks at me, blushing.

"Of course your Daddy loves you, Donny. Just because he died doesn't mean he stopped loving you." I say it softly so Joy can't hear. I feel bad for him.

Donny backs up from the window, his mouth hanging open. "What're you talking about? My dad's not dead. He's at home right now. Probably drunk already, but he's home watching the game."

My head is really pounding now. I put my fingers to my temples and rub. "Donny, I'm sorry. I must've got things mixed up. I felt your daddy's love and it was coming from . . . the other side. From heaven."

"You're crazy!"

Donny storms over to Joy and demands his money back. Joy yells at him. He runs past my box and around the side of the barn.

"One more, okay?" Joy hands me a quarter as bait.

"I don't know, Joy. I think I'm too tired. Donny's angry. I'm supposed to be helping people, not upsetting them."

"Oh, don't mind him. His daddy may as well be dead. He's a drunk and he beats Donny's mama. I think he beats Donny, too."

"But his daddy . . . oh, never mind. One more and that's it."

Shari Parker's tiny brown eyes are sunk so deep into her face they almost disappear

111

and her nose is shoved up like a piglet. Some of the kids call her Shari Porker. It's not hot out, but Shari has sweat dripping down both sides of her round face.

"Hey, Grace," she says in her out-of-breath voice.

"Hey, Shari."

"You look pretty."

"Thanks." I want to say so do you, but that would be a lie. "I like your pink blouse," I say instead.

She looks down, which makes her extra chin fold up over the real one.

"What do you want to ask, Shari?"

"Can I ask anything?"

"Sure. As long as it's about you."

"Okay. What's the most exciting thing that will happen to me this year?"

"Wow. That's a good one, Shari. Lemme see."

I close my eyes and concentrate. Joy and Chastity mumble in the background, probably making bad jokes about Shari. Then it gets real quiet. Too quiet. I open my eyes and I'm staring straight at Daddy's belt buckle.

When Daddy lifts the box off me I feel naked on the stool. Joy lied. A line of kids trails all the way out into the field, waiting their turn. When they see Daddy's face turning red as a tomato everybody runs off. All except Shari Parker. Her sweaty face keeps peeking around the edge of the barn, watching everything.

Daddy grabs the towel from my head and yanks the earrings off my ears. He throws them on the ground and orders me to stand up. Joy and Chastity start to sneak off, but Daddy calls them back.

"You both stay right here. You're all in this together."

Daddy looks like he's about to cry. "Now listen to me. What I'm about to tell you is very serious. You girls have opened up a path to the devil and it's up to you to close it. Get on your knees, all of you. I'm going to pray with you."

We drop to our knees in a circle in the dirt behind the barn, Chastity moving to make sure she lands on the towel Daddy threw.

Daddy bows his head. "Our Dear Lord in heaven, we come to you to ask forgiveness for the worst kind of sin: blasphemy against the Almighty God. My own daughters, Lord, children of a minister of the Holy Word, have forsaken You. They've reached into the belly of the earth and called upon the Beast in order to make a few pennies. I'm here to beg Your forgiveness of them and they are here to repent."

He jabs me with his elbow, but no words come. My head still hurts. Daddy elbows me harder.

I clear my throat. "Dear Lord. It's me, Grace, one of your children. I know it was wrong to use my gift to —"

Daddy grabs me by the shoulder. "Gift? That was no gift, do you hear me? What you messed with was the spirit world. Demons playing with you. That is not a gift!"

"But, Daddy —"

"Hush up and pray like I've taught you. Beg the Lord for forgiveness this very moment!"

When I close my eyes again Daddy lets go of me. "Dear Lord. Please forgive me for . . . doing what I know is not right. Help me to keep my body and mind a temple by always listening to the voice inside that reminds me what is right and wrong. And please help everyone to understand I was only trying to help. Amen."

It's the best I can do without disgracing God for the gift I know He's given me. Daddy leaves it alone even though I know he wanted something different. Something more.

To make sure he doesn't start yelling again, Chastity pipes up. "Dear Jesus, please forgive me for helping Grace do a bad thing. Help her not to play with demons anymore."

I flinch but keep my mouth shut and remind myself that this is for Daddy more than for God. God knows me better.

"And help me not to listen to Joy anymore when she comes up with one of her stupid ideas. Amen."

I can feel Joy's anger burning to my left.

"Joy? Your turn." Daddy says it softly like he always does to Joy.

"I'm praying quietly in my heart, Daddy."

Joy's eyes are closed, her hands folded like an angel as she perches on her knees. I roll my eyes and Chastity starts to grin but catches herself. She's mostly mad at me, not Joy.

"Well," Daddy says. "All right then. Just be sure to make it sincere."

He's always so easy on Joy, like she can do no wrong. She's his favorite. My only comfort is that I'm Mama's. She'd never say it outright, but she doesn't have to. I might look like my Daddy's side of the family, but Mama and me are more alike than any of my sisters. I think they know it, too. Probably why they treat me like a rotten apple when their plans go wrong. Like today. Like lots of days.

Daddy closes his eyes again. "I beg of you,

115

Dear Lord, to take pity on these children and hold for them a place on high with our Lord and Savior, Jesus Christ. Listen to their prayers and consider the ignorance of their youth. In His beloved name we pray, amen."

Daddy stands and we start to do the same. He holds up his hand.

"You aren't going anywhere. You're staying right here on your knees in prayer until the sun sets."

Chastity's eyes fly open wide. "But, Daddy, it's only three o'clock!"

"Jesus went into the desert and prayed for forty days and forty nights! The least you can do for Him is to pray until sundown. And there'll be no food until then. Jesus fasted the entire time he was in the desert."

He leaves us there all the livelong day. Every once in a while one of the neighborhood kids sneaks close enough to see us and points and laughs. When Chastity has to pee, she tries to sneak in the house. Daddy chases her back out. Tells her, "Jesus peed in the desert." Chas runs back and gets on her knees next to us. As soon as Daddy is out of earshot she whispers, "Jesus pees?"

I can't help but snicker. "Of course. He was in human form."

"So he pooped, too?"

Joy glances to her left and rolls her eyes. "Shush, Chas."

Chastity goes quiet. After about a minute she pipes up again. "I bet he didn't fart, though."

Eventually Chastity tinkles in the bushes at the edge of the driveway. I do the same thing after I can't wait any longer, but not Joy. She just holds it, like she holds most everything, from money to tears. Her bladder must be about to burst by the time Daddy finally comes out.

"I hope you've been praying," he says. "Because you're going to need God's forgiveness. You will pay everybody back. And each of you will put double that amount in the church offering plate."

I can see Joy doing the math in her head. It will mean no allowance until nearly the end of the year, three months away. I don't think I've ever seen her look so sad.

There's something about being outside alone after dark that clears my head. The fall air is crisp, yet not so cold as to keep you inside. The whole world smells like wet leaves and tree bark, and the moon puts a spell on everything within sight. An owl hunts mice in the meadow behind the barn. Every once in a while he lands in the tree and hoots, "Who cooks for you? Who cooks for you all?" He drags out the word *all,* like a record player that got turned down to slow speed at the end of the song.

Daddy has sworn my sisters and me to secrecy over the whole Amazing Grace thing, as if the entire town won't know by morning. It turns out Donny Workman's daddy, his real daddy, is dead. Apparently Donny went home crying and told his mama what I said. Mr. Workman, who had been drinking beer all day, blurted out, "Well, the little bastard finally found out." At which point Mrs. Workman called Daddy and told him I was an evil girl for telling her little boy that his real daddy had died.

Mr. Workman is actually Donny's uncle. His mama was in love with Francis Workman and they made a baby together. They were going to get married right away, but Francis was killed by a stray bullet in a deerhunting accident. His brother, Dean, the man Donny has always known as his daddy, married his mama to help her out. I guess she figured it was as close as she could get to Donny's daddy, even though Dean is a lot meaner.

When Donny asked me in his head if his daddy still loved him I was getting the answer back from Francis, his real daddy.

And it was so strong I couldn't believe it was wrong. Maybe if Donny had asked out loud I'd have gotten a different answer, although I don't think it would have been a better one. As I look up at the stars I can't help but think about Francis Workman and how much he loves a boy he's never seen, just like I love Isaac, the brother I've never gotten to see.

The grass rustles and I turn toward the barn. At first I think it might be Pippy, but Shari Parker walks quietly into the yard and stands still as a statue.

"You better go, Shari. My daddy's real mad."

"But you never answered my question."

I look at her, round face like the moon, waiting for her quarter's worth of knowledge.

"The most exciting thing to happen to you this year, right?"

She nods, expectantly.

I stand and put my hand on the doorknob. "It just did," I say, and walk back inside.

Lola is my new best friend. She used to homeschool, but her parents decided to send her to public school this year. She's a year older than me. The principal made her start a grade lower because she was behind in math. After word got around about the fortune-telling fiasco most kids have kept their distance from me. I'm not sure if they're afraid of me or afraid of Daddy. Lola hasn't been around long enough to be scared of either of us. On the first day she walked right up to me and said, "I like your hair." And she meant it.

Lola reminds me of a gypsy with her big eyes and thick, brown hair. She's different from the other kids. Sometimes she wears two different-colored socks on purpose. And she brings strange things like yogurt or goat cheese and bean-sprout sandwiches in her lunch. Yesterday when she asked if I wanted to sleep over at her house I was thrilled.

When Daddy said I could go I packed before he could change his mind, even though the sleepover isn't until Friday. I'm so excited I can hardly stand it. I've always loved sleepovers, but this one's special. It's not like staying with one of the church families who take us in from time to time. This is a real girlfriend, someone who invited me because she actually likes me.

Art class is at the end of the day and we're making Indian headbands out of leather with beautiful feathers in different colors. Mrs. Wick usually wears her long, gray hair twisted into a knot that looks like a frosted bun at the nape of her neck. Today two long braids fall down her back. When Glen Garvey complains that only boys are supposed to wear feathers, Mrs. Wick just says, "Hmmmph. All the more reason to make up for it now." The project seems a little babyish for sixth graders, but our teacher says art is supposed to keep us in touch with our inner child. Mrs. Wick is kind of weird.

Lola uses glue to make swirls in her headband that she decorates with glitter. She carefully places each feather and by the time she's done Lola looks like an Indian princess. My headband looks more like it fell off a dirty hippie. The paper kept ripping so it's taped together and the feathers stick out every which way. When nobody is looking I throw it in the trash barrel. Lola must have seen me do it because on our way out of the classroom she takes off her headdress and sets it on my head.

"It looks better on you," she says. Before I can answer she skips out the front doors and climbs up the bus steps.

I start for home proudly wearing my feathered headband until Billy Wolf rides by on his bike and knocks it off my head. I tuck it safely under my arm until I reach our house before putting it back on. I pause near the sewing room, where Mama is making flannel nighties and humming to herself. Every winter we each get a new nightgown. It's one of the few times I don't have to wear Joy's hand-me-downs. I want Mama to notice my headband, but I don't want to disturb her, so I watch quietly from the doorway. Mama has a rhythm to her sewing. She pushes the pedal with her knee and zips the fabric past the needle while chewing on her tongue, which she stows in the side of her cheek. Push, zip, chew all in one sleek motion.

People say Mama looks a little like Veronica Lake. She pins her silky hair back with bobby pins that match the yellow waves. Mama's no actress. But she sure can sing.

Aunt Pearl told me that Mama wanted to be a famous gospel singer before she met Daddy. Daddy says fame breeds pride, which is a sin. Even so, when he watches Billy Graham on the TV it sure looks like he'd love to swap places with him.

Mama's due date is a week away and she looks like if you laid a finger on her apron she'd burst. Her belly has grown so huge she has to let it rest on the chair between her legs. Any day now she might go to the hospital and bring home a baby. I still can't picture it. Every time I look at the bulge beneath her dress I just see it go flat, like air being let out of a balloon.

I move next to Mama and kiss her on the cheek. She smells like sewing machine oil and Tide detergent. I hug her from behind, my hand resting on her big belly. Beneath my palm, I feel my sister move inside the same home that used to be mine and Isaac's. It feels familiar, but different. I suppose when someone new moves in they take over the space, making it their own. But I'm suddenly homesick in a way that makes me want to cry.

"What's wrong?" Mama asks.

I pull my hands away. "Can I have a red-striped gown?"

"Hmmm. Not enough of that material.

123

How about green flowers?"

"Okay. But Chastity isn't getting a red-striped one, is she?"

Mama plucks a straight pin from between her lips and looks up at me. Her face has grown round, just like her belly.

"Of course not, Pocahontas." She grins. "You know I always make yours and hers to match."

"Yeah, I was just checking."

She waits to see if I've got anything else to say; then her knee leans into the pedal and off she goes again.

On Friday the school bus pulls to a stop in front of a shabby two-story farmhouse. Lola nudges me. "This is us," she says.

My mouth must be hanging open because she stands in the aisle with her hands on her hips and says, "Well? Are you coming or not?"

I grab my knapsack from under the seat. "Of course I'm coming."

Lola steps off the bus ahead of me. Two mutts race up the gravel driveway to meet us. Lola reaches down to scratch their scruffy heads. The dogs take turns sniffing my crotch, then trot alongside us as Lola leads me toward the barn. She pauses to pick up a couple of apples from under a tree in the yard and offers me one.

"Here. You feed Demeter and I'll feed Persephone."

Lola stands outside the wooden stall and holds her hand toward a white horse with splotches of black over her hindquarters. A spot near the horse's eye looks like a tear, giving her a sad-faced expression that is at the same time beautiful. Lola presses her cheek against Persephone's nose and strokes her neck as the horse gobbles up the apple.

"I love you, sweetie," she says, and I swear the horse nods.

I'm still clutching my apple when she looks up. "Your turn."

I look at my feet.

"Grace, your hand is shaking. Are you scared?"

She tugs at my wrist but I pull back. Lola looks into my face and tilts her frizzy head toward one shoulder. "You're so pretty, do you know that?"

It's not what I was expecting. And no, I didn't know that. Lately I feel like a chipped plate at a table set for company.

"She won't hurt you." Lola smiles, her full lips pulling back over perfect white teeth. "Trust me," she says.

I let Lola take my arm and she leads me to the shiny black horse in the stall to the right of Persephone. My hand is still trembling, but Lola's touch gives me confidence.

"She's lovely, isn't she?" Lola says.

Demeter looks me straight in the eye as I approach with my outstretched hand.

"Touch her first. With your other hand. Talk to her."

I hesitate.

"Go on," Lola says. "You can do it."

My heart beats in my throat. I've never been so close to an animal this big other than the Blue Rapids Zoo, where there was a steel fence between the animals and me.

"Hi there," I say, and reach out to touch the horse. Her neck feels like warm velvet. I lift my other hand to her mouth and she whinnies softly, then pushes forward so my head is against her throat. I slide my free hand over her mane as she kisses the apple from my palm with her slobbery lips. Her eyes widen and her mouth foams with delight. When she finishes chewing I raise both my arms and hug her neck. I love the earthy smell of her, the firmness of her muscles, the silkiness of her coat. A wave of emotion overtakes me and tears swell over my eyes as I stroke her.

"I know," I whisper. "You're safe now."

I feel Lola's hand on my shoulder. "Are you all right?"

"She was hurt."

"Yeah — pretty bad. We rescued her from the Humane Society. She was terribly abused. Wait. How did you know that?"

I look straight into Lola's face and tell the complete truth. "She told me."

I wait for her to laugh, but she doesn't. Instead, she purses her lips and nods. "Right on," she says.

Lola leads me to an art studio on the other side of the barn. I pause in front of two easels that stand side by side near the doorway.

"I did the one on the left," she says, pointing to a charcoal drawing of a ballet dancer.

"Wow. You're really good."

"It's just a sketch."

"I can't even draw a straight line," I say.

She takes me on a tour of the various art objects, mostly her mama's. The barn is filled with life-size exotic animals painted in exquisite detail, right down to the black-tipped toenails of a skunk. I can't take my eyes off a huge giraffe. Its head is in the rafters.

"How does she do it?"

"She makes them out of papier-mâché," Lola says. "She constructs the frame from chicken wire, then builds layers of skin with

127

newspaper and paste until they're ready to paint."

"I've never seen anything like it."

Lola laughs. "Neither had Sonny and Cher."

"What?"

"Sonny bought one for Cher. They came to an art show where Catherine was exhibiting. They were wearing dark glasses and hats, but Catherine recognized them. She didn't say anything, just acted all natural like they were no different than any other customer. I wish I'd been there."

Lola calls her parents by their first names. I try to picture myself saying, "What would you like for supper, Henry?" It just couldn't happen.

"And they bought one of your mom's sculptures?"

"Yeah, a fruit bat. But then while Cher was looking at other stuff, Sonny asked Catherine to make a zebra for his wife. He paid her five thousand dollars cash on the spot and gave us the address to ship it to. He sent another five thousand when he got it."

"Your mama got ten thousand dollars for making a zebra? You must be rich!"

"No way. It takes her almost a year to finish the big ones. And not many people are looking for a full-sized giraffe to put in their living room, so it's a specialty. But it did pay for this house and forty acres."

"You're lucky," I say. "You make things."

"So are you," she says, turning toward the house. "You know things."

We walk through the back door of Lola's house and into a mudroom strewn with piles of laundry in front of an old washing machine. Clothes dry on a length of twine running from one side of the room to the other. Several barn coats hang from hooks on the plaster walls. Lola kicks off her cowboy boots and wanders into the kitchen. A huge, striped cat sits on the countertop, eating kibble out of a homemade ceramic bowl. Lola scoops him up in her arms and motions for me to follow her.

The house looks like it's been a work in progress from the time the first nail was sunk. It has one big room separated by wooden beams because her parents knocked out most of the inside walls. A woodstove squats in the corner with chairs gathered around as if patiently waiting for the latest gossip. The dining room table stands only knee-high after somebody sawed off the legs. It's set with mismatched plates and surrounded by colorful sitting pillows. A window seat heaped with handmade afghans looks out over the horse pasture.

Lola's house feels like an art museum. An old beat-up couch with a patchwork quilt slung over the back slouches in the corner of the living area. Shelves line every wall, filled with books, papier-mâché puppets, clay pots, sculptures, handmade beads, and various other art projects. Every patch of wall is covered in watercolor paintings and pencil sketches. Some of the figures are naked. The rest of the space is absorbed by a black grand piano.

The Beatles' "Come Together" bursts out of two speakers hanging near the ceiling, and it sounds like the band is right in the room with us. Lola starts dancing across the room, her long braid whipping around like a spinning maypole. A woman with wild hair just like Lola's, except for a few gray streaks running through it, dances out of a side bedroom and playfully joins Lola. I'm sure this is her mama, but I can hardly believe it. She's so beautiful and she's like a hippie or something.

Lola's mama sees me staring and grabs my hand, pulling me into their dance. I feel awkward and self-conscious.

"You must be Grace. I'm Catherine," she says.

Daddy preaches that dancing is a sin, but

after a few whirls around the living room with Lola and her mama I can't help myself. The beat is wonderful and before I know it I'm stomping around the room with my eyes closed, forgetting that Jesus is watching. When the third song ends the three of us dance into Mrs. Purdy's bedroom. Lola pulls down the shade on the only window, which has a picture of blue mountains painted on it. She flips on a long light in a tube and suddenly barely-there designs jump to life, glowing from every wall. We flop onto the fur-covered bed and stare at the ceiling, which is painted with stars, planets, and a moon.

When the mattress sloshes beneath us my eyes pop wide open. Lola responds by lifting up her butt and letting it fall, sending me rolling into Mrs. Purdy, who giggles hysterically.

"A water bed!" I say.

Lola and her mama look at each other, then jump off the bed and start pushing on the mattress from either side, creating waves.

"Close your eyes, Grace," Mrs. Purdy whispers.

I force my lids shut and let my body roll with the water. Joni Mitchell purrs in the next room. The flannel sheet is warm beneath me. It feels like taking a bath without getting wet, except you don't have to worry about slipping under the surface if you fall asleep. I could just about drown in this place, this magical world of sleeping on water and glowing pictures and papier-mâché animals the size of life.

For dinner we eat Chinese egg rolls and Oriental noodles served with chopsticks instead of silverware. Nobody laughs when my food keeps falling off the sticks. I finally give up and ask for a fork. Lola's six-year-old sister, Brandy, fetches one from the kitchen. She and her twin brother, Buddy, talk like grown-ups because Lola's parents have never used baby talk with their kids.

Lola's daddy has curly, brown hair and a bushy mustache. He waves his hands when I call him Mr. Purdy. "No, no, Grace. Call me John," he says.

Mrs. Purdy also insists I call her by her first name. I tell them it's disrespectful and that my parents wouldn't like it one bit.

"We call you by your first name. Is that disrespectful, Grace? Would you prefer we call you Miss Carter?"

Lola grins at me, waiting for my answer.

I giggle. "No," I say.

"Well, it's settled then." He picks up his

chopsticks and delicately plucks a single noodle off his plate. Then he does what I sometimes do with spaghetti. He slurps until the end hits him in the nose. It's as if the kids are the adults and the grown-ups forgot to stop being kids in this house.

After dinner we make peanut butter fudge, then sit around the woodstove with our stockinged feet in each other's laps. Catherine moves to the piano and plays "Scarborough Fair." I like the way she plays it even more than Simon & Garfunkel's version. I tell her that the way she plays the song gives it little side melodies.

"Well, that would be the artist in me, I guess. Always having to add my own grace notes to make the song my own."

"Grace notes?"

She chuckles and calls me over to the piano. "See these, Grace?" She points to a piece of music on the stand. "Those are extra notes the composer added to embellish the piece. Make it fancier. Not everyone pays attention to them. For me the music would be flat without those notes. Of course, I also add some of my own."

As I lean over Lola's mama I wonder if this is what Isaac has been trying to explain to me all these years. He says the Knowing is simply a deep awareness. Does everyone smell the hint of lavender in Catherine's hair? They would if they were paying attention. They'd hear the extra notes and they'd see hidden pictures on the walls and they'd feel their mother's heartbeat long after they were born into this world.

Lola yawns. "I'm pooped. Ready for bed, Grace?"

I follow her upstairs to a room with a quilt-covered mattress on the floor surrounded by walls covered in graffiti. I decide right then and there I'm going to be a mom who makes finger and toe paintings with her children while listening to records on a real stereo. We'll visit national parks and go fishing on Sundays. We'll draw on the walls. I'll marry someone like John and we'll rock ourselves to sleep on a water bed with a leopard bedspread.

I wake from a dream about riding a paper giraffe to find my head in Lola's armpit. The sunlight trickling in through the window creates a star pattern on the curtain. Even the light in this house is artistic. One of the dogs, a floppy-eared mongrel named Chewie, is asleep on my leg. Downstairs John loads logs into the stove while Catherine hums in the kitchen. I feel a little guilty for thinking it, but boy do I ever wish I could trade places with Lola.

Her family is like something out of the movies, full of adventures and creativity. While I'm memorizing Bible verses they're learning lines to perform plays for each other. When I'm getting ready to go to church, they're getting ready to go to an art museum or a movie. Even their chores are more fun. I'd much rather take care of animals than iron choir robes or sort church bulletins. Somehow I can't picture Lola coloring pictures of disciples. She can probably draw better than the people who make the Sunday school papers.

When Lola stretches and moans I can see her breath. "I gotta go feed the horses." She pulls a sweater over her head and climbs into faded blue jeans, stuffing her bare feet into mismatched socks. "You can sleep a little longer if you want."

I wait until the house starts to warm before getting up. After a late breakfast of whole grain waffles and fresh-squeezed orange juice, Lola's daddy offers to give me a ride back to town. I don't want to go yet but I don't want to be rude, either. They probably can't afford gas for two trips.

Lola opens the front door of the truck and gives me a hug. "See you on Monday!"

I feel like crying. "See you then," I say, in

135

my most cheerful voice.

As Mr. Purdy backs out of the driveway, Catherine walks toward her studio wearing a fringed leather jacket and a red bandanna on her head. In the distance, Demeter and Persephone chase each other along the fence, whinnying. By the time we pull away I've already decided Lola and I will be friends forever.

When I get home Joy takes one whiff of me and says, "Pee-yew! You stink!"

I hold a few strands of hair under my nose and breathe in wood smoke to remind myself it wasn't a dream.

"I do not."

"You do too. I'm telling Daddy not to let you stay at that hippie house again."

"You don't know anything! They're not hippies, they're artists."

"Yeah, well, they're stinking artists. Go take a bath."

I walk away wishing Maxwell's Silver Hammer would go bang-bang on her head.

8

Daddy has invited one of the deacons and his wife over for dinner tonight. Mr. Franks teaches Sunday school, and Mrs. Franks leads the children's choir. We're sitting at the table eating pork chops when all of a sudden I hear milk spilling, but when I look around the table everybody's glass is still upright. Mama stands up real calm-like and says, "Well, my water broke."

Next thing everybody's running around getting Mama's hospital bag and talking excitedly about the Big Event. I crawl under the table and run my hand over the wet spot on the rug. When I lift my fingers to my nose they smell like puppy breath.

"Grace, get out from under there!" Daddy yells.

I don't move because I know he's focused on Mama. As I watch her swollen feet walk out the front door I feel like crying, but I'm not sure why.

First thing in the morning Daddy calls the four of us girls downstairs to the kitchen. I'm pretty sure we're all wondering what name he's gone and picked this time, but none of us is brave enough to bring it up. He stands across the table in a wrinkled shirt looking like he was run over by a tractor. I've never seen him look so tired. I'm more used to his huge presence, that voice booming down from the pulpit like thunder. Even when we're home I see him as the next one down under God. Today is the first time he looks just like anyone's daddy.

I already know what he's going to say. Mama isn't coming home with any baby.

"Your mama's okay," he starts. "She'll be out of the hospital in a few days. But your little sister isn't strong enough. There's a tiny hole in her heart and they have to wait to see if it will close."

Chastity grabs a box of Rice Krispies from the middle of the table and fills her bowl, seemingly unfazed by the weight of Daddy's news. A tear runs down Hope's pale face. She clasps her hands together and starts praying quietly. Joy runs back upstairs. I walk up to Daddy and put my arms as far around his waist as they'll reach, which is only about halfway. He smells like sweat mixed with Old Spice.

Daddy pats my head and says, "Okay, Grace. Go get ready for school now."

His words fall soft on me, like for a minute he's forgotten which one I am. I go to my closet to get dressed, but it feels so good in there I just sit down in my usual spot. He's here, too. I can feel him.

"Isaac?"

Yes?

"Why is the baby sick?"

It's part of her purpose.

I chew on his answer while I fidget with the lacy hem of one of Chastity's dresses hanging from the rod.

"I don't get it. Her purpose is to be sick?"

Partly, yes.

"What good is that? Living in that wonderful place all those months and then being born sick. She must be so disappointed."

No, Grace. She's content.

"Content? But Mama and Daddy will be so sad!"

I know. But they're learning a lot from this experience. Have you ever thought about how many parents of sick children your mama and daddy have consoled?

"No."

Now they can empathize with those people.

139

"Empathize?"

It means to be able to know how something feels. How someone else feels.

"Well I think that's pretty stupid. I feel sorry for Hope getting run over, but I don't want to be hit by an ice-cream truck just so I can empathize with her."

It's much more complicated than that. Mama doesn't know it, but she is prepared for this experience. And so are you.

"Mama still hasn't gotten over losing you! And now she has a sick baby, not to mention another girl."

I'm sorry this is so hard for you.

"Not as hard as it is for Mama. I think she'd be up to trading in that feeling for other mamas in exchange for having a healthy baby. A healthy *boy* baby."

Isaac sighs in my head.

"Is that why you died? So Mama could empathize with mothers of dead babies?"

I died because there was a change of plans.

"Whose plans? Yours?"

My plans are part of a much bigger plan. Just as yours are.

"I plan to help people so they don't have to suffer like Mama. I want to be a nurse."

I think that's great, Grace. It fits. There's a smile in his voice.

"Fits where?"

Into the big picture. The bigger plan.

"I bet you're going to tell me that I don't get to know what that plan is."

In time you will.

"I hate time. I just want to know now."

You already understand more than most people.

"You mean my knowing about things?"

It's a beautiful gift. Without it we wouldn't be able to talk like this.

"I'm glad we can talk but I wish you could just be here, sitting next to me."

I am.

I uncurl my finger from the bow on the back of Chastity's white pinafore and push my bangs out of my eyes. "I gotta go to school."

You know where to find me if you need to talk some more.

"Yeah, probably sitting on some cloud eating cotton candy."

Isaac laughs. I blow a kiss to the air and hope it lands on my brother. "Bye, Isaac."

Bye, Grace.

I rest my hand on the shelf next to me. Even though the furnace is off it feels warm, like someone's been sitting there. The closet door opens and for a moment I think Isaac did it until I see Daddy standing in the doorway.

"Who are you talking to in there?"

"Just myself," I say.

"You're lying. Do you know where liars go?"

"Yes."

Daddy jerks me out of the closet. He marches back and pulls all the dresses off the rod and throws them on the floor. He kicks every single shoe out into the room. Some of them fly under the bed.

"I've got enough on my hands without this nonsense. No more!" he yells. "Do you hear me? No more!"

I know better than to speak up, so I just try to stay out of his path. The next words out of his mouth devastate me.

"I'm calling off your baptism next summer, Grace. You're not ready."

"Daddy, no!" I burst into tears. I've been counting down the months until my baptism, which happens the summer when you're twelve. Partly because I want God's blessing, but mostly because I want Daddy's. Maybe that water really does turn holy. Maybe it will wash me clean of everything people say about me, once and for all.

Daddy ignores me. He stomps out of the room and down the hall, muttering under his breath. I carefully rehang Chastity's dresses and line her shoes neatly underneath them. I store my own shoes under my side of the bed and hang my three dresses on the hook on the back of the bedroom door. Before going downstairs, I peek my head inside the closet.

"Isaac?"

Nothing. I hope Daddy hasn't scared him away.

On the way to school I concentrate on Mama and my baby sister. In my mind that little baby looks perfect, like a brand-new baby doll. I see a nurse bend over her tiny face, breathing into her mouth until the doctor says to give up and walks out of the room. But the nurse keeps going because there's no reason for the little girl not to be alive. Then suddenly the baby gasps a deep breath and wails. Both Mama and the nurse cry out loud together. When the doctor comes running back the two women glare at him meaner than Billy Wolf's worst Evil Eye.

Lola is waiting for me outside our classroom when I walk down the hall, a fur wrap draped over her shoulders. When she sees my face her mouth drops to match mine. "What's wrong?"

"Mama had the baby. Another girl."

"You're upset you didn't get a brother?"

143

"No, not at all. I knew it was going to be a girl."

"Oh yeah. Stupid me. Of course you knew." She cocks her head to one side. "Then why do you look so sad?"

"She's sick. Something about her heart."

Lola grabs me in a hug. "Oh, I'm sorry!" She pulls back and grips my shoulders. "She'll be okay, right?"

"I don't know."

"But . . ."

"I don't know everything, Lola. Just some stuff."

Lola adjusts her wrap and I suddenly realize it's an actual bear skin. From a real bear. The front leg parts hang over her shoulder as if he's hitching a piggyback ride. The hood is actually part of the head. I reach out to pet it and this makes her smile.

"Somebody traded it for one of Catherine's sculptures."

My hand drops. "Poor baby," I say. My eyes well up but we both know it's not for the bear.

Mama's on the sofa when I get home from school on Thursday. All you have to do is take one look at her and it's obvious she has a hole in her heart to match my new baby sister's. No matter what Isaac says, it doesn't seem like this is a good lesson for Mama. She is just plain sad. Something else is different about her, too — a streak of irritability I've never seen in her before. When Daddy comes in and kneels beside her to pray she shoos him away. For once he is speechless.

Daddy wanted to name the baby Faith, but Mama would have none of it. While Daddy was away from the hospital Mama called for the nurse and filled out the birth certificate herself. Marilyn Elizabeth Carter is what she wrote on that piece of paper. My sister is named after a movie star and a queen. I think God gave Mama that name because Marilyn's going to get better and she's going to become someone important. And it will take a lot more than faith to get her there.

I sit on the floor by Mama's feet with my head resting against her legs. Tears run down her face, soaking the pillowcase one drop at a time. I want to tell her I can empathize with her, that I know how she feels, but I don't. Deep inside I know that creating a child, carrying her, and then facing the possibility of losing her is different from having your brother die, even your twin. Not worse or easier. Just different in the way that love feels when it's taken from you.

9

Marilyn lives at a special hospital for babies with health problems. Aunt Pearl is coming from Mississippi to stay with us for a spell, until Mama gets better. Besides being tired out from childbirth, Mama has something called baby blues. It means she's not feeling the excitement about having a new child, partly because the baby's sick and partly because of mixed-up hormones. She also sleeps a lot on account of her sadness. Daddy said the doctor warned it could take a long time to get better because of how many babies she's had. It's already been a month.

I begged Daddy to let me come along to fetch Aunt Pearl from the bus station. It's not really a bus station. Ralph's Car Service has a counter where you can buy tickets, and there's a chair next to the pop machine to wait for the bus. According to Daddy, Ralph is a heathen because he works on

Sundays. I like Ralph. His hands are usually black from car grease. His face, too, which makes his eyes look really white. Whenever I buy a bottle of pop he pries the cap off for me. I want to remind Daddy that Sunday is the day he works the hardest, but I don't think this is a good thing to point out after he's let me come with him to pick up Aunt Pearl.

Daddy uses the bathroom at Ralph's even though he just went at home. I know it's so he can leave religious tracts on the back of the toilet because Ralph won't let him put any up in the shop. When he comes out he motions me to follow him outside, where we sit on a bench that faces the road. Daddy buries his head in a newspaper to pass the time. I try to read the back page, but every time he shakes it out I lose my place. I study the buttons on his coat instead. They look like they'll bust right off if he eats as much as a peanut. Mama used to scold him about eating too much gravy. I don't think she cares now. The pile of mending in the laundry room has outgrown two baskets.

It's been three years since we took a trip in our station wagon to visit Daddy's family in Mississippi. Aunt Pearl is a widow who lost her husband in the war. She lives with her daughter Sue Ellen, Sue Ellen's husband, Larry, and their two boys. Our whole family stayed in their den, which is bigger than our entire first floor. Mama and Daddy slept on the pullout sofa while we girls camped on their soft carpet.

Mama disappeared in the middle of our second night there. I woke when I overheard Daddy and Aunt Pearl whispering in the kitchen. I slipped out of my blankets and hid next to the doorway.

"I never should have brought her back here," I heard Daddy say.

"You pulled her out of here too quick last time. She wasn't ready."

"Mind your own business, Pearl. The Lord called me to get back to my church and I followed His call."

"Twasn't the Lord talkin' and you know it. It was you thinking you could run away from the pain of losing your —"

"That's enough, Pearl! I'm going out to look for her."

The kitchen door slammed; then our car started up and backed out of the driveway. When the headlights shone in my face I pulled back behind the wall.

Aunt Pearl looked over in my direction. "That you, Grace?"

I stepped sheepishly into the light.

"Thought so. What you doin' up this late?"

149

"Something's wrong," I said.

Aunt Pearl sat at the kitchen table with her hands folded in front of her. She motioned for me to come over. I climbed into her lap and rested my head against her pillowy bosom.

"Nothing's wrong, shoog. Your mama just needed a little fresh air, that's all."

"I think she needed to go visit Isaac."

Aunt Pearl turned me around to face her. Bald spots showed through her bobby-pinned curls, like a bunch of Xs marking all the spots. "Oh, goodness no, Grace. Your mama wouldn't go to the cemetery in the middle of the —"

"That's where she is," I said.

The front bobby pins backed up when she raised her eyebrows. "How do you know that, child? Did she tell you?"

I shook my head.

Aunt Pearl pulled me against her, stroking my hair. "Don't you worry, Grace. Your mama's fine. She's just fine. Your daddy will find her."

Aunt Pearl made a pot of tea and we sat at the kitchen table sipping and looking toward the window over the next hour. Daddy finally came back with Mama about the time I licked the last bit of honey from my spoon. He'd found her sitting by Isaac's grave with a blanket draped over the spot where he was buried. We drove back home to Michigan the next day. Daddy wouldn't even talk to Aunt Pearl except to say good-bye before he rolled up his window and drove off. The last time I saw her she was standing in the driveway like a broken statue.

A motor sounds in the distance, pulling me out of my memories and back to Cherry Hill. I shield my eyes, straining to see up the road. When light flashes off the silver side of the bus I about jump out of my skin with excitement.

"Here it comes, Daddy!"

I wave madly at the bus driver in case he doesn't know to stop and leave Aunt Pearl. Daddy peers over the top of his paper, then folds it up real slow. The brakes make a sound like a roomful of teachers shushing noisy students as the bus rolls to a stop. I can see people moving around in the aisles but not well enough to make out faces because the windows are tinted dark.

When the door finally opens I recognize her feet first. Aunt Pearl wears slippers everywhere she goes. These ones are sky blue with black trim and a swirly design on the toe, the kind Orientals wear, though I personally have never seen an Oriental.

Aunt Pearl is round like Daddy but not much taller than me. She rocks back and forth when she walks, which makes her slippers lean to the outside. She takes the black-rubbered stairs one at a time, saying, "Lordy, Lordy," as if it'll take a miracle to get to the bottom step.

As soon as she hits the sidewalk she looks at me and grins, her front gold tooth sparkling like a little star. "Come here, shoog," she says, and opens her arms.

I bury myself in her hug. She smells like caramel corn. I don't want to let go, but when I do I notice a few Cracker Jacks stuck to her brown furry collar. She looks where I'm looking and flicks them off, after which she reaches into her huge flowered bag and hands me an unopened box of them. "Here you go, SweePea."

I thank her and wait to see if Daddy will tell me I'll spoil my supper, but he's busy getting Aunt Pearl's suitcases out of the side of the Greyhound bus.

"Hank, put those bags down and give your sister a hug."

Daddy stays put, holding her flowered luggage in both hands. She walks up and squeezes him real hard then lays her hand on his cheek. "You're still just as cute as when you were a baby," she says, which makes Daddy blush.

"Go on, Pearl," he says. "You don't remember when I was a baby."

"Oh yes I do. Changed your diapers many a time, ya little poopsqueak."

I laugh out loud hearing this, but Daddy glares at her. "Enough funny business," he says, and starts walking toward the car. "And don't call me Hank."

Aunt Pearl winks at me. "Never could take much ribbin'," she whispers. It feels good to be in on somebody's secret for once, instead of being the secret itself.

I wait in the Volkswagen while Daddy and Aunt Pearl talk in private on the sidewalk. Their conversation is hushed, but each word comes out in a huff of hot breath that turns into steam in front of their faces. Behind them, Ralph's tow truck pulls onto the lot with a brown car hanging from the back. The lady in the front seat of the truck is Rosalie Cutler's mama. Rosalie is one grade under me even though we're the same age. She had to repeat the second grade because she wrote her letters backward. Doing second grade over didn't help. She still writes backward letters.

Rosalie's mama climbs down from the truck all ladylike, a hard thing to do in heels. Mrs. Cutler is what they call a nervous person. Maybe because of Rosalie. Or maybe because she lost her husband to cancer and she's afraid of losing other things. She clutches her purse in front of her real tight as if somebody might try to take it. Halfway across the lot she nearly slips on an icy puddle. When Ralph reaches out to steady her Mrs. Cutler pulls away.

Aunt Pearl raises her eyebrows when she sees our Volkswagen, but Daddy gives her The Look so she keeps quiet about it. They get in the front seats and slam their doors at the same time. We wait while Daddy grinds the gears looking for the right one before he finally finds it. When he pulls onto the road I dig past the sticky popcorn and peanuts for my free surprise at the bottom of the box. Inside the package is a tiny magnifying glass. When I hold it over my fingertips the details remind me of the footprints on Marilyn's birth certificate we hung in the nursery. It seems like you could follow the swirls forever trying to get to the center and never find it.

Aunt Pearl leans sideways to look at me through the rearview mirror. "I think you've grown a full foot since I last saw you."

It's more like a foot and a half, but I don't want her to think I'm bragging since she's such a short person. I just grin at her and pop another caramel corn into my mouth.

Mama's on the sofa, right where we left her. She sits up when we walk in, but the top half of her body leans to the left and I worry she might tip over. Her messy hair is flat on one side and the zigzag design of the sofa has left a memory of itself on her cheek. I'm tempted to put my magnifying glass over it, but I don't.

Aunt Pearl kisses the top of her head. "Poor thing," she says. "You poor, poor thing."

Mama tries to smile but starts crying instead. When Daddy makes a move toward her she looks the other way. Daddy loves Mama almost as much as he loves Jesus and everybody knows it. Maybe even more than Jesus, although he'd never dare say it out loud. I think it just about kills him to see her this way. Eventually he turns around and walks out of the room, leaving his sister to comfort his broke-down wife.

Chastity and Joy walk home from school ahead of me. I stay and wait for Hope's bus. It's the last day before Christmas vacation starts. Hope goes to a school in Little Dune, but the bus drops her off at our school. I don't like her to walk home alone. If that molester is still out there she'd be an easy target. Hope will talk to anybody, even strangers. Especially strangers. The other reason I wait for her is because the kids tease her for being different. Sometimes they call her Hope the Dope, but I know better. Hope isn't stupid, she just has a hard time getting certain parts of her brain to work. She forgets things and she falls a lot. Mean kids like Billy Wolf like to trip her. Hope doesn't seem to mind when it happens. She never blames the person who tripped her. But I know what it's like to be picked on, so I walk her home most days.

When the bus pulls up, Hope skips down the steps and hugs me. "Merry Christmas!" she says.

"It's not Christmas yet," I say.

"I know. But it's almost Jesus's birthday and I'm so excited!"

Halfway home she starts shivering.

"Hope, where's your coat?" She was so happy when she got off the bus I didn't notice she wasn't wearing it.

"I left it on the bus!" She turns to me, panicked. "We have to go back."

Just then her bus passes us and she chases after it. I chase after her.

"Hope, stop!"

When the bus turns the corner Hope

shakes her fist at it.

"Here," I say when I catch up to her. "You can wear mine." I take off my coat and hand it to her. Even though she's three years older we're almost the same size.

"Really?" She sticks her arm into one of the sleeves. "It's still warm," she says.

"Let's get home before I freeze," I say.

Hope puts her arm around me. "Put on the other sleeve. We'll both wear it."

At first I think no way, but seeing Hope's grinning face makes me change my mind. I put my arm in the sleeve and my sister and I bumble our way down the sidewalk, falling twice, before working out a rhythm for walking while wearing the same jacket. When we come through the front door we're both laughing so hard we have a difficult time telling the others why we're both wearing the same coat. Aunt Pearl helps us out of the sleeves and even Mama giggles.

By the end of the day Mama seems a little better. By the end of the week, we're all feeling a lot better. For the first time since Marilyn was born we've had good meals, clean laundry, and a regular schedule. Not because Aunt Pearl does all the work, but because she makes us want to do the work. I don't know why, she just has a way of making you feel happy about making her happy. Our family is still broken, but the pieces don't feel as sharp with Aunt Pearl around. I hope she can fix things but not too quickly, because I want her to stay for a while. It sounds selfish, but I can't help it. She's like wax around a candle wick. Without her, it feels as if the whole family might just burn up into one big, hot mess.

10

Aunt Pearl shuffles across the kitchen and fetches two baby bottles out of the refrigerator. It's funny-looking milk, bluish with a little cream floating on top. The doctor says Marilyn will have a better chance if she has Mama's milk instead of the kind from a cow or formula. Mama's not up to traveling so she squeezes her milk into jars. Aunt Pearl and the church ladies have been taking turns driving a cooler up to Blue Rapids every couple days. Mama can't hold Marilyn right now, but maybe this is a way to love her from far away.

Aunt Pearl holds up one of the mason jars and smiles at me. "How's about a taste, SweePea?"

I shake my head, but she screws off the top and dips her finger into the milk anyway. When she sticks it in my face I shake my head like a wet dog.

"No, thank you!"

"Go ahead, Grace, take a lick. This here is mother's nectar."

Knowing Aunt Pearl, she'll stand there until I give in, so I close my eyes and open my mouth. I think I'll probably throw up when she plops that blue milk on my tongue, but I don't. It's about the sweetest thing I've ever tasted, laced with a memory of Mama's face looking directly into mine. I can even smell her, the part that's only breathable when you snuggle in real close.

Aunt Pearl's voice shatters the memory into tiny pieces. "Whatsa matter, shoog? You look like you're about to fall asleep standing up."

I open my eyes and wait until I'm back in the kitchen where I belong, although I feel like I belong in that other place, too. "Nothing's wrong," I say.

"You want to ride along with me to the hospital, Grace?"

There's no other place I'd rather be than with Aunt Pearl. Not to mention if I stay home Joy is apt to figure out a way to trick me out of my future allowance. We still have a few weeks of putting it into the Sunday offering plate as our punishment for the fortune-telling incident.

"Can I?"

"I don't see why not. I could use the

company and maybe you can help me find the gears in that confounded rig your daddy bought. From the Germans, no less." She mumbles a few more words under her breath then stops herself mid-mumble. "Oh, never mind, go get your coat and boots, honey child."

Aunt Pearl lets me shift the gears because I'm so good at it. It's not that hard since the Germans drew a map right on the gear stick. Plus you can pretty much feel where it needs to go, even reverse. I like the way the ball feels in my hand when it clunks into place. We make a good team, me and Aunt Pearl, even if she did have to add a block of wood on the pedals to reach them.

Aunt Pearl takes a wrong turn and we end up in a shabby neighborhood. She pulls into a snowy driveway to get her bearings. When a woman peeks out the front window from behind a torn curtain Aunt Pearl says, "Don't put the kettle on, Ma, we ain't stayin'." She backs out of the driveway and backtracks about six blocks before pulling into the hospital parking lot. She yanks the key out of the ignition. We hoist the Styrofoam cooler from behind the seats and slide the rolling door closed.

"C'mon, Grace," she says. "It's time you

meet your baby sister."

I follow her into roundabout front doors that sweep me around in a complete circle. Aunt Pearl grabs me by the collar on my third pass and rescues me from my spinning glass cave. She waddles past a tall lady pushing a cart full of food trays who looks down at Aunt Pearl's slippers. The lady winks at me before shoving her cart through the elevator doors ahead of us. Aunt Pearl taps the number 5 button and the tiny room shoots upward. It feels like my stomach stayed right where we started.

At the second floor the food lady gets out and an old man takes her place. As he moves to the back I can smell the sadness buried in the air he breathes out. Aunt Pearl waits until he grabs the rail before pushing the number 5 again. When the doors close his mind falls open like a dump truck, spilling his thoughts all over me.

How will I live without her? I can't sleep in that bed alone. Who will tend her flowers? Oh, Harriet, why did you have to go and leave me?

I plug my ears because it's too hard to take, but this doesn't help. When I look up at the old man he turns away. A tear travels down a crease next to his eye all the way to his chin, where it hangs on to a stubble of whiskers. Aunt Pearl is humming a cheery song and it feels like sprinkling sugar on rotten eggs. When the elevator bell finally dings for Marilyn's floor I practically run into the hall.

Aunt Pearl snaps her fingers behind me. "Slow down, Grace. You'll see her soon enough."

We follow a line of yellow arrows painted on the floor until a nurse stops us. She shakes a bony finger at Aunt Pearl.

"You can't take that child in there, Mrs. Gundry. You'll have to leave her in the waiting room."

Aunt Pearl shifts the cooler to her hip and grabs my hand. "Why not?"

The nurse folds her wrinkly arms across her chest. Her thin lips are squeezed so tight they barely move when she talks. "Germs. Children bring in germs."

Aunt Pearl grins. "You think she's gonna have less germs a couple years from now? This child has the same germs as me. We live in the same house."

The old woman tips her pointy hat toward the sign above the nurse's station. "No one under fourteen, that's the rule."

"If I can go in I expect she can, too."

Aunt Pearl marches off, leaving the woman in the white sailor hat with her mouth hanging open. We push through another set of double doors and then we're inside a room filled with bassinets. Along one wall, a couple of nurses sit in rocking chairs bottle-feeding tiny babies. Both nurses have socks on the outside of their shoes and masks over their mouths. One of them hums softly to the baby in her arms.

The bassinets look like little spaceships with their bubbled tops and beep-beeping machines. Aunt Pearl pauses as we pass a red-faced baby about the size of one of Chastity's dolls. She clucks her tongue. "Poor babe ain't no bigger 'n a minute."

I stare at each of the little bodies as we pass by half a dozen babies with tubes going every which way in and out of them. Some are crying. All of them look lonely. Aunt Pearl stops at the very last bassinet and sets down the cooler.

"There she is, Grace. Say hello to your little sister."

Behind the glass Marilyn is awake but quiet. She's beautiful and looks like a normal baby. She has blue eyes like my other sisters and a wisp of white-blond hair on her forehead. Joy, who gets all As in biology, says babies can't focus, but she's wrong. Marilyn is looking at me in the way you've known someone for a long time.

Aunt Pearl nudges my arm. "You want to touch her?"

I nod.

"See the holes in the side of her bassinet? You can reach inside there with these here mitts."

She helps me slip my right hand into one of the rubbery gloves. I slowly reach into the bubble and rest my hand over Marilyn's chest. As soon as I touch her I feel it. There's a hole for sure, a tiny hole, between the right and left side of her heart. My own pulse speeds up to match hers, faster and faster. I close my eyes and I can see her heart just as clear as if it's painted on the outside of her naked body. A tiny leak. So tiny. Tinier. My hand is tingling, sweating, buzzing, hot, getting hotter. I feel dizzy. The hole is shrinking, disappearing into itself.

"Get her out of here!" A familiar voice sounds from somewhere behind us, but I can't let go because it's not finished yet. I look up to find Aunt Pearl staring at me with bug eyes. My legs feel weak.

"You all right, SweePea?"

I turn back toward Marilyn, but the picture in my mind has disappeared and her eyes are closed. An alarm goes off next to her bubble. Bony Nurse bolts toward us, yelling. She's brought a big black man with her.

"Remove that child from here this instant!"

Aunt Pearl wheels around to face the two of them and holds her hand up like a crossing guard.

"Stay. Back."

The nurse stops so quick she nearly tumbles forward. She whispers something to the man, but her words echo on the edges of a dream. Aunt Pearl catches me just before my knees hit the floor.

I'm flat on my back on a sofa in the front lounge of the hospital. The lights are too bright. Aunt Pearl sits in a chair next to me. She strokes my forehead when I wake. "Hey there, SweePea."

I'm so tired. I can't believe how tired I am. It takes all my concentration to make words come out of my mouth. "Is Marilyn okay?"

"Oh, she's better than okay, shoog. They're sending her home tomorrow." Aunt Pearl crinkles her brow and brings her face next to mine. "Just what'd you do in there, Grace?" she whispers. "You fix that baby somehow?"

But I only remember both of our hearts

beating together and the buzzing in my hand. It was hot, I remember that, too. I haven't forgotten how mad Daddy got when I said Isaac helped us down from that tree and when I knew Chastity was sick. I bite my lip and keep quiet.

"Well," she says, "I saw it with my own eyes. Y'all got the healin' in you, child."

"Don't tell Daddy," I squeak out.

She smiles and kisses my cheek. "Don't you worry, shoog. Your daddy will be proud to know the good Lord works through his baby girl."

I try to sit up, but I'm too dizzy and have to lie back down. "No! Really, Aunt Pearl. Please don't tell him."

But she's grinning like someone holding the best secret they'll ever get to let out.

On the way home from the hospital I tell Aunt Pearl everything that's happened since I last saw her. I tell her about my conversations with Isaac and how the Knowing has gotten stronger. I beg her not to say anything to Daddy because he gets angry about such things. Aunt Pearl drives quietly for a spell before pulling into Thrifty Acres' parking lot. She turns off the engine. When she looks at me, her face is so full of love it could almost melt the ice on the car windows.

"I want to tell you a true story, Grace."

She turns to face the windshield, as if watching her tale play out on the glass.

"It was your mama and daddy's wedding day. We were all getting ready to go to the church, a little chapel about twenty miles east of Blue Rapids. Your mama picked it because she said it looked like it belonged on a picture postcard. Your daddy was intent on not seeing his bride in her wedding dress until she came up the aisle, so they were going to ride in separate cars. Well, I'll be doggoned if Isabelle didn't refuse to ride in her bridesmaid's car. Pitched a fit, she did. Wouldn't say why, just stomped her foot and said she'd ride with the rest of them and if Henry didn't want to see her dress he'd better just look the other way."

Aunt Pearl peels off hand-knitted gloves and huffs on her chapped hands before continuing her story. "So they rode together, Isabelle and Henry and her bridesmaid, Lana Bailey, all in the front seat. The best man, some skinny guy your daddy went to Bible College with, rode in the back with your aunt Arlene and me. It was July, so blasted hot we were nearly all stuck together by the time we reached the chapel."

Aunt Pearl pauses to pat my hand. "You listening, Grace?"

I nod. I'm hanging on to every last word. There's so much I don't know about my parents.

"What happened then, Aunt Pearl?"

"Well, I'm about to tell you that. Lana's younger brother found your mama's bouquet sitting on the kitchen table. He decided to drive Lana's car to the chapel so the bride would have her flowers. He took the back way on Garfield Road, which has more curves than a pinup girl, and ended up rolling the car when the brakes gave out. There was only about a foot of water in the ditch, but it drowned him because he was unconscious from hitting his head."

I start to shiver but not because it's cold. I'm shivering for Mama's sake. I wish I could tell her it wasn't her fault. That just because you know things doesn't mean you made them happen.

Aunt Pearl turns on the engine and puts the heater on full blast.

"Lana's brother, he was a good kid, but I didn't know him. God forgive me, but I was mighty glad he was in that ditch instead of your mama. Now, your daddy dearly believes the Lord spared his beautiful bride and maybe that's true. But he never did mention anything about her refusing to ride in Lana's car." She bows her head, slowly turning it side to side. "Never did."

We both sit quietly and ponder Aunt Pearl's story before I speak up.

"Daddy doesn't like it when people know things they're not supposed to. That's why you mustn't say anything about what happened with Marilyn today."

Aunt Pearl curls her lips inside her mouth and rolls them around as if she's evening out invisible lipstick before turning back toward me. "I understand, shoog. I didn't say nothin' when you told me where your mama was that night she visited the cemetery and I won't tell now." She bites down on her lower lip, as if sealing our pact.

"Isaac says we all have the Knowing, but only some of us welcome it. He says Mama turned away from the Knowing after having a vision of that ice-cream truck backing over Hope when she was little."

"That's what he tells you, huh?" She smiles and puts her arm around me, hugging me hard. "Well, if that's what the boy tells you, then it must be the truth, Swee-Pea." I can tell by the way she says it she's trying to convince herself by saying the words out loud.

She pulls back onto the highway and

drives a ways before speaking again.

"Doesn't matter if it was you or not, your sister's healin' came from on high. Our Lord still offers miracles, and it doesn't make a whit of difference how they come or who they come through."

11

Aunt Pearl never did tell Daddy the whole
story. Just said we were praying for Marilyn
when the commotion started at the hospital,
which in a way is true. Now that Marilyn is
home, Joy seems to think the baby is her
very own Christmas present. It's Joy, not
Mama or Aunt Pearl, who's first to pick her
up when she wakes. Joy carries her around
everywhere almost as if Marilyn is a part of
her body. Even when she's not holding the
baby she rocks back and forth like she's
forgotten her arms are empty.

It's probably a good thing Joy is such a
big help since Aunt Pearl has more than
enough work taking care of the rest of us
without adding a baby into the picture.
Aunt Pearl does the cooking and the laundry, as well as looking after Mama to see
she gets her medicine on time. Each of us
girls helps with one chore: Hope with cleaning, Chastity with laundry, and me with

cooking. It goes without saying that Joy's chore is Marilyn.

Daddy doesn't seem too interested in the new baby, maybe because this one wore Mama to the bone. Once in a while he'll carry Marilyn up to her crib, although he has to pry her out of Joy's arms to do so. Watching him hold her makes me go all soft inside. I don't know why, but something about seeing her little body cradled in his big old arms brings tears to my eyes.

Daddy spends most of his time watching Mama. She's here, but not here. Yesterday he found her in front of the barn, no coat on, holding an empty plate. She said she was meeting a friend for lunch. I pictured her like Chastity, who used to hold fancy parties with her play tea set for imaginary friends. I think the medicine makes Mama more like a child than us kids. And Daddy more like a father than a husband.

When the doorbell rings on the morning of Christmas Eve, Joy yells at me to answer it before it wakes the baby. As if her yelling at me won't wake up anyone within a block. I'm happy to be the first to greet Grandpa and Uncle Bill and Aunt Arlene, knowing what I'll get in return for putting up with her cheek torture. But Chastity has beat me to it. When she turns around after all the oohing and aahing her cheeks are red from pinching, but she's carrying the prized bag of Christmas candy they bring with them every year. Grandpa winks at me and hands me a butterscotch from his pocket.

Aunt Arlene is Mama's sister. We hardly ever see her and Uncle Bill because they live three hours away in a swanky place on Lake Michigan. Ever since Grandma died when I was only two, Grandpa has lived with them. Uncle Bill has an important position with the power company. He's a lot older than Aunt Arlene and also much quieter. He combs his white hair straight back and wears handsome sweaters. I've never seen Daddy in a sweater. Not even once.

Aunt Arlene sells Avon to all the rich ladies in Cedarwood. Every time she visits us her hair is a different color. Today it's the same as an overripe pumpkin with lipstick to match. I park myself on a stool in the corner of the kitchen while she sits at the table talking nonstop about all the houses she's been in and how nice they were decorated. She takes a sip of coffee, leaving a fat smear of orange lip prints on the cup. Aunt Pearl offers her an apron, but she just keeps right on talking. Aunt Pearl throws the apron on the kitchen table and turns back to the stove to baste the turkey.

I'm peeling potatoes over the sink when I sense Mama behind me. We all figured she'd sleep through most of Christmas like she sleeps through everything on account of the pills she takes, but here she is. I turn to see her putting on the apron that was meant for Aunt Arlene. It's the first time I've seen Mama wearing regular clothes instead of a nightgown since Marilyn was born. Her pink blouse is wrinkled and her slip is showing a bit, but otherwise she looks almost normal. I suppose something about having a bunch of women in her kitchen has given her a boost, even if one of them happens to be a lazy gossip.

We all try to act as if we're not shocked when Mama stands next to the stove and hums softly as she stirs jellied cranberries. Aunt Pearl cradles a big bowl full of mashed potatoes across the kitchen, whipping them to beat the band. When she sets the bowl on the table I'm surprised to hear Mama giggle before Aunt Arlene starts in, too. Aunt Pearl says, "What?" which only makes them laugh harder. I wonder what's so funny until I see it myself.

"Pearl got her titties in the taters!" Mama squeals, pointing.

Aunt Pearl peers down at the blob of white fluff on her chest. She looks around at all of us grinning, then lops the potatoes off her apron top and licks her fingers. "Mmm-mmm! Just makes 'em taste sweeter," she says. This sets everybody off again, including Mama, who laughs the loudest. I want to freeze this moment for as long as possible. It almost seems as if God has given us back our mama for Christmas.

When the table's all set I find Grandpa in the living room, bent over the hi-fi. He drops Bing Crosby's "White Christmas" album onto the spindle and gently sets the arm on the first groove. Whoever wrote the song obviously doesn't live in Michigan. We've never had to dream about snow in December. Sometimes we've had to wear snow boots with our Halloween costumes.

I follow Grandpa to the sofa and sit next to him even before his backside is completely on the cushion. I lift his three-fingered hand and lace my fingers between his. The two fingers between the index and the pinkie are missing except for a couple stubs. It's the same as one of the hand signals we learned in school this year. His hand says "I love you" in deaf language.

"Tell me again how you lost two fingers, Grandpa."

He looks at our big and little hands tangled up together and smiles. "Well, I was working at the furniture factory when the guy next to me left his blade running without a shield. He shouted something and when I turned his blade sheared off the last three fingers."

I cringe every time he tells it and yet I love the story. "Then how come only two are missing?"

"Because the pinkie was still dangling from the knuckle and the doctors were able to sew it back on."

"You went to the hospital?"

He grins because he knows I'm egging him on. "I did. Had the prettiest nurse in the whole wide world."

I point to the picture of Grandma and Grandpa atop the upright piano against the far wall in the living room. "And you married her, right?"

"You bet I did."

I hug him and settle back onto his flannel-shirted chest. I don't remember my grandma, but Grandpa swears I was her favorite grandchild, though I had to promise never to tell my sisters. It's been one of the hardest promises I've ever had to keep. What good is being best if nobody else knows it?

Grandpa pulls a pipe out of his pocket,

packs it with tobacco, and lights it with a match. He waits for me to blow it out, then sucks and puffs until the sweet smell fills my nose. Mama doesn't like the smell of Grandpa's pipe, but I do. Two Christmases ago I was sick with an earache and when he blew hot smoke into my ear, the pain went away.

Grandpa whistles along with the music between puffs. He can whistle just about every tune ever written. He sings a few of them, too. He once taught me "I'm Forever Blowing Bubbles," which Chastity and I sing in the bathtub when one of us farts underwater.

"Pa?" Mama calls from the kitchen. "You smoking in the house?"

Grandpa winks at me and we sneak out onto the back porch so he can finish his pipe.

I already know which presents are mine. They've been under the tree for nearly a week. We always open our gifts on Christmas Eve, when other kids are still writing love letters to St. Nicholas and setting out cookies and milk. We aren't allowed to believe in pagan idols like Santa Claus or the Easter Bunny. Daddy says if you mix the letters around, Santa spells Satan. I know better than to mention that if you mix the letters around in God, it spells dog.

Waiting to open our presents takes forever. When the last dish is wiped and put away we all gather in the living room, where Daddy reads the Christmas story from the Bible. He clears his throat and waits for us to quiet down before he begins.

"In those days a decree went out from Caesar Augustus that all the world should be enrolled . . ."

I try to listen but after a couple of sentences it just sounds like blah, blah, blah because I've heard it a million times. I stare at the fat red, blue, and green lightbulbs, then move my attention to a string of smaller lights shaped like candles draped near the bottom of the tree. Tiny bubbles float up to the tips and disappear. Bubble lights are the most magical thing about Christmas since we've never had Santa or the reindeer.

"And the shepherds returned, glorifying and praising God for all they had heard and seen, as it had been told to them."

Daddy closes his Bible and nods at Hope to hand out the presents. Being the oldest, she always gets to pass out the gifts even though she takes so long to read the labels we could scream.

Hope studies the pile under the tree. "Should we let Chastity and Grace open the music boxes first?" She slaps her hand over her mouth when she realizes what she's done.

Joy throws a fallen ornament at her. "Hope!"

Hope starts crying. "I'm sorry," she blubbers.

I look to see if Chastity's going to make a fuss, but she's already tearing into the paper.

"It's okay," I say. "We had a pretty good idea anyway."

Chastity and I open our packages at the same time. Besides the music box, I get a jigsaw puzzle, a pot-holder loom, and Silly Putty. I save the boring clothes box for last, halfheartedly tearing the paper and lifting the cover. Inside I'm surprised to find a handmade red-and-white-striped flannel nightgown with lace bodice and ruffled long sleeves. Chastity holds up a green flowered nightie. When I look at Mama she's grinning at me in a way that makes her tired eyes almost sparkle.

We got White Shoulders perfume for Mama and a vinyl zip-up case for Daddy to keep his Bible in so all the religious tracts won't fall out. Aunt Pearl gave us the money for their gifts since our allowance isn't enough. She says we earned it in hugs. I hand Aunt Pearl the package that Hope wrapped in glittery white tissue paper. Chastity and I made a card that reads, *Merry Christmas to a Pearl of an Aunt.* All us girls chipped in to buy Aunt Pearl a new pair of yellow slippers with red bows on the toes. Aunt Pearl starts bawling when she opens her gift. She sure does love slippers.

Snow falls outside the window as Uncle Bill drives away in Aunt Arlene's pink Cadillac, leaving fresh tire tracks in the driveway. Everyone is tired out except me and we tuck in early. When Chastity falls asleep I get up and gaze through the frosted bedroom window at the mounds of fluffy snow on the branches in the trees. Colored lights from a neighbor's house blink on and off, reflecting my face in the glass. When the house is quiet I tiptoe downstairs in the dark and find my way by smell to our tree.

Besides presents, having the scent of the woods in our living room is my favorite thing about Christmas. I plug in the cord and lie on the floor, waiting for the magic liquid inside the bubble lights to warm. Rubbing the soft flannel of my new nightie between my finger and thumb, I look upward through the tinseled branches. My thoughts turn to Lyle and I wonder where he might be sleeping tonight. With money saved from my allowance, I bought him a black comb in a plastic sleeve. I wrapped it in tissue paper and left it on the front pew in the loft. The last time I checked it was still there. It must be awful not to enjoy Christmas with your family.

I imagine Lola's family and the tree they cut down after snowshoeing to the back of their property together last week, now filled with artful ornaments and the handmade gifts beneath it. Their annual Christmas Eve tradition includes dressing up in costumes to put on a play even though there's no audience. Tomorrow their home will be filled with music and laughter and Chinese food. I would give anything to be part of it.

In the distance I hear bells jingle in the wind. I know it's the street-lamp decorations blowing around, but just for a moment I allow myself to imagine there really is a Santa. What if it was him, and not God, who gave us back Mama today? What if the only reason he's never stopped at our house is because no one here besides me believes in magic?

12

I thought having Marilyn home would keep Mama fastened to normal, but she's still off. After seeming almost like her old self on Christmas she's right back to how she was before. As much as Chastity can be a brat, I feel sorry for her this morning when she climbs into Mama's lap, then slides off like Jell-O. Not one to give up, she takes one of Mama's arms and puts it around her shoulder, but it hangs there like a wet dishrag.

Chastity pats Mama's face. "Mama?"

Mama slowly turns toward her. "Hmmm?"

"You wanna play old maid?"

Mama doesn't answer. She looks past Chastity at me standing in the doorway.

Chastity tries again. "Mama?"

It's like watching my sister put pennies into a machine with no gumballs left. I can't take it anymore so I tell Chastity I'll play Old Maid with her even though she always cries when she loses.

In her best baby voice, she says, "I don't wanna play wif you. I wanna play wif Mama."

When Mama doesn't take the baby-talk bait, Chastity cradles Mama's head in her hands and turns it back toward her. A bit of drool runs onto Chastity's hands. She quickly pulls them away and wipes them on Mama's robe. Aunt Pearl walks up behind me with Marilyn wrapped in the blue blanket Daddy bought, before he knew it was another girl. She looks from Chastity to me and shakes her head, mumbling under her breath as she moves toward Mama. Marilyn's eyes are wide open, but she's quiet as a prayer. That baby nearly never cries. It's almost as if she knows she's already more than Mama can handle without her adding to the fuss.

Aunt Pearl sets Marilyn on Mama's lap, lifting her arm off Chastity and making sure it stays put around the baby. She musses Chastity's curls, then glances in my direction.

"Shoo, girls. Your mama's gotta nurse now. She needs quiet."

I wander into the next room, but Chastity stays put. I hear Aunt Pearl talking softly before it goes quiet except for the sounds of

Marilyn suckling from Mama. Chastity walks past me and up the stairs with a nickel clenched in her fingers. I almost want to send her into the closet to talk to Isaac because he has a way of making everything better. But she wouldn't be able to hear him. Besides, I'm not about to share the one thing I don't have to.

It's bad enough that I've had to share Aunt Pearl. And now she's going back home tomorrow. Watching her pack this morning just about killed me. Daddy says Mama's feeling better and with the help of ladies from the church we can take care of ourselves just fine. Daddy's wrong. Mama still needs Aunt Pearl. I need her. She makes me feel perfect just the way I am.

After my morning chores I find Aunt Pearl in the kitchen with Marilyn over her shoulder, patting the baby's back.

"Let it go, SweePea," she says. "That air ain't payin' rent."

Marilyn burps and Aunt Pearl laughs. She hands the baby off to Joy and points to a chair. "Sit, young lady," she says to me.

Aunt Pearl brushes my hair into a fat, fuzzy ponytail. She pulls a rubber binder around and snaps it into place. "Don't worry, Grace. I'll be back to visit."

"Can't I go with you?"

185

"You have to stay here with your family, shoog. They need you."

"But I want to live with you!" I jump off the chair and turn to look into Aunt Pearl's green eyes. "Aunt Pearl, please . . ."

"Shhhh. Shush, child." She pulls me close, rocking back and forth.

Mama walks into the kitchen with a basket of ironing and dumps it out on the table. Half the clothes spill onto the floor. Aunt Pearl lets go of me and gathers them up. She sprinkles water on Daddy's Sunday shirts before rolling them up for the ironing basket. Mama starts humming a song I don't recognize, something about a wayward wind. Hearing her beautiful voice, Aunt Pearl nearly starts to cry herself. I know how she feels. Sometimes I wish I could catch Mama's voice in a jar and keep it beside my bed at night, let each note light the darkness like a captured firefly.

I leave Mama and Aunt Pearl in the kitchen and set out to look for Lyle. It's been over a month since I've seen him in the loft. I know he still comes around because sometimes the food I leave is gone, but more often than not it's still sitting there and I have to toss it out. When I reach the top rung of the ladder a cough sounds from the back of the loft. I don't see him until he sits up. From the looks of his hair sticking straight out you'd think he'd been scuffling across the living room carpet in Aunt Pearl's slippers. He's wearing a scarf around his neck and old wool gloves with holes where a couple of the fingers should be.

"Hello, Gracie."

"I've been worried about you, Lyle. Where've you been?"

"Oh, around," he says, getting to his feet. His knees crack when he stands up straight. Well, not too straight. Looks like he might tip over if you gave him a good nudge. I hand him a banana and he says, "Thank you, kindly," before shoving it in his pocket.

"You have a nice Christmas, young lady?" He asks like it was yesterday instead of a month ago.

"I got some neat stuff and Mama made me a new nightie."

"If your mama's sewing is anything like her cooking, you must have gotten a fine nightshirt." He slips the comb out of his shirt pocket and holds it up. "Had a pretty nice holiday myself."

I feel my cheeks blush. He spits on the comb and slowly slicks back his white hair, one hand smoothing it over, grinning at me.

"Actually, Aunt Pearl has been doing most of the good cooking. Mama makes the easy stuff like macaroni and cheese."

"Imagine that. Two mothers. You're one lucky gal, aren't ya?"

"That's the problem. Aunt Pearl is going back to Mississippi. Daddy says Mama is well enough to get on without her, but I don't think she is. I don't want Aunt Pearl to leave."

"Well, now. That is a problem, isn't it?" He retrieves the banana and peels it halfway. He's breathing hard through his nose, as though he's just run up a flight of stairs. I watch him eat the entire thing in silence, except for his loud breathing.

"Sometimes it's hard not getting what we want. Doesn't seem fair."

I nod enthusiastically, glad to hear someone is on my side.

"But your aunt Pearl might need a rest. She's quite a bit older than your mother, even older than your father, isn't she?"

I nod again. It's funny how he says mother and father, so formal-like for a hobo.

"Well, that makes her prit-near sixty. I imagine she's a bit tuckered out from taking care of you and your sisters plus your mother for the past month or two. You don't want to wear her out, do you?"

"Of course not. I don't want to do anything that would be hard on her."

"Then it's settled. Your aunt Pearl needs a rest." He rolls up the banana peel and slips it into his pocket. He pats my leg. "She'll be back. From what you've told me she loves you too much to stay away for long."

Lyle's right, but I still don't want Aunt Pearl to leave. My mouth folds into a pout before I can stop it. He puts his arm around my shoulder.

"She'll be back, Gracie," he says again, resting his head on top of mine. Lyle has never touched me before and I have to admit I never thought I'd like being this close to a bum, but it feels just fine.

By the time I wake up the next morning Aunt Pearl's all packed except for a pair of pink slippers I found under the sofa. I hold them out to her. "Here. You almost forgot these."

"Why don't you keep them, shoog. I expect they'll fit you. Try 'em on."

I drop to the floor and pull off my socks, then walk across the room to show how good they fit. "Perfect!" I say, ignoring the backs flopping at my heels.

"You might want to tuck a bit of tissue into the toes," she says.

We both laugh, which only reminds me how much fun we have together and that makes me sad again.

"Are you sure you have to go, Aunt Pearl?"

"I'm sure."

She backs herself onto my bed and pats it. I sit next to her and lean into her chubby arm.

"I want you to call if you ever need help, Grace." She pulls a piece of paper from her pocket with a phone number and address written on it. "And you better write and tell me how you're getting along, you hear?"

I nod, my eyes already burning with a cry that'll probably last for hours. She pulls me into her lap even though I'm way too big. I think I'd about like to die there.

Daddy hollers up the stairs that it's time to take Aunt Pearl to the bus stop. As we trudge down the stairway it's all I can do not to start crying again. I've been blowing my nose all day, and Daddy says if I don't stop sulking I have to stay up in my room when she leaves. I watch through the living room window as he throws Aunt Pearl's last suitcase into the back of our Volkswagen and slams the rolling door. Steam floats out of his mouth on account of how cold it is. Aunt Pearl buttons up her wool coat and grabs her big, black pocketbook off the dining room table. She goes down the line hugging each of us one at a time, starting with

Hope, who says, "God bless you, Aunt Pearl."

Aunt Pearl kisses Mama's cheek and then the back of Marilyn's neck as she sleeps over Mama's shoulder. Joy doesn't like to be hugged much, but she allows it out of politeness. I catch Aunt Pearl slipping a dollar into her pocket, which will make Joy's day for sure. She hugs Chastity, who hangs on her neck until it'd like to break off before Joy says to let go.

I made sure to be at the end of the line so I could have her last. All Aunt Pearl has to do is look at me and I burst out crying again. She folds herself around me, her wool coat scratching at my cheek. I breathe in as deep as I can to keep her smell memory with me after she's gone.

"Don't worry, SweePea. I'll be back to visit. You call me if you need anything."

She stands upright and surveys the lot of us one last time. "Y'all be good to your mama," she says.

Outside Daddy beeps the horn in one long honk. I feel like howling with it. Then before I can blink she's out the door. I run to the window and watch our green VW bus drive up the dirty-snow street with its two red-eyed taillights staring back at me.

"God bless you," Hope says again, as if

Aunt Pearl has just sneezed instead of off and left us.

13

Mama won't come out of her room anymore. Daddy says we should just do the best we can and take care of ourselves so he can care for Mama. He wants us to carry on as if everything is normal. Normal used to include Mama so it's a hard thing to ask. Plus he put Joy in charge when he's not here, making it even harder. When Joy told me to do the dishes tonight I wanted to throw a fit, but I said yes, even though it's not my turn. I feel a little sorry for her. She's got her hands full with Marilyn, which is a lot for a fourteen-year-old.

Chastity has been pouting all day, every day. Not only has she nearly lost a mother, she's also lost her favorite sister, who now ignores her because she's so busy with the baby. When Chas walks into our bedroom after supper and flops on the bed beside me I know she's getting desperate. She opens a book and starts flipping through the pages.

"What's Kotex?"

I tilt the cover to read the title. Oh brother. She's gone and found the book about becoming a woman in the back of Joy's closet. I can't believe she had the guts to go in there, let alone crawl around where there's bound to be dust.

"It's a sanity pad. You hook it onto a sanity belt when you have your period."

"What's a period?"

"It's what happens when you bleed from your crotch," I say.

She gasps. "Bleed? You mean real blood?" She clasps the book to her chest.

"Yeah, but it doesn't hurt. At least I don't think it does." I grab the book out of her hands and turn a few pages until I find the picture I'm looking for. "See this? Blood fills up on the inside of a woman's uterus — that's the womb — so a baby has a soft place to live. If there's no baby, then the blood comes out instead. That's why you need a Kotex pad."

Chastity wrinkles up her pudgy nose and groans. "Yuck!"

I point to another illustration titled *Your Changing Body* with a picture of a woman's insides. Not a photograph — more like a sketch with parts drawn in. The woman has her arms up to show hair under them. She

194

has squiggly hair on her crotch like Mama's and Hope's. And probably Joy's, but she keeps her body covered ever since she started growing boobs.

"Don't worry, Chas. It won't happen for a long time. Not until puberty, which is still a few years away for you."

Chastity sits up and drops her legs over the side of the bed, disgusted. "Not me. I'm not having it." She stands up and glares at the book in my hands.

"Maybe you should ask Joy to talk to you about it?" I say.

"Forget it!" she says, and marches out of the room, leaving me with the responsibility of having to sneak the book back into Joy's closet. I drop to my knees and slide it under the mattress just as Joy appears in the doorway.

"What's the matter with Chas?"

"Nothing."

"What are you doing on the floor?"

"Nothing."

Joy walks over and sits on the floor next to me. The two of us stare at our reflections in the glass bookcases without saying anything. After a bit, she breaks the silence.

"I'm sorry I got you into trouble with that gypsy thing last year."

It's not like her to apologize, even when

she's wrong. Especially to me. Maybe this being in charge thing has made her more mature.

"It's okay," I say. "I should have known better."

She nibbles on her index fingernail, takes it out of her mouth and looks at it, then moves to the next stubby finger.

"Is something the matter, Joy?"

"No."

"You sure?"

"Nothing's wrong. Well, except for this stupid assignment I have in Business Math."

I can't believe what I'm hearing. Joy gets all As in every subject. Especially math.

"It's too hard?"

"No, not really. It's just . . ."

"It's just what?"

She sighs and drops her hand into her lap, fingering the ironed crease down the center of her jeans. "It's just that I thought maybe you could help me."

Has she lost her marbles? Math is my hardest subject. "I don't think so, Joy." I laugh, which comes out like a snort. "You're asking the wrong person."

"No I'm not," she says. She leans back against the bed and walks her feet up the glass, leaving sock prints smudged on the surface of the bookcase. She stares at my reflection and speaks to it instead of me. "We're supposed to imagine we're investors in the stock market. Each of us has a pretend sum of money to invest and at the end of the semester we're graded on how well our stocks have done."

"So what's the big deal? It sounds like a fun assignment."

She turns to look at the real me. "I need your help. I need you to use your powers to choose what stocks I should invest in."

"You know I can't do that, Joy."

"I won't tell."

"No, I mean I really can't."

"Can't or won't?"

"It doesn't work that way. It's a rule that comes with the Knowing. I can't use it for profit."

She turns away from me. Spit hits the glass when she finally answers. "Oh please! Whose rule? Yours?" Back to the fingernails.

"God's. It's God's rule."

Joy leaps to her feet. "God's? What kind of mockery is that?" She folds her hands across her chest. "You think you can just toy with people, Grace? You think you're so special you can pick and choose who and how you help? That you can exclude your own family?"

"It's not like that!" I say. "Why are you so upset?"

"I want to use my own money, Grace. I want to invest my money so I don't have to be poor like Mama and Daddy. I figure if I invest it well now, by the time I graduate I'll be sitting pretty for college."

"I'm sorry, Joy. I can't."

When I start to cry she glares at me, breathing hard through her nose. "You know what? I was just making fun of you. I wanted to see if you'd go for it. You think I really believe in your stupid Knowing? The only thing you know is how to make this family the laughingstock of Cherry Hill."

She stomps out of the room. Her words feel like bee stings over every inch of me. I move toward the closet, then climb into bed instead. Sad and sleepy, I pull the covers over my head.

In the dream I'm standing with a crowd of people in the parking lot of our church. Suddenly a silver spaceship lands in the middle of the street and who should crawl out but the devil himself. Two horns stick out from his red temples just above furry eyebrows. His tail points upward behind him like a hunting dog on scent. He looks around at all the people frozen in their places, then focuses his cat eyes directly on me. A pitchfork appears in his right hand as he starts toward me. I try to run, but it feels like I'm moving through honey.

Lucifer is closing in on me fast. With nothing to lose, I turn to face him.

"What do you want with me?" I scream.

"Your Evil Eye, my dear."

He strokes his Snidely Whiplash mustache as he says it. I'm so scared I feel like I might pee my pants.

"My evil eye?"

"The one that sees. You're a little demon-child and you belong with me."

I look toward heaven, begging God to tell Satan I'm not evil, that I've been saved. But God's either busy or not listening, so I have to use my smarts instead.

"My eye can see that you're going to be swallowed up by a tornado," I say.

As soon as the words are out of my mouth a huge twister comes swirling across the horizon and sucks up the devil right before my eyes. His pointy red tail pokes out of the funnel cloud as it whirls past me. The crowd gathers around, amazed by my power but at the same time looking very afraid.

"Move it!" someone shouts, before they all run away.

"Move it! Everybody up!" Daddy raps on the wall at the foot of the stairs until he's sure no living thing could possibly be asleep.

I untangle myself from Chastity's legs and roll to my side of the saggy mattress. Pippy purrs beside my ear. I must have slept right through the night after Joy's hissy fit. Chastity tumbles out of bed, blond locks framing her pale face as if angels spent the night arranging them around her head. My crazy hair sticks out every which way like bent straw.

Each of us got one good thing from Mama. Hope got her perfect complexion, Joy got her smarts, Chastity got her wavy locks, and I got her intuition. On mornings like this I would trade my gift of Knowing for Chastity's beautiful blond hair in nothing flat. Untamed is the way Mama describes my frizzy red mess. "I don't know where you got that wild hair of yours, Grace Marie," she once said. "But no more use trying to tame it than you." She meant it to be kind, like taking my side against all those unruly hairs. I think she likes my wild parts. I'm a lion compared to her other lambs.

Chastity pokes me in the leg with her finger. She's already up and dressed in a jumper and penny loafers. "Grace, get out of bed! Can't you smell it?"

I take in a big breath through my nose and smile. CoCo Wheats.

When we get downstairs, Daddy is at the stove in his work pants and a loopy undershirt. The outline of his belly button pushes against the thin cotton like when Mama was pregnant with Marilyn. He carries the pan of CoCo Wheats around the table and plopplop-plops a spoonful into each of our bowls.

"Daddy," Chastity whines, "they're lumpy."

"Hush up," Joy hisses through her teeth. She turns back to Marilyn and spoons another tiny teaspoon of strained apricots into the baby's mouth. Marilyn grins so big at my sister that the orange goo dribbles out of her mouth and runs down her chin.

"Do you have any idea how lucky you are?" Daddy says to Chastity.

Uh-oh, here comes the Starving Children in India lecture.

Chasity interrupts. "But, Daddy —"

"You sit there and eat every bite, young lady. And you think about how many children aren't even going to get breakfast today."

Chastity quietly spoons the lumps out of her bowl and hides them under her napkin. I miss one of the lumps and gag as I bite into a squishy ball of mush. I quickly shove a piece of peanut-buttered toast into my

201

mouth followed by a gulp of milk, wiping up the drips with the back of my hand. Daddy's busy scraping the dark parts off the next batch of burnt toast as if the bread won't still taste like charcoal. By the time he finishes, the sink is coated with blackened crumbs he'll probably try to use in tonight's casserole.

It's no secret that Daddy's a cheapskate. He talked Mr. Norberg into giving him a clergy discount at the grocery store. Ever since then he's had to do the food shopping because Mama was too embarrassed to go down there anymore. Daddy cuts coupons out of the Sunday paper that he gets for free on Monday because it's a sin to buy anything on the Lord's day. He takes the whole wad with him to the store. One of his favorite things is to brag about how much he saved on top of the ten percent clergy discount.

About the time the rest of us are finishing breakfast, Mama wanders into the kitchen wearing her light blue nightie and sits glassy-eyed at the end of the breakfast table. Her big, brown nipples stare at me through fabric that's worn thin from too much time in bed. Daddy plants a kiss on her sleepy cheek and sets a cup of coffee in front of her. She smiles at us from very far away.

■ ■ ■ ■

After I'm sure Daddy has left for his office I run up to the closet and close the door. The dream is still fresh in my mind.

"Isaac?"

Yes?

"Is there really a devil?"

Not with horns and a tail, no.

"But Daddy says . . ."

Your daddy is just passing on what he's been taught. There's no such thing as a pitchfork-wielding demon, if that's what you're asking.

"Then who is Satan?"

It's more of a what than a who.

"I don't get it."

Satan represents all the evil in the world. It's the dark side in all of us, our temptation to serve ourselves at the cost of others. You can probably think of some good examples.

"Like war? And stealing?"

Those two are usually the same thing, aren't they? Most wars are started over greed, someone taking what's not theirs. Satan is just the human personification of evil. People need a picture, something scary that they can relate to.

"Satan, demons, the devil . . . they all

scare me. Sometimes people call me a devil for having the Knowing."

You're not evil, Grace. You're human and all humans have the capacity for good and evil, but you've chosen to serve the former.

I pause, worried about the next thing I want to ask. If Isaac's right it'll be okay, but if not, I might get struck down just for thinking it.

"Is God . . . real?" I flinch as soon as the words are out in case lightning is about to hit.

Very real.

"Have you seen him?"

It's not like you think, Grace. God is in you. God is in all of us. To people like your daddy he is human-looking. Others recognize God in a river or a tree.

"But Jesus is the son of God, right?"

We're all children of God.

"I'm so confused."

I know it's difficult to understand. That's why we create so many myths around God. What matters is that you experience God in the way that feels true to you.

"The closest I ever felt to God was before we were born."

God is love in all its forms, but there is no greater love than a mother for her children.

"Even before they're born?"

Even before they are conceived.

"I feel like my head might explode."

Understanding God is one of life's biggest questions. Always has been and always will be. God exists in the wondering. The fact that you're asking just means you're normal.

"I would never call myself normal."

You're right, you're not normal, Grace. You're exceptional. One day you'll know how extraordinary you are, a blessing to the world.

"Ha."

I mean it, Grace.

I can tell by the way he says it he does. I'm just not sure if I believe it myself.

14

It feels as if we've lost Mama for good. The pills she takes for her sadness keep her in a world nobody can reach, not even Daddy. She mostly stays in her room reading magazines or pretending to read them. Sometimes she just turns the pages. Today it's more than I can bear. She's propped up in bed with her bare feet crossed at the ankles, staring at a photo of Grace Kelly. She points at the magazine.

"We should give you a pixie."

I lean in and look closer at the photograph. "I don't think I'd look good in short hair, Mama."

Mama has always trimmed our hair, but when she started taking the medicine for her condition we all ended up with crooked bangs. The last time was a disaster. When she pinched my jaw in her hand I squeezed my eyelids shut, fearing one of those blades would miss their target. I heard a crink,

crink sound and when I peeked open one eye Mama was scrunching up her nose, looking at the scissors.

I gasped. "Those are pinking shears!"

"Oops."

"Oops?" I shook loose from her grip and ran to the bathroom mirror. My bangs looked like one side of a zipper.

"Mama!"

"Don't worry, I can fix it," she'd said, following my wails into the bathroom. Behind me, her face drooped in the mirror, like the nursing home residents Daddy calls on. When I turned around she was holding the regular scissors.

"Be careful, Mama," I whispered, as she crunched through my bangs again.

"Ta-da!" she cheered after her second attempt, meaning to shove the scissors in her apron pocket but missing by an inch. I jumped out of the way before the point could hit my bare toes. When I turned back to the mirror a neat edge of bangs traveled up one side of my forehead, exposing only my right eyebrow. Mama smiled behind me, obviously pleased with herself. I decided not to make a fuss since if my bangs were any shorter, I couldn't really call them bangs anymore. And I vowed never to let her cut my hair again.

207

I give Mama's hand a squeeze before climbing off the bed. "I'll think about it, Mama."

But she's gone again, to wherever she goes when she stares at you without really seeing. I back out of the room and head for the kitchen, where Joy sits at one end of the table sorting bank checks and piling them into separate stacks. Marilyn is propped in a plastic walker, delicately picking through a tray of stale Cheerios. Her toes barely reach the floor and the only way she can scoot is backward. When I stop to grab an apple from the bowl on the kitchen counter she grins, a soggy Cheerio stuck to her cheek.

"What are you doing, Joy?"

Miss Busybody doesn't even look up to answer me. "Helping Daddy get ready for his tax appointment."

"How come?"

"Because he's too busy. I do all his banking now."

"But you're only fourteen."

"It so happens that some of us mature faster than others." With one foot, Joy hooks a leg of the walker and pulls Marilyn, who has flopped like a drunk to one side, back to the table. She adjusts Marilyn's position and tucks a blanket on each side to help keep her upright. "Besides, I enjoy it. It's like being the banker in Monopoly."

Everyone knows Joy lives for numbers, especially when they have dollar signs in front of them. A couple years ago she shoved a wallet in the back pocket of her jeans, just like a man does. Ever since Mama got sick Joy's started walking heavier on her heels, like she has somewhere important to go.

"We should ask Daddy to take us to the roller rink," I say. "We were supposed to go on my birthday, but I think he forgot."

She stares at me through straight bangs that hang over her serious eyes. Joy cuts her own hair.

"I said I have to sort the checks for Daddy. Why don't you call your hippie friend?"

"Daddy grounded me from the phone after he caught me in the closet again."

"So go use the pay phone at Ralph's."

"Can I borrow a dime?"

Joy reaches into her pocket and throws a coin on the table. "I want it back with interest."

"Can I have fifty cents for skate rental?"

She sighs. "Here's a dollar. Now go on and stop bothering me. I'm trying to count."

Joy goes back to tallying a column of

numbers on a notepad, ignoring me in the way grown-ups ignore little kids when they're concentrating on important stuff. She licks her thumb just like a pro, then picks up another stack of checks from the piles in front of her. I beat it out of there before she tells me to bring back the change.

Lola answers on the first ring.

"Hey. I was hoping maybe we could go do something today."

"Hi, Grace. I thought you were grounded from the phone."

"I am. I'm at a pay phone."

"You want me to ask Catherine to come pick you up?"

"Actually, do you think she'd take us to the Roller-Rama? Joy gave me a dollar."

"That sounds like fun. Hang on."

Lola puts her hand over the mouthpiece, but I can still hear her muffled voice.

"We can pick you up in half an hour. Catherine says she'll put in some time at the food co-op while we skate."

"What's a food cop?"

"Co-op. It's like a grocery store, but the customers own it and take turns working so they can get better food for less money."

"Oh."

"Where should we pick you up?"

"I'll be on the bus bench in front of Ralph's service garage."

"Okay, see you soon!"

On the way to the Roller-Rama Catherine asks me about baptism. Apparently Lola has shared about Daddy not letting me get baptized this summer.

"It's a ceremony," I say. "We get baptized to prove our love for Jesus in front of witnesses. The water washes away our sins and we're purified."

"So before baptism you're impure? Forgive me, Grace, but I'm not a religious person. I'm not judging you, I'm just curious."

It's weird talking to people who aren't Christians. Almost everyone I know goes to church, even if it isn't our church.

"Well, once you're born again God forgives you for your sins. The baptism is more of a ritual."

"Born again?"

Lola leans forward and rests her chin on the back of the front seat. "Catherine, stop grilling her!"

"It's okay, Lola," I say. And then to Catherine, "That's what we call it when you get saved. Your first birth is your regular family and then you're reborn into the family of God."

"I think I get it. Becoming a Christian is the application and baptism is the initiation, right?"

"Sort of."

"And why won't your father let you get baptized?"

Lola slaps the back of the seat. "Catherine!"

"Sorry. None of my business."

I'm glad we've arrived so I don't have to answer her. Catherine hands Lola a five-dollar bill. For people who live in a dilapidated house with broken furniture they sure seem to have a lot of extra money. Lola even has her own skates. They're painted two different colors, red and blue, with yellow puff balls on the toes.

I close the car door and wave to Catherine as she drives away. I hope she doesn't get in an accident. I hate thinking about my best friend's mama suffering in hellfire just because she wasn't raised in a godly family. I say a silent prayer as we head toward the building.

"Sorry, Grace. I should have kept my big mouth shut."

"Don't worry about it. I like your mom."

I wait in line at the rental counter for plain white skates that are scuffed and stinky from all the feet that wore them before me. When the pimple-faced kid hands me my change I join Lola on a bench near the rink's edge.

"Was that your allowance?" I ask as we lace up our skates.

"We don't get an allowance. My parents give us money if we need it. They call it discretionary expenses."

"Do they ever say no?"

"Of course. I asked for a trampoline last year, but John said no. He claimed he could build one from scratch, but he never got past digging a humongous hole before deciding to turn it into turtle pond."

"You have a turtle pond?"

"No, just a hole. That's the thing. My parents have lots of great ideas, but most of them never get finished."

The organ music combined with all those wheels rolling across the wood floor makes it almost impossible to carry on a conversation without yelling.

"Let's skate!" Lola says.

"I'm not very good!" I yell back.

She just smiles and peels off the bench. It takes me a minute to steady myself before taking the first awkward strides. We skate around the rink, me slowly, Lola skating backward so I can keep up with her. I fall at least once every few times around. I am such a klutz while Lola is like a speed demon, parting her legs to skate over tiny kids and whizzing by older teens and adults.

When I fall for the umpteenth time we decide to take a break. Lola buys us each a blue moon ice-cream cone from the food counter. We sit at the balcony tables licking our cones and laughing at the people doing the hokey pokey below us. Next up is the Couple's Skate. The organ music is replaced by "Stand by Me" on the loudspeakers. The regular lights dim and a disco ball lights up, throwing colorful shapes across the wooden floor. Two by two, teenagers begin pairing up and moving toward the floor.

Lola grabs my hand.

"Wait, no," I say. "This is just for girl-friends and boyfriends."

Lola laughs. "No, it's for couples. We're two people, aren't we?"

"Yes, but I don't think that's what they mean."

Lola pulls me by the hand, prying me off my seat. "Screw them. It's the last skate and I want to get my money's worth."

I have two choices. I can go with her or fall flat on my face trying to get away and probably end up tripping a bunch of people. Either way I'm going to be embarrassed. And I'm right. As soon as we start around

214

the rink, the not-couples sitting in the balcony start laughing and pointing. I hear "Get off the floor!" and "It's for couples, not queers!" And "Look at those dumb girls!" I try pulling away from Lola, but she's got one arm hooked around my waist to keep me from falling.

"Don't pay any attention to them," she says.

My face flushes hot. I can't wait until the song is done and we can get out of here.

On our third time around the corner on the balcony side I hear two distinct words. *Look up!* The warning comes from inside me, not from the crowd. I instinctively jerk my head toward the ledge where a little boy is climbing on the wrong side of the railing, using it as a monkey bar. I let go of Lola and fly toward the side of the rink with my arms in the air. A moment later a woman screams from the balcony. And then he's falling, just missing my arms. I slam into the wall and spill face-first onto the wood floor, arms still outstretched. The boy bounces off my legs and onto the floor with an ugly thud.

A crowd gathers in a circle around us. The little kid is sprawled next to me, a small trickle of blood snaking out from behind his head. A lady not on skates races across the wood floor toward us and kneels by the boy. The lights go up and the music stops with a *skreeeeek* across the vinyl record.

"Jimmy! Oh my God, Jimmy!"

He doesn't answer at first, but then his eyes come open. He looks up at all the faces hovering over him and starts screaming his head off. The lady scoops him up and runs toward the front door. The others skate behind her, leaving Lola crouched next to me on the floor.

"Are you okay?"

"Yeah," I say, rolling onto my back. "I think so."

"You knew he was going to fall, didn't you?"

I don't answer her. I don't have to.

Lola and I lean against the metal outside wall of the Roller-Rama, waiting for Catherine to pick us up. The sun has warmed the igloo-shaped building and it feels good on my back. I can still feel the vibration of wheels under my feet even though I'm back in my tennis shoes, an invisible rumble beneath me. As people leave they glance back at me nervously, then shake their heads, mumbling between themselves. I bury my head in my hands.

Lola grabs my arm. "Why are you crying?"

"I missed him."

"It's a minor concussion, they said. He's going to be okay. It would have been a lot worse if you hadn't padded his fall."

"But if I wasn't so clumsy he wouldn't have gotten hurt."

"Grace."

When I ignore her she pulls my hands apart and stares me in the eye. "Grace!" she says again.

"What?"

"You can't save everybody. You aren't superwoman."

"I know." I wipe my wet face with the hem of my blouse. "But sometimes I wish I didn't have this stupid . . . thing."

"Clairvoyance. I looked it up."

"Whatever it's called, I hate it."

"Don't say that."

"I just want to be like everybody else."

A woman walks past us, dragging two girls behind her. She glares at me and makes a wide circle around us. Lola gives the lady the middle finger before turning back to me. "No you don't," she says.

By Monday morning the last dirty splotches of snow have melted after a heavy rain. Even though Lyle spends less and less time in the loft these days I always check the barn after supper, hoping to find him. Every night I put plastic Baggies in my pockets and sneak from the dinner table things that aren't too gooey or runny. Nobody ever sees me do it, I'm that careful.

After washing tonight's dishes I sneak up to the loft with meat loaf and a couple slices of bread in my pocket. My heart goes soft inside when I see Lyle curled up in the straw on the floor behind the last pew. His eyes are closed, but he isn't sleeping.

"Are you hungry?"

He opens his wrinkled eyelids. "I guess I am."

He raises himself and moves to sit cross-legged in front of the legless front pew, pretty limber for a man his age. I scrape his food on a paper plate and sit on the bench facing him.

"Where did you used to live, Lyle?"

He pulls a fork out of his pants pocket. "In the U.P., just south of Sault Ste. Marie. Most beautiful place on God's earth."

"So why'd you move here?"

He finishes gumming a mouthful of meat loaf before answering. "To look for work, same as everybody else. Not many jobs up there."

"Did you find one?"

"Yep, but it didn't last long. A little

218

problem with the bottle made me late for work one too many times."

"The bottle?"

He smiles his toothless smile. "My mistress," he says, patting his breast pocket. "Miss Ginny."

I must look confused because he says, "Gin. I like gin from time to time."

"Oh," I say. "So how do you get by?"

"Nice people like yourself, Grace," he answers. "And a small government check."

"Where do you stay when you're not here?"

"Under the stars. Sometimes in the orchards. There used to be an old school bus down by the tracks, but the village had it hauled away."

My stomach tightens. My voice trembles when I try to answer. "Oh . . ." is all that comes out. I glance toward the stairs. Lyle looks at me with a long, sad face.

"It's not like they said, Grace. I was takin' a leak, that's all. Those kids happened on me relieving myself and claimed I was exposin' my private parts to them." He wipes his stubbly chin with his sleeve.

My gut says he's telling the truth, but I don't tell him so.

Lyle sets the plate on the floor next to him. He licks the fork clean and puts it back in his pocket. "I don't blame you if you don't believe me," he says.

"I believe you," I finally croak out.

He walks slowly to the back end of the loft and stretches out in the straw, pulling a blanket over himself. "You have yourself pleasant dreams, Gracie."

I want to convince him I really do believe his story, but the words stick in my throat until it's too late. Lyle is already taking deep-sleep breaths so I leave quietly, promising myself I'll make it right with him tomorrow.

15

Daddy's sitting at the kitchen table wearing navy-blue slacks and a white undershirt. From the side I can see where he says God sprayed freckles on his shoulders. He hasn't shaved yet and the patch of dark whiskers around his mouth makes him look like Fred Flintstone.

"Your toast just popped up." He points with a paring knife to the four-slice toaster without looking up from the mound of potatoes in front of him. Mama is supposed to bring a dish to the mother-daughter banquet tonight, but Daddy is the one who got stuck making it. None of us know how to make scalloped cheese potatoes and since Aunt Pearl left he's had to step in on some of the mothering duties.

I slather peanut butter and grape jelly on my toast, licking the extra off my fingers before joining Daddy at the table. I love watching the potato skins roll off in ringlets.

Daddy gouges out an eye with the pointy end of the knife and drops the lopsided potato into a pan of water, which sloshes over the side of Mama's blue-and-white speckled kettle. She has a whole set of matching pans that look like they were left out under a bird's perch.

"Put in a few more slices for your sisters," Daddy says.

I drop two more pieces of bread into the slots and push the lever down until it catches. Daddy grabs another potato and starts over again. When my toast is gone I get a second peeler from the drawer and start in on the rest of the pile. Daddy nods at me and it feels like a little extra sunshine sneaked into the room. When the last potato is stripped of its skin he rolls the peels up in the soggy newspaper and heads for the backyard. I run upstairs to pick out a dress for tonight.

Mama always sits with Hope at the mother-daughter banquet because she's the oldest, so the rest of us have to eat with one of the church ladies who has chosen us to be her companion for the evening. Joy tried to talk Daddy into letting her take Marilyn as her "daughter" to the banquet, but he said no. When she threw a fit he agreed to let her take Chastity instead of having to go with church ladies.

Last year I had to go with Edna, the fat lady. This year Mrs. McBurney has picked me to be her little darling. Mr. McBurney digs wells for a living, but Daddy refused to let him redo our well when the old one went dry because he uses a stick shaped like a Y to find water in the ground. Daddy says the devil points the way. Mr. McBurney never comes to church with his wife. I felt bad when Daddy hired someone else. Mr. McBurney only works in the months when the ground isn't frozen, so they don't have much money. Also because their life is kind of sad. Their only daughter was killed in a car accident a few years back when her drunk husband ran them into a tree. The McBurneys wanted to adopt their two grandsons, but the kids' daddy wouldn't let them go. Everybody knows he only wants the boys to work his farm so he can sit around and drink beer. Mrs. McBurney drives out to the farm to feed them whenever their daddy's on a binge, which is practically every day.

It's not that I don't like Mrs. McBurney. She's actually a really sweet old lady and I feel sorry that her daughter died. The problem is how she smells. She has bad breath and wreaks of Old Man McBurney's stinky cigars. Plus I don't think she bathes too regularly. On Halloween Mrs. McBurney gives out apples so most of the kids skip their rickety old house. "That's the crispest, juiciest apple you'll get tonight," she'll say, as if everybody else is handing out apples, too.

I always smiled and let her make a big to-do over my costume, which was usually a ballerina or a princess since Daddy won't let us dress up in any pagan costumes like monsters or witches. Now that I'm twelve I'm too old for trick-or-treating. I hope some other kid takes my place and shows up at her house next fall.

It's still hours before the banquet, but Hope is already dressed. She gets to quote verses during the program and she's practicing in front of the dining room mirror. Her white-blond hair is in two thin braids tied with red ribbons that match her red dress. She even has a red Bible to coordinate her outfit. Hope probably has a dozen Bibles. People give them to her all the time. I have a hard time keeping track of just one.

I've decided on a white blouse and a yellow skirt for tonight's banquet. I brush my hair into a ponytail and pull on a cardigan sweater with pearl buttons. Hope is sitting on her bed when I pass by her room, her mouth moving but no words coming out. She's holding her Bible in her lap as her feet kick at the bed rail.

"What's the matter, Hope?"

She startles when I speak, her feet freezing in mid-kick. "Do you think Mama will make it to the banquet tonight?"

Mama's usually late for everything these days, or worse, just doesn't show.

"Of course she will," I say, but I'm a little worried for Hope. She's been looking forward to this night for months. I think of all us girls, Hope has suffered the most on account of Mama's illness. Mama tended to hover over Hope like an umbrella, trying to protect her from harm. I imagine it's because of the car accident when Hope was little. Ever since Mama got sick, I've done my best to be nice to Hope, but we don't have much in common. Even though she's three years older than me, she seems younger in the way she gets overexcited about stuff or angry and frustrated when things don't go her way. I just hope Mama doesn't do anything tonight to upset her.

I go searching for Mama and find her standing in front of her dresser mirror wearing a pink crepe suit and matching heels. I didn't really think she'd be able to pull it off. She looks beautiful, even though her outfit is getting too big for her with all the weight she's lost. She seems more awake than usual, so that's a good sign.

"You ready, Mama?"

She spritzes a bit of her favorite White Shoulders on her wrists and neck. I hand her my lace-tipped hankie and she sprays a tiny bit of perfume into it. She hands it back to me, smiling.

"Just about," she says.

I wait for her to tell me how pretty I look, but she's smudging pink lipstick with a tissue, which takes all her concentration, so I go wait on the front porch for my chaperone. When Mrs. McBurney arrives at our house I can't help but smile. She's wearing a veiled hat with a black dress. I pin a pink corsage to her collar, holding my breath so as not to smell her.

"Thank you, Joy," she says. People always get our names mixed up even though we're really different. "I'm Grace," I say. "Shall we go?"

Despite looking like she's dressed for a funeral, Mrs. McBurney's face beams as we walk across the street together. I don't think she even notices when I scoot my chair a bit farther away from her at the banquet table. We're sitting across from Donna Sue Brady from my Sunday school class. I'm still mad at her for that time she ratted on me last year, but at least I have someone besides adults to talk to.

Donna Sue leans forward and taps me on the hand. "Did you hear about that blind girl?"

"No. What happened?"

"Nobody's seen her for a few weeks."

"Really?"

Donna Sue nods. "I heard her grandma sent her off to some special school for the blind."

Donna Sue's mama smacks her daughter in the back of the head. "That's enough!"

I'm dying to hear more, but Mrs. Brady starts in about how gossip is a sin and we shouldn't be spreading rumors about the Anderson girl. I head to the banquet table before I say something I might regret.

The food is mostly casseroles. I fill my plate with mashed potatoes and cake and start shoveling it into my mouth while several church ladies read mother-themed poems and stories. Hope says her verses without missing a single word and gets lots of applause. After dinner they give away the table decorations to the person who has an X under her chair, as if anyone would actually want an ugly piece of Styrofoam with a glittery MOM and fake flowers sticking out of it. But when Hope gets the *X* at our table she cradles her prize as if it were made of real gold. She shows it to Mama, who drops it, spilling glitter all over the white paper tablecloth. Hope looks like she's about to cry until another lady trades hers for the one she got.

It's finally time to announce "Mother of the Year." Last year when they chose Mama I just about fell out of my chair. She'd stood on the podium bawling until Mrs. Franks went up and helped her back to her seat. I guess they felt obligated to choose her since she's the pastor's wife, but last year was definitely not an award-winning kind of year for Mama. Even before Marilyn was born, she was already starting to slip away from us.

I drop my forkful of chocolate cake when Mrs. Franks announces this year's winner.

"Violet McBurney," she says into the microphone.

I look over at my temporary mother-for-a-night to watch her reaction. She just sits there gazing sweetly at Mrs. Franks, who is wearing a satisfied smile.

"You won!" I say, reaching over to jiggle Mrs. McBurney's wrinkly arm.

She startles out of her glazed-over stare and looks at me. "Me? No, you must have heard wrong, honey."

"Violet?" Mrs. Franks repeats her name. "Come on up, dear."

I watch as my "mother" slowly removes the napkin from her lap and sets it on the table. She rises from her chair and hobbles up to the platform. One of her legs is shorter than the other so when she walks it looks as though she's climbing over something with each step. By the time she reaches Mrs. Franks everybody in the place is clapping. I'm clapping so hard my hands burn. I feel proud, even if I'm just her pretend daughter for tonight. I look toward Mama, who has fallen asleep in her chair. Not even a room full of clapping wakes her. Hope's pretending not to notice, but I catch her kicking at Mama's leg with the toe of her red shoe.

Mrs. McBurney accepts the wooden plaque from Mrs. Franks and holds it close to her body. She chews on the side of her mouth like she always does when she's nervous. She stands in front of the crowd with her slip hanging below her old dress and holes in both her stockings, too bewildered to speak. After all the women settle down she tilts her chin toward the microphone and squeaks out a crackly, "Thank you."

When Mrs. McBurney sits back at our table, tears run down her cheek and I realize mine are wet, too. I scoot my chair next to hers and put my head on her shoulder. She takes my hand and strokes the top of it with her callused thumb. Beneath the layer of cigar smoke and perspiration a cross between homemade biscuits and Ponds moisturizing cream breaks through the surface of her wrinkled skin.

When we get home from the banquet I sneak out the back door and climb the steps to the loft two at a time. I've decided I can't wait until morning to talk about the banquet and to tell Lyle I know he was telling the truth the other night.

"Lyle? Are you back there?"

No answer. I look everywhere, even under the pews, but the place is entirely empty of all his things. No paper plates, no jacket, no blanket. Not even the fork he leaves on the pew for me to wash. The only thing left of Lyle is the shape of his body in the pile of straw.

16

On the last day of school Lola steps off the sidewalk and climbs the stairs of the bus. I feel like the best part of my life is about to disappear. What if she ends up not liking me anymore like most everyone else in school? What if she makes a new best friend over the summer and I'm all alone again? Now that Lyle has disappeared it feels like I'll be completely alone. They are the only two people around here who I can be myself with and not feel like a weirdo.

Lola pulls the latches and slides the bus window down so we can talk. "Don't look so sad, Grace. It's not like we can't still chat on the phone." The bus doors close and the wheels start to roll. I chase after it, waving wildly. "Call me!" Lola grins, throwing me the peace sign. Just as the bus reaches the far end of the lot I catch sight of her two white butt cheeks pressed against the window of the emergency doors at the back of the bus. I love her so much.

I walk back inside the school and stand with my hands on my hips watching Chastity slowly empty the cubby outside her third grade classroom. She checks both sides of a piece of paper, then carefully folds it into a neat square before tucking it into a pocket folder. Knowing Chas, she'll organize everything to take home, right down to the last eraser.

"Hurry up, slowpoke," I say. "School will be starting again by the time you finish."

"I have to clean everything out. Miss Burmeister said so."

"Fine. You can walk home by yourself."

When I start to turn away she dumps everything into a paper bag and runs up the empty hallway.

"Wait up!" She catches up to me at the front doors. "Did you pass sixth grade?"

"Of course, dodo bird. Only dummies don't pass."

"So did you pass?"

"Shut up, Chas."

"I'm telling Daddy you said shut up."

"Yeah, well, how about I tell him you were on the monkey bars in your dress again with boys staring up at your underpants?"

"Was not."

"Were too."

I push through the double glass doors and Chastity runs out ahead of me. A wave of dread passes through me before I recognize what it is. The tiny red hairs on my arm stand straight up and my feet refuse to move. My sister calls to me from the sidewalk.

"Why are you just standing there? I thought you were in a hurry." When she turns around to look for me she busts out laughing. "Your hair!" she says. "You look like you stuck your finger in a light socket."

"Look up," I say, pointing.

Above us a sticky wind plays roughly with the American flag as it smacks against our yellowed sky. The air feels thick with raindrops hanging just out of reach, waiting for permission to let go. Up and down the street, people start spilling out of their houses, gazing toward heaven. They step softly, as if the ground might give way beneath their feet.

"C'mon, Chas. There's a storm coming."

Joy rolls up on her new Schwinn 3-speed. "You guys better hurry or you're going to get sucked up by a tornado," she says, grinning.

"Tornados don't really suck people up," I say.

"How do you know? Oh yeah. You know

233

everything." She straddles the powder-blue bar and pats the seat behind her for Chastity to hitch a ride. "The rest of us listen to the weatherman."

Chastity tosses her bag into the front wicker basket and climbs up, holding on to Joy's waist with her chubby arms.

"Say hello to the Wizard of Oz for me!" Joy says.

"Look out for that house falling on you!" I shout as they speed away. But the wind carries my words the wrong way, slapping me in the face with a picture of Joy's brown shoes sticking out from under our front porch. I shake the image from my mind. As much as she bugs me, I love my sister. The thought of losing another person is just too much *much*.

The train whistle blows in the distance as it chugs through town. Leaves swirl around my feet, then catch a ride into the air before chasing down the street. I run all the way home. When I reach the house, Joy's bike is on its side with the wheels still spinning. Mama stands in the front yard, a flowered housedress dancing around her bare legs. Her crinkled forehead relaxes a bit when she sees me, then folds again as she peers up the road.

"Hope's not home yet," we say at the same time.

Mama glances at her watch. "The bus should be here by now."

The bus driver has started dropping Hope off in front of our house. She says it's on her way home anyway, and this way she can make sure Hope doesn't leave anything behind.

"Let's go inside, Mama. You can watch from the porch." I tug at her arm, but she refuses to move.

"Go on, Grace. I'll be right in."

As soon as the screen door slams behind me the sky opens up. Within seconds Mama is soaked to the bone. I run back out and grab her hand, pulling her into the house just as the town siren starts to howl. Somebody has sighted a funnel cloud.

"I've got Marilyn," Joy hollers on her way to the basement.

I pull two blankets out of the linen closet and hand them to Chastity. "Here. Take these downstairs. I'll be right back." Climbing two steps at a time, I run to our room and pull Monopoly and Scrabble from under our bed. I stop to watch the rain gushing from the eaves past our window. As I head down the basement stairs I utter a silent prayer. *Please, God, let Lyle be okay.*

We take our place in the northeast corner of the basement, just like always. My heart thundering inside my chest seems almost as loud as the storm outside.

"I get to be banker," Joy says, setting up the board. Chastity and I don't even try to argue with her. Joy always gets to be banker. She dumps the playing pieces into the lid of the box and grabs her favorite. "I'm the car."

"I'll be the dog," I say. I like the dog. Daddy won't let us have one. The only reason he allowed Pippy is because Mama fell in love with the kitten I found in the barn when we moved here.

Chastity picks up each of the silver-colored pieces one by one, studying them. She tucks her feet under her blue dress and chews on her lower lip.

Joy sighs. "For crying out loud, Chas, just pick one or I'll pick it for you."

"I'll be the iron," Chastity finally says.

Joy and I both giggle. Only Chastity would pick the iron.

I glance toward the stairs. "What do you think is taking Mama so long?"

"She's still waiting for Hope. Stop worrying and roll the dice to see who goes first."

I roll snake eyes, which means I'm last. While my sisters take their first turns I run up the stairs to see what's keeping Mama. I find her at the front picture window, shivering. A brilliant jagged line lights up the darkened sky outside, immediately followed by a *crack!* that makes us both jump.

"Mama?"

She doesn't move. I close my eyes and make a picture of Hope in my mind. I see her huddled on the floor with her hands clasped over her head, praying to beat the band. "Mama, she's still at her school."

Mama turns to look at me. "She's okay?" she whispers.

I nod.

We both look toward the phone just before it rings. It's one of the other mamas telling us that Hope's school is keeping the kids until the threat of tornado is over. Mama's hand trembles as she sets the receiver back on the cradle. I know she's thinking about that ice-cream truck and how she almost lost Hope once before.

In the window behind Mama, I glimpse Daddy holding a newspaper over his head as he bolts from the church parking lot toward our house. It's strange to see Daddy run. I've never even seen him walk fast before. Just as he reaches our yard a gust of wind wrestles the newspaper from his hands and carries it up the street. He crashes through the front door staring at us like a wild-eyed dog.

"Why aren't you all in the basement? There's a tornado over Lake Michigan headed this way!" He says it through gasps, his chest heaving. Mama moves back to the window, twisting the hem of her wet dress with her fingers.

"She's worried about Hope," I say. "The school's keeping the kids until the storm passes."

He walks up behind Mama. "She's safer there, Izzy." He tugs at her arm, but she resists.

I touch her other arm. "She's gonna be okay, Mama."

She relaxes just a bit and lets Daddy lead her toward the basement stairs.

"Grace, get going," he says, nudging me with his hand against the middle of my back.

In the basement, Mama keeps her ear glued to the weather reports on a transistor radio while the storm howls outside. Daddy holds her hand, squeezing every now and then to let her know he's still there. A curtain of rain pelts the glass until the window wells fill with muddy water. My sisters and I pass the time trying to scare each other and sneaking past Boardwalk.

"I heard it sounds like a train roaring overhead," Joy says, as she steals a fifty from

Free Parking. She adjusts Marilyn, who has fallen asleep, to her other arm.

A huge crack of thunder booms above us, rattling the windows. Chastity scampers over to Mama and Daddy and I follow. The lights flicker on and off twice before the room goes completely dark. Above us our whole house shakes, the wind leaning it one way and then the house fighting its way back to center. Mama starts humming "A Shelter in the Time of Storm," which is meant to comfort us but for some reason makes me even more scared. Chastity climbs onto Daddy's knee and I lean against Mama's shoulder. Even when the next bolt of lightning hits a tree in the yard, Joy stays silent in the corner holding Marilyn. The light throws itself over the shape of my sister, her blanket like a superhero cape around her narrow shoulders.

Half an hour passes before the wind finally quiets down and the rain becomes light finger taps on the windows. A voice from Mama's radio announces that the twister touched down on a farm about two miles west of Cherry Hill and then disappeared. When the weatherman gives the all clear, Daddy says we can go upstairs.

We stand outside in the aftermath of the tornado that has missed us by three hills.

Roof shingles dot the yard between broken branches that carpet the wet ground. It looks like there's enough of them to make up a whole tree. A telephone pole rests across the cab of our neighbor's truck. I glance toward the barn. If only Lyle were in there, safe and sound. When Daddy follows my gaze I look away.

"Thank God it jumped those hills," Daddy says, shaking his head at the mess.

He sends me to fetch the trash barrel and we all start picking up the smaller branches. "Might as well not waste any time pouting," he says.

Mama's gone back to staring up the road. About the time the barrel is heaped full, Hope's bus pulls up in front of the house. She trips on a branch and lands with both palms out, but scrambles right back up. Mama runs over and hugs her like you do someone you haven't seen for years. The bus pulls away and a TV van from WCHR takes its place in front of our house. A man I recognize from the six o'clock news jumps out. He and Daddy talk in hushed voices before the man waves for his cameraman to join them. The next thing I know Daddy's standing on the sidewalk with a bright light shining in his face.

"Reverend Carter," the man says, "were

you afraid?"

Daddy looks straight into the camera. "No, sir. If God had seen fit to take me and my family to be with Him, then so be it. As it was, He spared us. That just means the Lord has more work for me to do here." Before the interviewer can ask the next question, Daddy pulls the microphone toward his face. "And for those of you listening, you may want to show up in church on Sunday and show your gratitude for His mercy."

The man in the trench coat wrenches the mike from Daddy's grip. "Thank you, Reverend," he says, and makes a "cut" sign under his chin.

When nobody is watching I sneak up to the loft. Still no Lyle. I sit on the front pew and close my eyes. I try to picture where he might be, but my mind is like a blank chalkboard. The Knowing isn't like a ghost that can go through closed doors. If someone doesn't want me to see them, I can't. But I can feel him. I feel his loneliness and his sadness as if they are my own. Maybe they *are* mine. Maybe the reason we get along so well is because we know exactly how the other feels.

His fork sticks out from under a pile of straw. I pick it up and wipe it off on my shirt. Some part of Lyle is still on the fork because I can feel him here, even though he's not. I put the back of the prongs against my cheek and close my eyes. I see a boat a tiny ways off from an unfamiliar shore. Pine trees line the bank with a little cabin set back into the woods. A barefoot woman walks out the front door and down to the shore. She has a handsome face, like an Indian princess. She waves excitedly to the man on the boat. He stands, shades his eyes with his hand, and smiles in a way that takes up all the light from the surface of the water.

I open my eyes. Is that where Lyle used to live? Was the woman his wife? He's never told me about her. We've talked so much about me, but he rarely tells about himself. There's so much more I want to know. If he ever comes back I'll ask him about her. I'll ask him about the boat and that place and why on earth he would leave it.

Daddy lets us stay up late to watch him on the news, but they show an interview with Mr. Lewis instead. Their Plymouth is upside down on top of their house. He says he hated the car anyway because it was a lemon. And then he burped right on TV in front of the whole world. I guess cars rest-

ing on roofs are more exciting than grateful
preachers.

17

Mama's doctors sent her to Woodlands Rest Home for the last half of July. She missed this year's baptism service, but so did I. I pretended to be sick so I wouldn't have to watch other people get baptized when it was supposed to be my turn. Daddy brought Mama back home two days ago. She doesn't seem very rested if you ask me. She still naps a lot and when she is up and around she bumps into the walls. Joy won't let Mama hold Marilyn unless she's sitting down. Mama reminds me of a Dilly Bar from the Dairy Queen, like there's only a thin shell covering what's melting inside.

With Mama sleeping so much we're mostly on our own. Hope goes to summer school during the week. I don't like to swim, so Joy and Chastity usually take Marilyn to the beach during the day. I once slipped through the middle of an inner tube and swallowed a lot of water. I thought I was drowning for sure until I stood up and everyone laughed because the water was only up to my armpits.

I spend a lot of time riding around on the ugly bike Daddy got at the Salvation Army for five dollars. After forgetting about his promise to bring us to the roller rink for my birthday he came home with the bike a couple weeks later. He bragged that they were asking ten dollars, but he talked them into a clergy discount. I painted it black with Rust-Oleum because I thought it would be cool. It turned out uglier than it started. I don't even care. The feel of the wind in my face after I pump up the hills, then race down the other side more than makes up for its looks.

I'm practicing popping wheelies in the church parking lot when I spy Billy Wolf out of the corner of my eye. Before I can get away he pulls into the lot and starts following me around in his red car. He's sixteen but he still picks on kids half his age. He knows I'm scared of him. Who wouldn't be? One look from those half-closed snaky eyes of his gives me the heebie-jeebies. I've heard rumors that maybe he's the one who molested that girl last year. They still haven't found the culprit.

"Hey, weirdo," he says out the window.

"Where'd ya get such an ugly bike?"

When I don't answer he pulls up right next to me and chuckles. He cups one hand over his mouth and spits into it, grinning. "Here's a special kiss," he says. Billy sticks his arm out the window and slaps the side of my face, smearing my cheek and knocking me off balance. My front wheel hits the curb and I fly forward over the bike, sliding along the ground until my shirt is up to my neck. I hear him laughing as he circles the lot one more time before peeling out, throwing a shower of dirt in my direction.

I sit up and peer inside my shirt to inspect the damage. My right nipple is peeled partly away from my skin, bits of gravel in its former place. I try pushing it back onto my chest, which is striped with bloody scratches, but it just hangs there. The sight of it makes me dizzy. When my head finally clears I grab hold of the handlebars and run alongside my crooked bike, hoping Billy doesn't ambush me again on the way home.

Standing in the kitchen, I lift my shirt to show Daddy the damage. He pulls in a breath, then turns away.

"Joy should be home soon. She'd be better at that." He keeps his wide back to me.

"But, Daddy, look. It's coming off! I don't want Joy to fix it, I want Mama."

His shoulders flinch at the mention of her name. "You know your mama can't do it, Grace." He grabs a pile of mail off the counter and busies himself opening an envelope with a butter knife that has strawberry jelly on it.

I run to the bathroom, afraid to put my shirt down where it will stick to the blood again. "Fine! I'll do it myself."

Normally I'd get smacked for talking to him with disrespect, but he doesn't say a word. I close the door and rummage through the medicine chest to find the Mercurochrome and Band-Aids. I don't make a sound when dabbing the scratches with a soaked cotton ball, even though it hurts like Hades. But I let out a scream when I try to pick a piece of gravel out of my chest.

Daddy knocks on the bathroom door. "Uh, you okay in there?"

I'm trying my best not to cry, but a worm of tear tracks makes a path through the dirt on my face.

Another light tap. "Grace?"

I feel his hand on the outside of the door before it opens. He takes a step inside, looks at his shoes. "You want me to fetch your sister from the beach?"

"No!" I clutch my shirt in front of me,

holding it away from my skin. He raises his gaze to meet mine, then slowly lets his eyes fall to my battered chest. I drop my arms at my sides, then collapse on the edge of the bathtub, sobbing.

He moves toward me, a wave of Old Spice one step ahead of him. "Okay, now. We'll get you fixed up."

One by one, he plucks sharp stones with tweezers held between his fat finger and thumb. He accidentally pokes me with the sharp end of the tiny tongs and I half expect my nose to light up and a buzzer to sound.

"Sorry," he says.

Once the gravel is out, he dabs my nipple with iodine and tapes it back into place with a square piece of gauze and white tape. I flinch just a tiny bit, but keep quiet.

"There," he says, handing me my shirt. "Good as new."

Even though he's just seen my girl parts up close, I turn away to put my top back on. When I turn around again, he's gone.

I wanted Daddy to call Mrs. Wolf and tell her what a bully her son is, but he refused. He says he doesn't want to make any trouble. What about my trouble? I think, but I don't say it out loud.

I've decided to do it myself. I call Mrs.

Wolf and tell her what happened.

"My Billy would never do a thing like that," she says.

I inform her that yes, he certainly would — and did — but she just poo-poos me as if the whole idea is ridiculous. Some people are totally blind to their kids. Joy told me Billy was adopted and that's why he's so mean. I have a pretty good idea why his real parents gave him away.

I slam down the phone and march into the living room, where my sisters are watching *I Love Lucy.*

"I wish Billy Wolf would die!"

"Get in line," Joy says, without turning away from the TV.

After supper I go to work on a jigsaw puzzle I've been putting together for a month. It's a picture of a herd of buffalo in a snowstorm. With all that white, it's the hardest one I've ever tried to finish. I've only snapped three new pieces into place when Joy races into my bedroom and knocks half the sky off the card table. She's all out of breath.

"Joy! Look what you did!"

She sits on my bed. "Joey Wolf got hit by a car."

My mouth drops a mile. "What happened?"

"He didn't look before riding his bike out of their driveway. A car ran him over."

"Is he going to be okay?" My voice is shaking.

"He's dead, Grace."

"Dead? Are you sure it wasn't his brother Billy?"

"It was Joey, all right. I saw Billy on my way home."

My heart feels like it just folded in half.

"Get out of my room!" I scream.

"What's the matter with you? It's not like you and Joey were best friends or anything. Sheesh."

"Get out!"

Joy whirls around and I slam the door behind her. Kneeling beside my bed, I lace my fingers together and pray harder than I've ever prayed in my life.

Dear God. I'm so sorry for wishing Billy was dead. I'll give you anything I have in trade for my horrible thoughts. Please forgive me.

I'm still hiding in my room three hours later when Daddy hollers up the stairs for us all to go to bed.

The next day during Vacation Bible School we're making plaques shaped like open Bibles with John 3:16 written on them.

250

Every August we try to scoop up as many kids in the county as possible and expose them to Jesus. I think most of the parents send their kids to get rid of them for a while because they're bored and sick of each other. I'm looking for the brown paint when one of the girls from the trailer park whispers, "I heard he bit his tongue off when he got hit and the ambulance guy just picked it up off the road and stuffed it back in Joey's mouth." She pours plaster of Paris into her mold while the rest of the kids all suck on their tongues, checking to make sure they're attached.

I feel like I'm going to throw up. Leaving my project on the table, I push through the heavy front doors of the church and head toward home. A loud car roars up behind me as soon as I cross the street. I turn just in time to see Billy Wolf's mean face in the window when he whizzes by in his red Chevelle. He swerves toward the shoulder of the road as he passes our house, nearly losing control of his car before speeding up the hill out of sight.

When I reach our sidewalk I find Pippy's flattened body lying in a puddle of blood and fur in front of our house. Squatting, I stroke her limp body, still so warm. Tears burn my eyes. I carry her to the meadow

251

behind our barn and dig a hole. I lower Pippy's body into the ground, crying so hard I can't stop hiccupping. I fall asleep in the grass until Chastity's voice wakes me, calling for Pippy from the back door of the house. I keep quiet. This secret is between God and me.

18

The Coopmans own most of the orchards in Cherry Hill. Their fruit stands line the road coming both ways into town with signs that lead up to them. Each sign has only one word on it, I guess for slow readers or fast drivers. *Fresh. Cherries. Just. Ahead. Best. Prices. Sweet. Sour. Red. Black. Yum!* First thing after breakfast this morning I head into town with fifty cents Daddy gave me to buy a quart. My bike is a little crooked thanks to Billy Wolf. Ralph at the service station did a pretty good job of fixing the frame. The wheels are still a bit bent, but it gets me places faster than my two feet. I ride up to the white-painted cherry stand near the lake.

Mrs. Coopman is not typical of rich folks. She doesn't get her hair done at the Bee Bonnet like most of the other ladies. Instead, she wears her graying hair tucked up under a big straw hat with strands falling out around her face. I figure it must be near to her elbows, which is pretty long for someone in her sixties. She's beautiful for her age, with high cheekbones and eyes that smile before her mouth does.

Mrs. Coopman watches as I run my hands over the piles of ruby-red cherries. I want to pick the container with the most fruit because I plan to eat a few on the way back. The more I start out with the less likely Daddy will notice a few missing.

"Would you like to taste one first?" She winks at me from under her huge brim.

"Sure."

Mrs. Coopman hands me a few black cherries, plump as all get-out and dark as blood. I roll one around in my mouth, cool and slippery, before biting into it. The flesh is just-right chewy and sweet as candy, still warm from the sun.

"Good, huh?" she says.

I nod, not wanting to talk with a pit in my mouth and not wanting to swallow it either.

"I'll fill you up a fresh quart."

She turns her back to me while I suck the last bit of fruit off the pit. I figure on spitting it out once I leave since it wouldn't be ladylike to do here. But I must've eaten too fast because I get the hiccups and I'm worried I might choke on the pit. Sweat starts to drizzle under my arms as I try to banish thoughts of my grisly death by cherry pit from my mind. Just as Mrs. Coopman turns back around I spit the pit, full force, and watch in horror as it lands on top of her wrist. I gasp, mortified by my cloddish act.

Mrs. Coopman looks down at the pit stuck to her arm and smiles. "You should enter the annual Pit-Spit in this year's Cherry Festival, Grace. I believe you might have a shot at winning."

"I'm sorry," I say. I now think I might die of embarrassment instead of choking.

Mrs. Coopman flicks it off her arm. "Don't worry about it." She pops a cherry into her mouth. In one slick motion she maneuvers the pit to the front of her lips and *floof,* lets it fly. It pings off the handlebar of my bike. "Your aim is good," she says. "You just need a little work on distance."

I laugh my head off. Mrs. Coopman is nothing like most of the ladies in this town, even the not-so-rich ones. She dumps my quart of cherries into a paper sack and I hand her two quarters.

"Say, Grace," she says. "You're twelve now, aren't you?"

"Yes, ma'am. Twelve-and-a-half." I wipe my sweaty hands on Joy's hand-me-down shorts.

"Would you be interested in working for us? We could use a few extra hands."

It's the best thing that could have happened today, save for Mama snapping out of her low-down mood.

"You bet I would!"

She waves at a couple of tourists approaching the stand, then turns back toward me. "You'll need permission from your father."

"No problem. When can I start?"

"Well, you can come on Monday if you like. We begin at seven a.m. in the east orchard behind the high school. Can you meet us on the truck up at the house around a quarter 'til?"

"Sure I can."

"Bring a sack lunch and a note from the reverend."

"Okay. I'll be there."

I fold the top of the bag over the handlebars, then pedal my ugly bike home as fast as I can, forgetting all about the cherries I'd planned to stop and eat on the way. The screen door bangs behind me as I race through it.

"Daddy?"

No answer.

"He's still at work," Chastity answers from in front of the TV.

"Hey, you're not allowed to watch soap operas, Chas."

I set the bag of cherries on the coffee table and watch as a beautiful nurse in a short, white uniform kisses a man in his hospital bed. She doesn't look anything like the nurses I've ever seen in real life. Chastity turns her head toward me, the rest of her body flat out on the floor in front of the screen with her chin in her hands. She doesn't see very well, but she won't tell anyone because she thinks she'll look ugly in glasses. Chastity would look beautiful in a garbage bag and diving flippers.

"Who's gonna tell?"

"Well, at least back up a little. You're going to hurt your eyes."

"Too late," she says, and turns back to the screen just as the nurse pulls the curtain around her patient's bed and the romantic music starts up.

Across town, the six o'clock whistle blows at the fruit processing plant, sending half the town home for supper. I'm making grilled cheese sandwiches with applesauce and tomato soup, one of Daddy's favorite meals. He walks into the kitchen with a day's growth of whiskers and saggy eye bags but brightens when he sees what I'm cooking. I pull out the end chair, his spot, and holler for everyone to come to supper. Mama doesn't come to the table, but I set aside an extra serving for her and one for Lyle just in case he's come back.

The first two sandwiches go to Daddy, along with a scoop of applesauce that I've sprinkled with cinnamon to make it fancier. When I turn back to the stove, smoke is rising from the griddle. I carry the sandwiches to the sink and scrape them off as fast as I can. I shovel one burnt-side down onto Chastity's plate just as she comes through the door.

"Let's bow our heads and say Grace," Daddy says.

My sisters point at me and mouth my name, grinning. They used to do it out loud, but it made Daddy mad, so now they just pretend to say it. It's getting old.

"Bless this food to our bodies that we may use it to serve the Lord Jesus Christ our Savior. Amen." We say it all together, though Joy's voice is barely above a whisper. She doesn't like to pray out loud.

We're almost finished eating by the time I get up my nerve.

"Daddy, would it be okay if I picked cherries for the Coopmans?"

He wipes his mouth with a square of

paper towel. I know what he's thinking. They're Catholics.

"Daddy?"

He takes a swig of milk. "Let me finish in peace while I think about it."

Joy practically swallows her sandwich in one gulp. "I've gotta babysit for the Pooles," she says, pushing away from the table. Joy has recently cut her blond hair short, like Twiggy. It looks cute on her, in a boyish way. As she passes the table she stops and kisses Daddy on the cheek. "I'm taking Marilyn with me," she says.

She tosses her paper plate into the garbage and places her glass in the sink. He watches her leave, then goes back to chewing. Hope pulls a hair out of her applesauce, studies it, then holds it up to her head. It's the same length as hers, just past her shoulders. She hides it in her paper napkin and goes on eating quietly.

"What do they pay you?" Daddy finally asks.

"Mrs. Coopman said we get fifty cents a bucket."

"No wonder they can afford a new truck every year. They charge us fifty cents for a measly quart."

"It would help with school clothes, Daddy. I could buy some of my own."

259

Chastity makes a whining sound from her side of the table. "Hey, my grilled cheese is burnt!" She turns her sandwich over and dangles it over her paper plate like a dead fish.

"It is not, Chas," I say. I lean closer to her and whisper, "Wanna be a patient at *General Hospital*?" She shuts up after that.

Daddy takes a bite out of his second sandwich and chews even slower than usual. He finally swallows. "You can work for them on three conditions."

I feel my pulse pump an extra beat.

"One: No Sundays."

I figured on that one.

"Two: You tithe ten percent in the offering plate."

I forgot about that, but I should have seen it coming.

"And three . . ."

He takes another bite without finishing his sentence. Waiting is agony. Finally, he clears his throat.

"Three: Stay away from the migrant workers. I don't want you talking to them, not that they can speak English anyway. They're dirty and they like white girls. Stay away from them, you hear?"

I resist the urge to start singing "Jesus Loves the Little Children," a Sunday school song with a chorus that goes, "Red and yellow, black and white, Jesus loves them in his sight." It's the first time I realized that they left out brown.

"Thank you, Daddy," is all I say before clearing my plate.

At 6 a.m. Monday morning I slip into a pair of cutoffs, a sleeveless T-shirt, and my old tennies. I tie a red bandanna over my hair and tiptoe downstairs as quietly as I can. I grab the lunch I packed last night and head out the door with a banana to eat on the way. I hop on my bike, passing a group of white-coated workers walking toward the processing plant. By the time I reach the Coopmans' driveway, the back of the flatbed is already full of people, most of them migrant workers. I recognize Doug Lewis and his sister Sally.

I set down my bike and climb up next to them.

"Hi, Grace," they say.

"Hi," I say.

Doug says something else just as the truck starts up, so I can't hear him. Sally pulls thin strands of long, dark hair out from behind her ears self-consciously, but they poke through anyway. She looks at me and I smile at her as we bump along the driveway. The migrant workers say nothing, not one word. Our truck travels up Fourth Avenue and out Bing Street to the two-track dirt path leading to the orchards. When we reach the top of the hill the truck jerks to a stop. Doug hands me a bucket from a stack on the side of the truck.

"Grab a harness, Grace. There's never enough to go around so it's first come, first serve."

I lift a burlap strap with buckles and hooks hanging off it from the pile and jump down from the end of the truck. Mr. Coopman points to a row and I follow Doug and Sally down a path between two lines of trees.

"Look for a full one," Doug says. "The trick is to find a tree with lots of clumps of cherries. Otherwise you'll spend most of your day moving the ladder."

I watch him strap on his harness and hook his bucket on the front of it. I do the same with mine, but the pail hits my knees.

"Here," he says. "You need to adjust it." He yanks on the back and the bucket slides up. I start to follow him to the tree he's chosen. "No more than two to a tree. Sorry, Grace. You can work the one next to us if you want."

Doug and Sally begin plucking cherries from the bottom branches and dropping them into their buckets. The tree next to the one Doug has chosen is sparse with a few cherries hanging in scattered clumps. I venture farther down the row until I find a tree bursting with fruit and earning potential. Not to mention eating potential. This has got to be the best job ever.

Every time I fill a bucket I carry it to the end of the row. One of the supervisors dumps it in a huge crate, then punches a card with my name on it. At the end of the week we'll give the card to Mr. Coopman to tally up. It takes me about an hour to fill a bucket. This is because I have eaten nearly a quart and practiced spitting pits. I never knew cherries tasted so much better when you eat them straight off the tree. I do the math in my head and figure I can make about twenty-two dollars a week. That's more money than I've ever had at one time.

After dumping my third bucket at the truck, I climb the tree to get to the cherries near the top. Most everyone else uses a ladder, but I feel safer in the branches. From up here I can see the lake, nearly the whole town of Cherry Hill, and the railroad tracks running through the middle of it. Below me the migrant workers call out to one another. Their language comes out in a rush of syllables. I like the musical sound of it.

I'm leaning out to the edge of a branch with my bucket nearly full, when a horn blares, nearly startling me out of the tree. Next thing I know, everybody floods out of the orchard and walks toward the truck because the Coopmans provide lemonade to go with your lunch.

I sit down under a tree with Doug and Sally and pull out my egg salad sandwich.

"How many so far?" Doug asks.

"Four." I take a bite of my sandwich, but I'm not very hungry. I may have eaten a few too many cherries.

"That's pretty good for your first day. I'm only one bucket ahead of you. I think you're tied with Sally."

Sally nods as she goes back for a second glass of lemonade. She doesn't talk much.

"Say, you want to have a contest? See who can get the most buckets by the end of the week?"

"What's the winner get?" I ask.

"How about an ice-cream cone from the Dairy Queen? Triple scoop."

"Dipped in chocolate?"

"Deal!" he says.

"Deal," I say, even though the thought of eating anything else right now makes my stomach swirl.

■ ■ ■ ■

By lunchtime on Wednesday I'm five buckets behind Doug. I hate the thought of giving up an hour's work to him. Especially since he rubs it in every chance he gets.

"Five and a half so far this morning," he says as he shoves a handful of Fritos into his face.

I get up and move farther down the row.

"Hey, you're not getting sore about losing, are you, Grace?"

"No," I call out behind me. "I just want to claim this other tree I saw earlier."

I lean back against the tree next to a family of migrant workers and unwrap my PJ sandwich. A Mexican woman with a baby in a sling on her back slathers a gooey mixture onto tortillas and hands them out to several children sitting patiently on a blanket. The older children watch the younger children while the parents and elder siblings work. Some of the babysitters are younger than the kids Joy sometimes babysits.

One of the toddlers wanders closer to me and smiles. *"Cabello rojo?"* she says. I can tell it's a question by the way her voice goes up at the end. I open my mind to find hers already open.

"Would you like to touch it?" I ask it in English, holding a handful of my bushy red tresses out toward her. She toddles closer and I lean forward. She takes a couple more steps and gently runs her fingers through my hair. She squeals before running back toward the other children. The mother scolds the girl, but I shake my head and smile.

"It's okay," I say.

She smiles back, throwing her hands up as if to say, "Kids!" She mumbles something and the next thing I know I'm surrounded by a slew of barefoot children, all taking turns touching my hair. They jump back at first, as if expecting red hair to be hot, then come back for another feel. I love being surrounded by so many beautiful children. I wonder if Mama felt this way with all of us scrambling for her attention.

The woman calls out in Spanish and the children run back and lay down on blankets. She puts the smallest baby to her breast and sings softly. Despite the noisy trucks and forklifts, most of the children fall asleep within minutes. I rub my eyes and fight the urge to find a place on those blankets, but the sight of Doug heading back into the orchard forces me to my feet. This isn't

266

about ice cream anymore.

When I finish the tree I started before lunch I move to the back of the orchard to look for another full one. I find a tree bursting with so many cherries that it's more red than green. I charge up to it, claiming it as my own. Out of the corner of my eye, I watch a young Mexican man under the tree next to me work his fingers over a branch, cleaning the cherries off in one sweep. He catches me watching and grins. *They like white girls.* I quickly look away, but the urge to figure out how he picks so fast gets the best of me and I find myself studying the movements of his hands. He sets his ladder against a branch closer to my tree and starts in on it. He's holding his body away so I have a better view.

"Would you like me to show you?" He says it in Spanish, but I hear him in English.

"Sí," I say, one of only two words I know in Spanish.

He drops his hands and walks over to me. Putting his hands over and just above mine, he strips the cherries off at about half his normal speed. His fingers play over the branch like an angel plucking a harp.

He backs up. "You try," he says.

I clean most of the cherries from the branch but get all the leaves with them. I pick them out of my bucket. We get yelled at for too many leaves.

"No, no," he says. "Feel. Pull only where there is light resistance. The cherries will come to you. The leaves want to stay behind."

I try again on a new branch. This time he puts his hands over mine and mingles our fingers together. I don't feel scared at all. In fact, I like the way his hands feel over mine. They're strong but small and delicate for a man's hands. Much smaller than Daddy's and gentle like rain as they flutter over the cherries.

"Close your eyes," he says. "Let your fingers decide when to pull."

I squeeze my eyes closed. He lifts his hands away and I let my fingers work along the branch, hearing only the dull thud of the cherries hitting my nearly full bucket. I open my eyes to find the branch cleaned of cherries and only one leaf in my bucket.

The man grins and pats me on the shoulder. *"Bueno!"* he says.

"Manuel?" a voice calls from the other end of the row.

"Sí!" he calls back. *"Aquí!"*

"Gracias, Manuel," I say. The only other word I know in Spanish.

"Have a good day, señorita." He tips his

straw hat, before jogging up the row.

By the end of the day I'm only two buckets behind Doug and by the end of the week I've passed him by six.

"You must have cheated," he says when I show him my punch card. "You had that Mexican guy helping you."

"I picked every cherry myself," I say. Doug knows I don't lie.

"Oh, all right. I guess there are worse things than getting beat by a girl."

"Yeah," I say. "Like marrying an ugly one."

We laugh together in the way you do when you're so tired you could cry.

19

Daddy steps down from the pulpit and stands behind a table at the front of the sanctuary. A white cloth covers the table under shiny silver domes that hold the tiny communion glasses and little squares of bread. Daddy nods at the deacons. They walk down either side of the middle row of pews, passing the plate and the tray of tiny glasses while Daddy reads a passage from the Bible. The glasses have grape juice in them because drinking alcohol is a sin. Serving actual wine is another reason Daddy thinks the Catholics are wrong.

Only people who have been baptized get to take part in the ritual. Mama holds a little glass in one hand and a square of bread in the other. I didn't think she'd get out of bed this morning, let alone come to church, but she surprised us all. Maybe the new medicine is working. Hope and Joy each get the bread and juice, too. I once asked

Daddy if the bread was really Jesus's body and the juice his blood. He said no, it's only symbolic. I was relieved to hear that. Once everyone is served, Daddy reads the next verse. "Take, eat: This is my body which is broken for you. Do this in remembrance of me."

Daddy pops the bread into his mouth first, then everyone else does the same. Joy turns to me and opens her mouth as she takes the bread, rolling her eyes like it's chocolate fudge instead of stale bread. She chews slowly, then sticks out her tongue just to get my goat. I do my best to ignore her, but she knows I'm jealous.

"After the same manner also He took the cup, saying: 'This is my blood, drink it in remembrance of me.' "

Everyone with a glass throws back their juice, then sets the tiny glass in a rack that hangs on the back of the pew in front of them. *Clink, clunk, clink, clunk,* rings all across the church.

"For as often as you eat this bread and drink this cup, you honor the Lord's death until his return."

Momma dabs at her lips with a hankie as Daddy walks down the aisle, praying, holding his Bible over his head. When he reaches our pew, Mama steps out and joins him at the back of the church to help greet parishioners after the service. Chastity and I set to collecting the glasses and putting them back in the silver container, which is our job. When we've collected them all we carry them down to the kitchen and leave them for the church ladies to wash later.

"Let's go home," Chastity says. "I'm hungry."

"I'll be right there," I say. "I'm going to rinse these out so it will be easier for them to clean."

When I turn my back to her she runs off. I wait until her shoes *clap clap clap* across the tile floor to the carpeted stairs before lifting the lid from the bread. I dump the leftovers in an empty bread bag. I take the cover off the other serving piece that holds the tiny glasses. Each one sets in its own hole. Most of them are empty, but four or five unused ones are still full. I peek through the serving window to make sure nobody's there before plucking one of the full ones and drinking it. Welch's tastes way better than the watered-down off-brand that Daddy buys for home. I drink one more. Then the other three. I open the fridge and find the half-empty bottle of Welch's concord grape juice on the rack and guzzle the whole thing. Just as I set it on the counter I hear him in the doorway.

"Come to my office," Daddy says.

He motions for me to follow him. My heart is in my chest. I wait for him to move behind his desk filled with books, papers, and a picture of Mama from before they had kids. A huge map of the Middle East is pinned to the wall behind his desk. It's marked with the journey of the Israelites to the Promised Land. A second smaller map shows the apostle Paul's missionary journeys. We're mostly not allowed in here so right away I know I'm in a heap of trouble.

Daddy points to the steel folding chair in front of his desk. "Sit down."

"Daddy, I was thirsty . . . ."

"What are you talking about?"

"Nothing. I was just . . . nothing."

He points to the chair again. The metal feels cold against my bare legs when I sit.

"Grace, have you been feeding that old drunken hobo?"

"What?"

"You heard me. The truth, Grace. Sheriff Conner and I had a little talk."

"I was, Daddy, but not anymore. He left last spring."

"Right about the same time as that poor Anderson girl disappeared. Do you have any idea the danger you put yourself in?"

"But Lyle didn't have anything to do with that! He's a good person. I heard her grandma sent her to a special school for blind kids."

"Lyle Miller? Creeps like that get away with murder because they convince little girls that they're sweet as honey. You should know better."

He opens a drawer and tosses an envelope into my lap. I hang my head, fingering the crisp paper.

"Open it."

I tear open the envelope and immediately recognize the camp insignia for Camp Blessing. "Bible camp? The last week of summer? Daddy, no!"

"This retreat is a chance for you to let the Lord work through you and recommit your life to Christ."

There it is, his true feelings, right here in the open like a big ugly rock. I'm an embarrassment to Daddy and this family. All I've ever wanted is for him to be proud of me, to smile down on me with that sweet grin he saves for Joy when she gets another A or for Chastity when she curtsies for company and for Hope when she rattles off a slew of Scripture verses. I could get all As, dress like a beauty queen, and memorize the entire New Testament and it wouldn't matter. I don't know why I keep aiming to prove myself worthy of his approval, but I can't seem to stop trying. Maybe I'm just stubborn like Aunt Pearl says. She once told me I'd cut a hole in the wall before admitting it wasn't a door after I ran into it.

"But I am committed. Why don't you believe me?"

"I'll believe it when your actions match your words. Now go help your sister get dinner on the table."

I run out of the office and smack dab into Harold Weaver, knocking a stack of hymnals out of his arms. I immediately start crying.

"Whoa, what's the hurry?"

"I'm sorry. I'm such a klutz!"

He draws me close in a hug. "It's okay, honey. It was an accident. Don't cry."

When I pull away and start to pick up the song books he shoos me away. "I've got it. You go on home."

"I'm sorry," I say again, before running out the front doors of the church.

The following Saturday morning I find the old brown suitcase on the basement shelf above rows and rows of canned green and yellow string beans that Mama and Hope put up before Marilyn was born. I blow a layer of dust off the top and drag it upstairs to my room. Years of musty storage hits me in the face when I throw the suitcase on my bed and unsnap the tarnished latches. Borrowing a bottle of Chastity's Jean Naté spray cologne, I baptize the suitcase thoroughly, hoping the citrus scent will hide its smelly secrets.

It takes me less than fifteen minutes to fill the suitcase with dresses, shorts, tops, and one pair of patent leather shoes. In the back pocket goes my bathing suit, white cotton underwear, socks, and the bra that Aunt Pearl sent me for my birthday that I still don't fill out. I stuff my diary into a zippered compartment on the inside of the suitcase along with my favorite pen, one that writes in three different colors depending upon which part of the cap you push. I love to write in green. It feels like words growing out of the paper.

Maybe going away won't be so bad, even if it's for a week of Bible camp. Maybe when I get back Mama will be better. Maybe without having me around to remind her of Isaac will lessen her pain. It won't lessen mine. Not having Mama as part of our family is like having the thread slip from the needle. She pulled us all into this world and we need her to keep us sewn together.

Daddy drives me to Camp Blessing in the

old station wagon because the bus is on the fritz. The camp sits on a branch of Cherry Lake that's surrounded by pine trees. He signs me in at the lodge, where everyone knows him because he sometimes gives guest sermons. I hope Daddy's not coming this year because I've heard all his sermons at least a dozen times. Plus he always goes into overtime. According to Mama he's the longest-winded preacher in the county. Probably the state.

"Behave yourself," he says before climbing back in the car. Since we only live two miles from Camp Blessing it doesn't seem like a long goodbye is necessary. I drag my heavy suitcase and bedroll toward Miracles, the cabin that I was assigned to. I grab a top bunk against the wall. As I spread out my blankets and pillow a voice floats up from below.

"Hi there."

I hang my head over the side to find a girl with straight, black hair parted down the middle, sitting Indian-style on the bottom bunk. Her dark eyes are just shy of being crossed.

"Hi," I answer.

"I'm Wanda. From Illinois."

She doesn't blink. I feel a hole forming in

the middle of my forehead as she stares into me.

"I'm Grace. I live on the other side of the lake."

"I used to be a witch," she says.

I don't know how to answer that so I don't say anything.

"But I'm a born-again Christian," she adds. "I only use my talents for God now."

"Oh," I say. Looks like I've got me a kook for a bunkmate.

"You're a witch, too," she says.

"No, I'm not a witch." Definitely a kook.

"Yes. You. Are." She separates her words to give each one single weight. "I can feel your power."

"Hmmm," is all I say. I don't want to be rude because I'm going to be sharing a cabin with her for a week, but I don't really want to have this conversation either.

"It's nothing to be afraid of, Grace. As long as you use your powers for good, of course."

Her big, dark eyes suck me in. My head feels dizzy. I don't know if it's from her words or if I've been hanging upside down for too long. I shake my head and slide off the top bunk. My shirt catches on the coil frame and turns it inside out over my head. I'm trapped with my arms straight up and

278

my head inside my sleeves, my button breasts keeping eye contact with Wanda.

She climbs out of her bed and unhooks my shirt, pulling it gently back to my waist. As soon as she touches me, a buzzing sensation zips through my entire body. Maybe she really is a witch. And maybe like me, she has a tough time making friends.

"You wanna play tether ball?" I ask, trying to change the subject.

"No, thanks. I like it here."

"Okay. See ya later." I run out of the cabin, letting the screen door bang behind me. The next time I see Wanda is when all the campers gather for a welcoming service in the chapel, which is built out of knotty pine and has a clean, wood smell. The air is hot and muggy and my dress sticks to my back. I slide in next to Wanda, who sits completely still with her eyes closed all through the sermon. Not once does her head nod or her body lean, let alone topple over. I wish I could learn that trick.

I pass the time letting my fingers trace the beautiful markings in the smoothly varnished pew until we're finally excused and sent to get ready for bed. The boys' cabins sit up the hill in the pine trees just beyond the two bathhouses, one for boys and one for girls. The girls aren't allowed to go higher than the rest rooms, and the boys are supposed to stay fifty feet from the girls' area.

The bathroom smells like pine cleaner. I find an empty stall and listen to the mix of high-pitched voices filling the room as I pee. When I go to wash my hands I can hardly edge them under the faucet because so many girls are crowded in front of the mirrors. I wedge myself into the flurry of pajamas and slippers, mouths foaming with toothpaste that dribbles down their chins as they try to talk.

"Ginger, what cabin are you in?" asks a stubby girl with almost no chin.

A tall blonde who looks like she belongs on the cover of *Teen Miss* flips her long hair over her head and begins brushing it slowly. From under the curtain of yellow silk she says, "Miracles. With a bunch of snotty-nosed kids. But I'm going to complain until they move me."

She whips her hair back and shakes it out. "They should go by age, not grade." She glares at one of the counselors standing by the door.

"We can't change the rules for you, Ginger," the lady says.

Ginger pulls a pink satin robe around her waist and parades out the door with all the girls wishing they were half as beautiful as she is.

Nine girls are assigned to my cabin, including me. Besides Wanda there's four girls from the Christian Reformed Church in Cherry Hill. They remind me of bowling pins, the way they cling together. If you bumped into any one of them, I expect they'd all tumble over. Next to my bunk is Carrie, who is redheaded like me but wears her hair in two braids. She's quiet and usually has her freckled nose stuck in a mystery book that she hides inside her Bible. I wish I'd thought of that. Beneath Carrie is Tina, a chubby girl from Indiana who was immediately shunned after being caught biting her toenails under the covers.

And there's Ginger. She's fourteen, but just finished seventh grade. She claims it's because her daddy is in the army so she had to change schools a lot, not because she's dumb. Ginger's the only one of us who fills out her bra. She wears a slip with lace cups to bed instead of pajamas and has a pink sleeping bag with matching pillowcase. A fluffy, white, stuffed cat sits in the middle of her bed that she brushes in the same slow way she brushes the hair that hangs down to the middle of her back. Her hand mirror matches the hairbrush, also pink. A plastic pouch filled with assorted headbands sits on the dresser in which she has claimed all but one drawer, the bottom one.

Our cabin counselor, Edith, looks somewhere between thirty and sixty, depending on the way the light hits her face. After we're all in bed, she tells us to say our prayers to ourselves rather than out loud like you're supposed to. I get the feeling Edith is getting a little tired of adolescent girls.

Swimming lessons are from two until four in the afternoon between Bible classes. We're instructed to always cover ourselves when walking to and from the lake. No two-piece bathing suits are allowed, which is fine with me because I'm so skinny and still an A cup. Ginger, of course, stretches the rule to the limit. She wears a hot-pink bathing suit that's cut out on the sides and has little peekaboo rings from her navel to her bust-line. Her perky breasts form a perfect V and look as if they'll leap right out of her suit every time she moves. The back is cut out, too.

I love watching her walk down to the water. She oils herself up in the cabin first so her tan skin shimmers in the sunlight. Ginger uses a bath towel instead of a beach towel, wrapping it around her hips like an exotic miniskirt. Even though the boys are way down at the other dock, they all stop and watch while Ginger walks to the beach for her lesson, which she obviously doesn't need.

When she reaches the water she stretches and drops her towel in the sand before walking slowly to the end of the dock, posing for several long seconds before doing a perfect dive. She pops up way out in the lake, then swims back to the dock and pulls herself up onto it. With her hair slicked back and droplets beading up on her browned skin she looks like a wet Barbie doll. Across the way there's a dock full of boys wishing they were Ken.

On the third day of camp I'm walking behind the girl's bathrooms when I hear a noise in the woods. I stop dead in my tracks. The boys aren't supposed to come near here. A branch snaps, then a giggle that I immediately recognize.

"Lola? Is that you?"

She peeks out from behind a tree. She's wearing a sundress over army boots. I look around to see if anyone is watching. "You're going to get me in trouble!"

I run into the woods and pull her farther

out of view. I'm worried about getting caught, but seeing Lola I can't keep from grabbing her hands and jumping up and down with her.

"How'd you get here? And what in the world are you doing here?"

"I hitched a ride. I've obviously come to rescue you," she says. "I've been spying and this has to be about the most boring summer camp I've ever seen in my life."

"It's true," I say, lowering my head. "I'm being punished."

"For what?"

"For everything. Telling fortunes, feeding a hobo, wishing Billy Wolf was dead, talking to Isaac."

"Seriously?"

"Shhh! Someone will hear you." I look behind me to see if anyone has spotted us. "Daddy has been watching me like a hawk lately. I think he believes it's my fault that Mama's depressed."

"Grace, that's ridiculous. You told me yourself your mother was depressed even before you were born. Isn't that what your aunt Pearl said?"

"Yeah, I guess. But she got worse after Isaac died. And then even more so after Marilyn was born."

"You want to know what I think? I think

she wishes she was more like you. I think she feels trapped in her life with that stupid church and your dad and your god."

"Lola, don't say that!"

"Why? If I'm condemned shouldn't I be struck down?" She looks up through the canopy of pines. "Yoohoo! Come and get me! I'm right here!"

Tears well up in my eyes. "Lola, please stop. I couldn't bear it if . . ."

She wipes a tear with her finger and tilts my chin with her hand, but I look away.

"I'm sorry, Grace. I just get so mad."

"It's okay," I say. "We were raised different."

"Thank God!" she says, which makes us both laugh.

"You better go," I say.

She hugs me, then pulls away and kisses me on the forehead before sprinting into the woods. Her gauze sundress flutters as she runs, catching light between the trunks until she finally disappears. I start back toward camp, but stop when I hear screaming in the distance. At first I think it might be Lola, until I realize the noise is coming from my cabin. I run down the hill and into Miracles.

"How dare they touch my things!" Ginger shakes her hairbrush at Edith.

"Calm down, Ginger. You were given a list of rules when you enrolled."

"I didn't enroll! My grandmother sent me because she thought this place would be good for me. I didn't want to come and I hate it here!"

When she starts crying Edith reaches out to touch her shoulder. Ginger knocks her hand away.

"You tell them they better give me back my things or they'll be sorry!"

Edith tries to stop her, but Ginger wriggles out of her grip and runs up the hill toward the bathroom.

I had a feeling I wouldn't see her in Bible class the following morning and I was right. The next time I see Ginger is after lunch on Thursday when all the campers and counselors gather on the lawns to meditate on the Scriptures during quiet period. I sit on the wooden dock, watching ripples form on the surface when the fish poke their noses out of the water. Ginger has her back to a tree, a Bible in her lap. There's a boy sitting on the opposite side of the tree and I can tell they're back-to-back even though there's a tree trunk between them. The guy is one of the other cabin counselors. He has his head down pretending to read his Bible, but

I know he's whispering to Ginger. She smiles, pulling blades of grass from the ground and running them over her tanned calves like feathers.

Wanda told me that the lady who runs the camp not only confiscated Ginger's makeup and nail polish but also let the hem out of all her dresses. Wanda shared this while we were standing in the inspection line early this morning. Thanks to Ginger we now have to pass Edith's "fingertip test" every morning before breakfast. If your hemline is higher than where your fingers touch your leg, you have to let it out. Ginger threw a fit, but from the looks of it she's found someone to take her side.

The next morning word spreads like swimmer's itch that Ginger is being sent home. They can't even hold out one more day until camp is over. Ginger was caught in one of the boy's cabins with Ricky, the guy from the other side of the tree. Wanda says they were "petting" and she's pretty sure they would have gone all the way if the janitor hadn't walked in on them. I try to imagine him petting her hair, her face, and her long legs. I'm pretty sure he probably petted her breasts, too. Truthfully, I'd like to pet them just once to see what they feel like.

Right after lunch Ginger's mama pulls up in a white convertible. Ginger gets in and slams her car door. I bet she'll have her own convertible one day, probably pink. Something tells me she's pretty much destined to get whatever she wants in this life. As the car spins out, Ginger turns to face the camp one last time. Through the cloud of dust I see her middle finger sticking straight up in front of her gorgeous face.

Wanda and I have actually become pretty good friends over the days we've shared a bunk. During free time she'd sit under a tree in her bell-bottom jeans and bare feet, strumming an old guitar and singing songs about Jesus and love. She told me all about her "Jesus Freak" friends, which are like hippies for Jesus. She taught me a few guitar chords and I'm getting pretty good. I even made up a song about how the wind feels like God blowing in your ear. Wanda liked it so much she made me play it for her all the time, but I know it was her sneaky way of making me practice. I now have calluses on the ends of all my left fingertips.

We haven't talked about the witch thing since the first day I arrived, though we both know about the other. I think Wanda has the Knowing, but it's thinned out, like the watered-down orange juice that Daddy stretches a mile to make it last longer. She offered me a peek one night while I was lying in my bunk above her. She sent her thoughts up to me and I saw how she's ashamed of her gift. She thinks she's damaged, that the Knowing is a curse that needs to be controlled. Unfortunately this belief has ended up controlling *her*. It takes a lot of energy to try to be what you aren't, but even more not to be what you are.

Wanda hugs me before climbing into the back of her parents' sedan. She's wearing a tie-dyed headband around her black hair and a T-shirt that reads "Jesus Is Far Out" on the front. I wish she lived nearer so we could visit each other. We exchange addresses and promise to write, but we both know we never will.

Joy pulls up in our station wagon and rolls down the window just as Wanda's car disappears from sight. "C'mon, Grace. Get your stuff and get in."

"Hey, you're not old enough to drive yet."

She just stares at me so I run back to the cabin to get my things. I skid to a halt at what I find. Wanda has left her guitar on my bed with a note:

Dear Grace,

Sing your heart out. (Don't worry, I have a better one at home.)

Peace, Love, and Jesus,
Wanda

I throw my suitcase and sleeping bag into the way back of the station wagon, then gently rest the guitar on the floor behind the front seat before climbing in. Joy drops the shifter into reverse, then looks behind us for stray campers. She steps on the gas and the engine dies.

"Bus still broke?"

"No, Ralph fixed it. Daddy gave me the station wagon so I can go to the store and stuff."

"Daddy gave you a car?"

"I got a special license exception that they usually only give to farm kids. They call it special circumstances or something. I need to run errands for Daddy now that Mama . . ." She glances toward the back seat. "So where'd you get the guitar?"

Something is different about Joy, but I can't put my finger on it. When she runs her hands through her fine hair, her bangs fall back over her eyes, which have dark circles underneath them. Joy's face has gotten older in the week I've been gone. Maybe acting like a grown-up makes you look like one.

She restarts the car then steps on the brakes and turns to face me. "You want to show me your cabin?"

"Nah."

"You sure?"

"I'm sure."

We ride home in silence, me not wanting to ask about Mama and her not wanting to talk. Joy drives past our house and pulls into Dairy Queen down by the lake. She buys me a hot fudge sundae. With her own money. That's when I know something's up.

We sit on a picnic table facing Cherry Lake. The last batch of tourists dot the water with white sails and bikinied skiers behind speedboats. An ongoing battle has always separated the two. Sailors want the powered boats banned because they go too fast and the ruffled wake tips them over. And the speedboaters think the sailboats get in their way. Personally I side with the sailboats. They're prettier. Plus the fast boats scare me when they come too close to the beach where people are swimming.

Joy and I both laugh when a skier loses his balance and flips before slamming onto the surface. One of his skis floats toward the middle of the lake, but he's obviously saved what is most important. He holds his beer out of the water, whooping. It's our laughing that finally breaks the silence.

"Nobody was home when Mama passed out," she says. "The doctors aren't sure if she mixed her pills wrong or took too many. They took her back to the rest home."

I want to ask her if Mama did it on purpose or if it was an accident, but I don't think either of us could face the truth, whichever way it happened. Why can't Mama stop hurting, stop hurting herself and us?

"Can I go see her?"

Joy takes a lick off her cone. "Not for a few weeks at least. Maybe longer."

Joy won't look at me. She just keeps licking away at her cone as if she might uncover something worth saying. Finally, she throws the last couple of bites in the trash can next to the picnic table.

"Let's go home," she says.

When I tell her I want to stay for a while she doesn't argue. She wipes her hands on a paper napkin and walks toward the car. I grab my guitar out of the backseat and throw it over my shoulder before she drives away. Wanda left the embroidered leather strap attached that makes it easier to carry. Sitting on top of the picnic table, I pluck and strum until my fingers are too tender to hold the strings down anymore. I take the long way home around the fruit processing plant and over the railroad tracks, letting the past week gently blow away like drifting sand before turning back toward home.

I'm almost asleep when the side of the bed sags next to me. I pretend to be sleeping, hoping to feel Mama stroke my face the way she used to when I was a little girl. She reaches out and tucks a few stray hairs behind my ear then pulls the covers around me and pats it. Through the slit between my eyelids I see Joy's nail-bitten fingers smoothing out the quilt.

"G'night, Grace," she whispers, in a way I know not to answer.

20

A lot has changed around here in the last few months. For one thing it's quieter. Hope started a new project — she's trying to read the entire Holy Bible in a year. She's a slow reader to start with, plus she's underlining as she reads to keep track of how far she's gotten. Sometimes she stops to memorize a verse, which bogs her down even more. It'll take her a lot longer than a year to finish, but I admire her determination. I can't even eat a Tootsie Pop without biting into it after three licks.

Mama was in the rest home for six weeks. They changed her medications, but it hasn't helped much. She sleeps even more than she used to and rarely gets dressed. Joy picks Marilyn up from Mrs. Poole's house every day on her way home from high school. Mrs. Poole already has a toddler so she offered to take Marilyn during the day to help us out. Joy keeps a bunch of storybooks and toys in her room so she can study while watching Marilyn. My job is to make dinner. I don't mind since that means Chastity has to wash dishes. I think she actually likes doing them. Sometimes she stares at her reflection in the dishes and pretends she's a movie star. But she still refuses to put her hand in the sink and pull the plug when she's done. Chastity can't stand soggy food coming into contact with her hands.

Tonight I'm making SpaghettiOs with hot dogs cut up in it. Daddy bought the family-size cans, but I still have to open two in order to feed everybody. Daddy buys the economy size of everything to save money. Our creme rinse comes in a pink gallon jug. We probably have enough to untangle a whole congregation's worth of hair.

Daddy took a part-time job at the Rexall to help with paying Mama's and Marilyn's hospital bills. The church can't support us even though he's doubled the congregation since we first moved here. Daddy has a way of convincing people to come to church. Earl Felt never used to attend with his family because he didn't have Sunday clothes. Daddy told him if he'd come the next Sunday he'd wear overalls in the pulpit. I couldn't believe he actually did it. I loved watching Daddy that day wearing overalls while he preached. I think it made him seem more like a real servant of the Lord. Earl has attended with his family almost every Sunday since that day. I wonder if Mama would come to church in her nightgown next Sunday if Daddy promised to wear his pajamas in the pulpit?

Daddy walks into the kitchen wearing his white jacket from the drugstore with a pocket on the front. He stocks shelves and waits on customers in the afternoons. I think he likes his job because he can witness to people, although the owner had to talk to him about it last week. Some of the customers were complaining that Daddy preaches at them. Daddy agreed to stop, but he still slips a religious tract into every single bag that leaves his register.

I set paper plates around the table and noisily pound a spoon on the side of the cook pot to bring the family to the kitchen. Daddy lifts the cover and peers inside. He doesn't smile, but he doesn't frown either. His face is just flat. Maybe he'll get tired of my cooking and let Aunt Pearl come back.

After supper I head upstairs to work on homework for my current events class. I'm supposed to write about something important going on in the world. Most of my seventh-grade classmates are writing about the Vietnam War, but that's one thing I can't think about. If I concentrate too hard on all those people I hear them wailing in my head. I've decided to write about Janis Joplin. I'm not supposed to listen to rock and roll music, but sometimes I sneak the dial on my transistor radio over to WOKY out of Milwaukee. I think Janis has the Knowing, too. I want to write about Janis because she understands what beauty is in an ugly kind of way.

I've just started the second page of my report when the phone rings and Joy hollers for me to answer it. Chastity is grounded from the phone after calling a modeling agency in California last week. Daddy threatened to yank the phone out of the wall when he got the bill. I run downstairs and grab it on the fifth ring. For once it's actually for me.

"Hi, Lola!" I drag the phone into the hall closet so we can talk without Miss Big Ears listening to every word.

"What're you doing, Grace?"

"Working on my essay."

"Will you write one for me?"

"You know I can't do that, Lola."

"What'd you say?" She yells it into the phone.

"What's that thumping noise?"

"Just a minute." Lola puts her hand over the receiver and yells even louder, "Catherine! Can't you wait until I'm off the phone to practice your congas?"

The thumping continues. She comes back on and says, "I'm going to have to call you later, okay?"

"Okay," I say.

When I finish my homework I decide to write Aunt Pearl a letter and beg her to come back.

Dear Aunt Pearl,

It seems like forever since you left and I sure do miss you. You would not believe how big Marilyn is getting. She's walking all over the place and she can talk some, though she can't pronounce her r's too good. She calls me Gwace.

Ever since Mama went to the hospital Joy elected herself head honcho around here. Daddy makes us do everything she says even though she's only two years older than me. Yesterday she ordered me to change all the bedding while she took a nap with Marilyn.

I was wondering if you might come back for a while. Daddy won't ask for help because he thinks if we pray hard enough Mama will snap out of her depression. Sometimes I wonder if she'll ever be normal again.

It's okay if you can't come, but I hope you do. Joy's driving me crazy. Write me when you can.

Love from your Sweet Pea,
Grace Marie

I fold the letter and tuck it into one of Mama's pretty envelopes that match the stationery. Little pink roses line the edges of the paper and the inside of the envelope. I spritz a little perfume from a dusty bottle shaped like a bell that I borrowed from Mama's dresser. As I'm going out the door Daddy asks me where I'm headed.

"I wrote Aunt Pearl a letter," I say.

"You shouldn't bother her. She just had surgery and doesn't need you crabbing about how much you miss her and making her feel worse."

"What kind of surgery?"

He blushes. "Woman stuff," he says.

"Maybe a nice letter is just what she needs to cheer her up."

He frowns but fishes two quarters out of his pants pocket. "Here. Pick me up eight stamps."

On the way to the post office I tear up the letter. Daddy's right. Aunt Pearl doesn't need me whining about my problems. I buy eight stamps and spend the change on a Tootsie Roll at Norberg's. As I pass the blind girl's house I pause at the rickety gate in front of their sidewalk. I keep hoping she might come back, but the place looks completely empty, right down to curtainless windows. A fat red maple leaf rests on the wooden seat of the tree swing. Part of me wants to climb over the fence and go for a ride, the part that still feels like a girl. But the part that's starting to feel more like a woman won't let me. I close my eyes and picture the blind girl. Something bad happened to her, but I can't see what. When I try harder to get inside her head my mind goes cold and flat.

By the time I get back from town, Daddy's in the bathroom doing some last-minute cramming for his sermon tomorrow. It's one of his favorite places to think. Unfortunately, if one of us needs to pee we have to walk over to the church because he's not coming out anytime soon. Even if he did, nobody would want to go in right after Daddy's been in there. I fast-walk across the street, rushing past the church janitor and into the girls' bathroom. Somebody has scratched *Jesus Loves You* into the back of the bathroom door. I wonder if whoever wrote it considered whether Jesus would like her vandalizing His holy house.

On my way out I stop near the big meeting room in the basement where the kids sing before Sunday school. Mr. Weaver is buffing the floors with a machine that twirls the wax into a shine so glossy you can almost see your reflection in it. It's a little like that commercial for dishwashing soap. "Look, Marge," one lady says to the other, "you can see yourself." And sure enough Marge's face is right there on the plate, red lips smiling away. As if either of those fancy women actually does dishes.

Mr. Weaver startles me when he hollers across the room.

"What?" I yell back.

He leans over and turns off the buffer. "You wanna try it? It's fun."

I grin at him. "I suppose next you're going to ask me if I want to whitewash a fence, Mr. Weaver."

"Now, Grace, you know you can call me Harold."

"Daddy says it's disrespectful to address adults by their first names."

"Well, I'm not just any old adult. I'm your friend, right?" He digs into his pants pocket.

He might have quit drinking but he still has a beer belly bulging over his belt. "Here," he says, holding out a plastic bag of peppermints.

I hold back from taking his friendship offering. Partly because Daddy doesn't like it when we beg candy off Mr. Weaver and partly because I'm not a little kid anymore.

He shakes the bag, sending the minty smell my way. "Go on, have a couple."

I take a step toward him. "Well, okay. I am kind of hungry."

"Need to fatten you up a little anyway, Grace. You're too skinny." He looks me over and smiles. "Although you're starting to fill out some, aren't you?"

My face heats up. I'm embarrassed and pleased at the same time. At least somebody has noticed.

"So you wanna give it a whirl?" He nods toward the buffing machine.

"Okay," I say. It does look kind of fun.

"Here. Put your hands on the bar and hold tight. When I turn the machine on, just follow it around the room."

I grab the handle and brace myself.

"Ready?"

I nod. When he bends over to flip the switch his butt crack shows above his baggy work pants. I concentrate on the machine instead. The vibration feels weird under my hands, as though it might jiggle the skin right off my arms. He comes up behind me and puts his hands over mine to steady the buffer. His belt buckle digs into my back and when he pulls back on the handle, his knuckles push against my chest. I let go of the whole business and duck out from under him.

"Grace!" he yells, then chases the buffer, catching it right before it slams into the piano. He kicks the switch off with his foot. His face gets even shorter when he furrows his brow.

"What'd ya go and do that for?"

I stare at him blankly. "I don't know. It scared me, I guess."

His forehead relaxes a little. "It's okay, honey. You go on back home now. Tell Pastor Carter the floors will be slick enough for the Lord himself to eat off when I get done with them, you hear?"

I bend over the drinking fountain on the way out. The warmish water tastes like iron. When I stand and wipe my face on my arm, the janitor is leaning against the handle of the buffer with his eyes closed, smiling. He sure does love his job.

Most people don't like school, but I look

forward to it. Our little elementary school goes from kindergarten all the way through eighth grade. The classes are small, with some combined into two grades. The high school, where Joy is a freshman, sits across the street from the K-8 building. I'm glad Joy and I don't go to the same school anymore, but the teachers still compare us. "Your sister was so quiet," they say when I make too much noise. Or, "Your sister is a whiz at math. Surely you can do better." Next year will be my last year here. In a way I will miss it, but I'm also ready to stop being treated like a child. Chastity is probably counting down the days until she's the only Carter at Cherry Hill Elementary.

When Monday comes around Lola and I walk to the field beyond the campus during lunch hour and lay with our heads on a rock. The ground is cold and damp, but the sun warms our faces. We both get bored with the way the other seventh-grade girls walk around whispering to each other about boys. We'd rather watch clouds drift by and discuss the world and stuff. Sometimes Lola reads aloud to me from one of her poetry books, but she has to explain most of them. Sometimes I talk about how much I miss Mama. Lola listens without ever getting sick of me. And sometimes we don't say anything, just lie side by side and stare at the sky.

"Did your family go on vacation last summer?" I ask her, pulling my hood down over my ears.

"Yeah, we went to a music festival in Colorado."

"Wow. That must've been amazing."

"It was. But I wish I could have planned for it. When our family does something it's usually spontaneous and my parents never tell us until the last minute. One time they got us up in the middle of the night to drive to Canada so we could fly into Churchill to see the polar bears."

"You saw polar bears?"

"Yeah, they were really cool. But I had to call the neighbor from a pay phone to get him to feed and water the horses while we were gone. Catherine never thinks of things like that when she gets an idea in her head."

"At least you get to go somewhere. We've never even been on vacation."

Lola props herself on one arm. Her freckles have doubled in number since we left the school building. "Never?"

"Nope. Unless you count the time we drove down to Ohio to see Billy Graham preach."

In the distance the school bell rings. I sit

up, but Lola doesn't move. She's chewing on a blade of brown grass, stroking the soft tip with her long fingers. In her faded bib overalls and barn boots, she looks like a female version of Huck Finn.

"We should go in," I say.

"You go ahead. I think I'll stay here for a while."

"But, Lola, you'll get in trouble."

"I'm already in trouble for drawing a mermaid on the chalkboard, remember?"

"Oh, yeah." I feel sorry for her because it's obvious Mrs. Humphrey has it in for Lola. "It was beautiful," I say.

"Thanks."

"I wish I could draw like you." It's the truth.

"I wish I could know things like you."

"Maybe you should have put a bathing suit top on her," I say.

"Mermaids don't wear bathing suits, Grace."

"That's true."

I lay back down beside her. We don't say any more, even when Mrs. Humphrey comes out and hollers our names. We both know she's too lazy to walk all the way out here to try to find us.

Lola and I end up having to stay after

306

school and each write "I will not be a troublemaker" five hundred times. I write the first word all the way down the page and then the next word. This way seems to make the punishment go faster. It takes Lola twice as long because she's so mad her pencil lead keeps breaking when she pushes it into the page. When we finally finish, Mrs. Humphrey hands me a note to give to Daddy. I open it in the school parking lot.

Dear Rev. and Mrs. Carter,
   Grace has been exhibiting worrisome signs of rebellion. I believe she's being influenced by spending time with children who share few family values. I suggest you monitor her friendships more closely.

Sincerely,
Marjorie Humphrey

I crumple up the letter and toss it in the trash can next to the school bus stop. Daddy already thinks Lola's parents are low-lifes. I convinced him they only dress like they do because they're poor. I told him I've been witnessing to the Purdys and that I'm pretty sure they might visit our church very soon. I make a mental note to invite Lola to church with me the next time I see her.

As I walk down our street I imagine Mama in the kitchen making pork chops and cabbage for supper. She'd be wearing her favorite flowered apron, singing happily as she waits for her children to arrive. After dinner she'll sit on the edge of the bathtub and pour a pitcher of water over my hair to rinse the shampoo. We'll talk about girl things, mother to daughter, while she washes my back. I'll pull a handmade nightie over my head before she follows me to bed, petting my face until I fall asleep. By the time I reach the house my daydream feels so real I almost call out her name before seeing her bedroom door closed like it always is when she's tucked away in there, far away from us.

I climb up to the loft, but of course Lyle isn't there. I haven't seen him since that evening when I doubted him about the kids and the school bus. I walk to the back of the loft and lay down in the straw where he used to sleep. Something shiny catches my eye under the pew in front of me. I stretch out on my belly and strain to reach the object. Sometimes when Lyle drinks he drops things. For once I'm glad since this is the first thing I've found of his besides the fork he left, but that wasn't really his, it was one of ours.

It's a locket. The silver is partly blackened and bent on one side, like it was left in the charcoal grill. The chain is similar to the one we have on our bathtub plug. I used to see Lyle fiddle with that chain in his pocket sometimes. I always figured it was connected to a watch. I try to pry the locket open, but it won't budge. I bite it with my teeth. No luck. I set it on the straw, then pick it up again. I fold my hands over the locket and close my eyes.

That lake again, and the bow of the boat cutting a path through the water. He's paddling furiously. The water splashes against the oars as he plunges them into the water over and over. *No, no, no, no, no!* The smell of smoke and the sound of branches crackling. And then his voice, wailing, before everything goes black. The locket burns in my hands and I drop it. It lands on the floor and pops open. On one side is a younger version of Lyle. On the other an unfamiliar face. She stares back at me, smiling, but the smile isn't meant for me.

21

I thought it would never happen. As I sit with my underpants around my ankles staring at the dark splotch it's obvious that this is blood and it's coming out of me. The stain is shaped like a jellyfish, dark in the middle and faded on the edges. When I touch the spot and lift my finger to my nose, it smells like rust. I find a box of Kotex pads under the bathroom sink and pull out what looks like a tiny mattress with sheets hanging off both ends. I stick it in my underwear and head toward my bedroom to retrieve the sanity belt from my dresser that Mama gave me a couple of years ago.

The huge napkin keeps my thighs too far apart and I'm walking like Aunt Pearl. This woman thing is not as cool as I thought it would be. Joy has Tampax and I know where to find them. I tiptoe to her room as gracefully as I can with what feels like a diaper in my underwear. Joy's asleep with her head at the wrong end of the bed. It's one of the few times I've seen her face recently without a furrow in her brow. I quietly steal two tampons from her closet shelf and waddle back to the bathroom.

This is even worse than the pad. I've tried every position they show on the stupid box. I'm getting blood all over my knuckles, poking around where I know it's supposed to go, with no luck. The box says "slender," but the cardboard cylinder feels like it was made for an elephant. I wiggle it around some more until finally the thing moves inside me. I really, really hate this. I can't possibly suffer this every month.

Chastity follows me with her eyes as I walk toward the refrigerator to get milk.

"Why are you walking funny?"

"I'm not."

"You are. You're walking like a duck."

I fill my bowl with Cap'n Crunch and add milk. Daddy must have had a coupon. Usually it's Cheerios or Corn Flakes or some brand we've never heard of. Either that or Chastity threw one of her fits in the store.

I start to sit, but the cardboard thing pinches inside me and I jump back up.

"Whatsa matter wif you? You fall down or sumpin'?"

Even though she's ten, Chastity has

started talking like a baby ever since Mama got back from the rest home.

"No, I didn't fall down or sumpin'," I say, mocking her.

Joy walks in dressed in neatly-pressed jeans with a blouse tucked into the waistband.

"Hey, Joy, lookit Grace. She hurt her butt and now she walks funny and can't sit down."

A fire rises in my cheeks. "I didn't hurt my butt, you infantile. I got my period, okay?"

Chastity's blue eyes widen and her mouth drops open, exposing a mouthful of half-chewed cereal. "Really? Wow. I can't wait to tell everybody!"

"You better not, Chas. I'll make your life miserable. I promise."

"You alweddy do," she says, making a face.

Joy looks at me, then Chastity. "Leave her alone."

I can hardly believe my ears. Joy doesn't say anything else, but I can feel her watching me as I move awkwardly around the kitchen.

"Hey, Chas, go get my purse, will ya?" Chastity bounds out of the room. Joy's request means chewing gum for her.

As soon as Chastity is out of earshot Joy

whispers through her teeth, "You stole some of my Tampax."

"I'm sorry. Those pads are so awful and that stupid sanity belt for hooking them up is impossible."

"*Sanitary* belt, Grace. It's called a sanitary belt." She's trying to be nice, but I can tell she's choking back a laugh.

"Oh," I say, even though I think mine is a better name for it.

"Just don't do it again. You really shouldn't use tampons the first time anyway."

"I know. It hurts like crazy."

"That bad?"

"Yeah, the cardboard keeps digging into my insides."

Joy spits out the milk she was just starting to gulp. "You left the cardboard inside?" Joy laughs so hard her face gets even redder than mine. "That is the dumbest thing you have ever done, Grace. In fact, it's so dumb I'd be too embarrassed to tell anybody."

She's clutching her stomach. I want to punch her. I feel my chin start to quiver and I burst into tears. I hate being a woman and I hate having my period. But what I hate most is that I do such stupid things.

Joy stops laughing and eyes me with something like sympathy but more like pity. "I should have explained it to you." She motions me to follow her to the bathroom. She slides a hidden blue box from behind the stack of towels in the linen closet and unwraps a tampon. "Like this, see?" She pushes the cotton out of the tube in one swift motion and it falls on the floor with its string trailing along like a dead mouse. "The cotton stays inside. You pull out the cardboard and throw it away."

I just stand there.

She hands me the box. "Don't worry. You'll get it after a couple of tries. Or you can switch back to the pads."

I grab my belly. "Why does my stomach hurt?"

She shakes out a couple of white tablets from a blue bottle in the medicine cabinet. "Take these. The cramps will go away after a few hours. If it gets bad just go to the sick room at school and ask for a heating pad."

The only good thing about this period so far is Joy being halfway nice to me. I pop the pills into my mouth and chew them up. I love the way aspirin fizzes my tongue and makes my whole mouth tingle.

Chastity jiggles the door handle. "What're you guys doing in there?"

"Nothing," Joy says. She unlocks the door. "Let's go, Chas. I'll walk you to school."

Joy takes her small leather shoulder bag

from Chastity and starts fishing for gum. I'm left with a box of tampons in my hand, a knot in my gut, and the knowledge that my life has changed big-time.

"Isaac, if you can see me, go away." I say it out loud, but I mean it as a joke.

Of course I can see you.

"Isaac? Oh man, I can hear you! It sounds like you're talking into a tin can. What are you doing here?"

You spoke to me.

"Yeah but . . ."

You didn't think I'd answer? We don't have to be in any special place to talk, Grace. Not anymore.

"Why not? I thought . . ."

Exactly. You thought you had to be in the closet. You believed it, so it was true. But I distinctly heard you speak to me just now.

"I know, but I was kidding."

Were you?

I sit on the edge of the bathtub. "No, I guess not. Actually I was wishing you could somehow help me. I don't mean physically help me but, like . . ."

I'm stuttering like an idiot.

No need to be embarrassed, Grace.

"I'm not." I quickly shove the tampon into my pocket.

Grace?

"Yeah?" I stare at my white tennis shoes. There's a spot of blood on one of them.

I don't see you in the way you think. I'm not watching you. I'm watching over you.

"You mean like a guardian angel?"

Something like that. Think of it as soft vison. I'm able to picture you as a red-haired girl in blue jeans if I choose to, but those details aren't important to me. Right now I sense someone I love going through a range of feelings from joy to anger to sadness to . . . embarrassment and frustration.

"But I thought . . ."

Things have changed, Grace. You've reached a point in your life where your gift has deepened and will continue to do so. You'll need me less and you'll grow to trust yourself more.

"No! I do need you. I'll always need you."

And I'll be here when you do.

"Promise?"

Promise.

His voice echoes in my head, then fades, and I know he's gone. I close the bathroom door and get to practicing this new womanhood thing.

Isaac was right. It's not just the period or the cramps or even the hormones flooding my body. It's as though a secret channel has suddenly flung its doors wide open. Everything feels stronger and deeper than before. Sounds are crisper and the images that come to me are more colorful. Even my teacher's voice is like a knife the way it slices away on a distant part of me, the part that hears without listening.

Mrs. Oberman is lecturing us about the natives who lived here before the Europeans moved in. It's why nearly every Michigan county has an Indian name. I glance down at the history book on my desk. The wrinkly-faced Indian in the photograph looks sternly at the camera, like those guards who aren't allowed to smile when standing in front of a palace. When I trace the black and white photograph with my finger, his eyes seem to soften. It feels as though he's looking at me. Not just in the way a portrait sometimes appears to follow you with its eyes but actually seeing me. I slam the book shut. I must have gasped out loud because suddenly the room is quiet and Mrs. Oberman is staring at me along with everyone else in the room.

"Is there a problem, Miss Carter?"

"No, ma'am," I say. But I can feel him, that Indian guy, warm under the covers of my book.

I stop at Ralph's on my way home from

school to buy an Orange Crush. Ralph's feet are sticking out from under an old blue Chevy. I hear a thunk as his head bumps into metal and then the F-word that I've only heard Lola say one time and under similar circumstances when she dropped a manure shovel on her bare foot. Ralph rolls out from under the car, rubbing his forehead. When he sees me he grins.

"Sorry, Grace. I didn't know you were standing there."

"It's okay," I say.

He stands and wipes his hands with a dirty blue rag that doesn't seem like it's doing much good.

"I haven't seen you in a while. You doing okay?"

"I'm all right."

He frowns. "How's your mom doing?"

I picture Mama drooling on her pillow or shuffling to the back stoop, where she sometimes sits for hours. I'm about to tell Ralph she's okay, just like I tell everyone when they ask about her. Before I can open my mouth the picture of her scrambles in my brain and instead I see her slumped behind the wheel of our car.

"Grace? Honey, you look pale." Ralph leads me to a greasy chair. "Why don't you sit down for a minute."

I try to shake the image of Mama from my mind, but it won't go away.

"Can I use your phone?"

"You need a ride? I'll take you home."

"No." I run behind the counter and dial our house.

Hope picks up. "Carter residence."

"It's me, Hope. Where's Mama?"

"Grace? I don't know. Probably in bed. Why?"

"Go look and come back."

"Okay."

I hear her footsteps pad toward the bedroom, then farther away. She calls for Mama. Half a minute later she's back.

"She's not in her bed or on the back porch."

"Who else is there?"

"Everyone. Joy and Marilyn are in the kitchen. Chas is watching TV. Daddy's in the bathroom."

"Tell Joy to check in the barn for Mama."

"Why would she —"

"Hope! Do it now!"

She drops the receiver and I hear it swing back and forth against the wall.

"Joy! Chastity!" I scream into the phone. "Somebody go help Mama! She's in the barn and she needs help RIGHT NOW!"

Ralph looks at me like I've lost my last

marbles but keeps his distance. I hear muffled voices, the back door slam, then Daddy's voice. He picks up the receiver.

"Who is this?"

"Go to the barn!" I yell.

"Grace? What's going on?"

"It's Mama! She's not breathing. Daddy, please go to the barn!"

The receiver drops again, this time hitting the floor.

■ ■ ■ ■

Part Two

■ ■ ■ ■

For the Lord has poured over you a spirit of
   deep sleep.
He has closed your eyes and covered your
   heads, you prophets, you seers.
                              — Isaiah 29:10

Part Two

22

Over a year has passed since Mama went into the coma. Between the carbon monoxide fumes and the pills she took, the doctors say her prognosis isn't good. What they mean is, she might never wake up. Daddy hasn't let any of us come to the hospital because he doesn't want to upset us kids any more than we already are. But this week they told Daddy he should let us visit. They think we'd feel better if we could see Mama sleeping peacefully. I heard about a man who was in a coma for ten years and then just popped his eyes open one day. Maybe they secretly hope we might be able to bring her out of it since they haven't been able to.

I read in a magazine that people in comas can hear you even if they can't respond. I want to tell her about all the happy things she's missed, like Marilyn's first time on the potty, Joy getting her actual driver's license, that we filled two more Green Stamps books and we're halfway through a third. I'll leave out the sad stuff, like missing my thirteenth birthday, and probably my fourteenth since it's only a couple weeks away. I'll tell her about the day Daddy let Joy trim his hair with the electric razor and she carved a huge bald spot in the side of his head. He tried covering it up with shoe polish but it rained, turning his collar black and his face red. I think she'd laugh at that. I could probably fill an entire notebook with the things she's missed.

Hope and I slide into the back seat of our bus. Daddy has Joy drive to Blue Rapids so he can spend the time last-minute studying for his sermon tomorrow. I brought my math homework. Hope brought her Bible. She's up to the book of Jude in her quest to read the whole thing, about a year behind schedule but almost there. Chastity refused to come along. Threw the biggest fit I've seen since she was seven years old and her favorite dress shrunk in the clothes dryer. I think she doesn't want her heart broken twice. The tantrum worked. Daddy let her stay home to watch Marilyn.

When we get to the hospital Daddy takes Hope and Joy into Mama's room first because they let only three people in at a time. I wait in the visitor's lobby, where a little boy with the darkest face I've ever seen stands directly in front of me, staring. There aren't any black people in Cherry Hill so it's hard not to stare back. He has an Afro like on the Jimmy Hendrix album at Lola's house. I want to touch it so badly I have to hold one hand with the other one to keep myself from feeling that kid's head. A little girl with a bazillion barrettes in her hair comes up and stands next to him. The two of them look at each other and giggle with their hands over their mouths, but I can still see their dazzling smiles.

I busy myself with an article in *Good Housekeeping* about how to look good for your man when he comes home from work. According to the magazine, no man wants to be greeted by a wife in curlers. A kiss is welcome, but she should not talk at him as soon as he gets in the door. Fix him a drink, the article says, and let him unwind before serving him dinner. It doesn't make sense to me. Seems like the husband should be the one who brings the wife a drink after running behind kids all day, shopping for groceries, doing laundry, and cooking meals. Maybe if Daddy had helped Mama more she wouldn't have needed those nerve pills. Maybe she wouldn't have tried to kill herself. And maybe she wouldn't have ended up in this cold, ugly hospital.

Daddy taps me on the shoulder, startling me. "You can go in now."

When I walk into the hallway he points toward a room where Joy stands sideways in the doorway, one foot in the room and one in the hall. He motions for me to go in. "I'm going to call on some of the other patients. Joy will stay with you."

Ever since Mama's "incident" he's been watching me with an eagle eye. When he asked how I knew about her being in the barn with the engine running, I said God told me. He can't get too mad at me because if I hadn't made that call Mama might not even be alive. But I know he's rattled. He stares at me when I walk into a room, brows furrowed, like he's trying to read a road sign from too far away without his glasses on.

I stand in the hallway with my feet frozen in place. My legs are trembling. I want to see Mama, but part of me is afraid. Daddy puts his hand in the center of my back and pushes me across the hall. Joy moves aside and I feel myself stepping over an invisible line between two worlds. I glance toward Joy lingering in the doorway, picking at a hangnail. Hope remains on her knees on the other side of Mama's bed, praying quietly, her head resting on the sheet near Mama's feet.

Mama's skin is pale as baby powder and her body like a limp doll. She's not in this world at all. Her breath is here but that's about it. I force myself to pull a chair up next to her bed and reach for her needle-bruised hand. As soon as I touch her I'm lost in a different place. There's no hospital room, no sisters, and no more sounds from the bedside machines. Yet here's Mama, smack-dab in front of me, sitting on a porch swing, a slight breeze blowing the hair back from her face.

"Mama?"

"Grace . . ."

The way she says it is like a prayer.

"What are you doing here, Mama?"

"I'm just resting, that's all. Isn't it a lovely day?"

Dandelions and butterflies flood a meadow beside us. Each time the wind blows it ruffles the grass, turning it a new shade of green. The sky above us is the color of a lagoon with cloud bubbles swimming by. I can smell lilacs blooming somewhere close by.

"It's beautiful, Mama. But where is this? Where are you?"

Mama smiles so big her eyes almost close.

327

She grips the chain that supports the hanging swing and nudges with her feet. The swing creaks as she moves, but I can't see up to where the creaking starts. Even the clapboard wall behind her looks like just the front of a house on a stage set. If I walk up and push on it, will it fall over? Is there anything behind it?

I take a step closer. "Is this heaven?"

Mama tilts her head and looks at me in a way that loves me out loud. I smile back at her.

"Look around, Grace. What do you think?"

I take a moment to inspect her world. Everything is beautiful, perfect.

"Well, I don't see any mansions or streets of gold and we seem to be the only two people here, so I guess this isn't heaven. That means you can come back, right?"

Mama doesn't say anything. She closes her eyes and sings softly. The song is familiar. It's from my *Carpenters* album.

Mama opens her eyes and looks right at me as she sings. Is she talking about the day I was born or how the angels helped create the world she now lives in? She stops singing.

"Mama?"

"Shhhh!" she says. "They're coming."

"Who's coming?" She's fading out right in front of me along with her voice. "Mama? Hey, Mama!"

Joy's hand on my arm brings me back to the chair. I open my eyes to find Mama back in her hospital room. No porch, no swing, just the bed and all the noisy machines.

Joy glares at me. "Who were you talking to, Grace?"

"I was talking to Mama."

She sneers at me. "You're crazy, you know that? Just plain crazy."

Hot tears spill onto my cheeks. "But I saw her! She's in the most beautiful place. And she's happy again."

"Like I said. You're crazy." She squints at me as if by looking close enough she'll find a way to prove it. "I'm going to go find Daddy. I think we should go now."

Hope continues praying with one eye open, peering at me. "And help Grace to stop dancing with the devil and having visions and lying to people and —"

"Shut up, Hope," I say. "Just shut up."

"And saying shut up and . . ."

I can't take it in here anymore. The room feels hot and stuffy and sickening. I kiss Mama softly on her cracked lips. There's the tiniest hint of a smile on her face.

"Bye, Mama," I whisper. "I'll come back

and see you again."

Maybe she can't answer, but I know she heard me.

Joy drives us home with Daddy in the front seat going on about my wild imagination. No matter what he says I know Mama saw me, just like I did her. Maybe he's upset at the idea of me knowing Mama in a way he never will. What bothers me more than Daddy's yelling is wondering whether she'll ever come back after being in such a perfect place. Where she doesn't have to be Mama to five children in the way that uses you up until nothing's left.

"I don't get it. How can Mama be in between worlds?" I'm reclining on the lowest branch of the tree in our backyard, looking up through the leaves at the sky, which is the color of a robin's egg. Ever since I got my period, Isaac and I can talk in other places besides a closetful of Chastity's stinky shoes.

The same way I can, Grace. The Universe is much more navigable than people think. Once a person finds the door it's very tempting to cross over.

"Can I cross over?"

You already have. You saw her, spoke with her. There are very few barriers for someone like you.

"Then, can I . . ."

You live in a physical world for now. Be patient.

"But I want to come visit you, Isaac."

You do visit with me.

"But I can't see you!"

You don't need to, Grace. There's nothing to see. I know it's hard to understand, but I'm not a human being anymore. I'm just . . . being. I took human form just as you have and now I'm —

"Dead. You're dead."

I hate it when I cry, but my eyes begin to burn and blur with tears. I can't stop myself.

Grace . . .

His voice is a comfort and a sharp pain at the same time. I turn and rest my face against the rough branch, letting my legs dangle like a lazy sloth. The day is perfectly still, but in the next moment the leaves above me rustle with an invisible wind. All at once it feels like I'm underwater. Warm water. I hold perfectly still.

"Isaac? Is that you, Isaac?"

A rush of love both fills and surrounds me as Isaac passes through me. The word that comes to my mind is rapture, like Daddy talks about in Revelations. I feel engulfed in a wave of tenderness. Or like I *am* the wave,

awash in love beyond what I've ever experi-
enced, even from Mama. After a moment
the gust settles and he's gone. I'm left weeping like a newly crowned beauty queen. I
think I finally understand what they mean
by a *good* cry.

Lola agreed to come to church with me,
but only for a Sunday evening service
because they're the shortest. And also
because I promised to help write her English
paper in trade. A thunderstorm has been
brewing all day and the clouds over our
house keep getting darker and darker. About
the time Lola's parents drop her off on their
way to a folk concert in Blue Rapids, the
sky opens up and dumps all that rain on
our heads. We race across the street to the
church. Lola and I shake off the water in
the foyer before finding a spot in the pew
behind Edna Warber. Edna is the church
treasurer. She's never been married, what
people call an old maid. I have a feeling that
her being such a big woman might have
something to do with it.

Lola and I look like a couple of drowned
rats as we settle in. I glance over at the
empty pastor's family pew and remember
the last time Mama was here. She had to sit
all by herself because Chastity pretended to

be sick so she could watch *The Wizard of Oz* on TV. Joy stayed home to look after Chas, and I sat with my youth group that night. When I'd turned around during the service it looked like part of Mama was already off somewhere living another life. Sort of like she is now.

I once found some poetry in the basement that Mama had written in college, where she studied music before meeting Daddy. According to Aunt Arlene, Mama has always loved to write poems and songs and she was real popular in high school. Grandma sent her to Bible College hoping she'd meet a nice preacher, which is exactly what happened. Mama dropped her dreams of being a famous gospel singer and songwriter to become a pastor's wife instead. At least she got to sing in our church. People are deeply moved by Mama's singing. The last time she sang, it was a song called "Brother Ira" about an old man who gets kicked out of the choir because he sings off-key. Even Joy sniffled a little when Mama sang that one.

After Mama came back from staying at the rest home the first time, she wouldn't sing in church anymore, not even when people begged her. She claimed the medication made her throat dry. I think those pills made her forget the words to the songs and she was too stubborn to use a crib sheet. Mama has always prided herself on being a professional even though she dropped out of college. Now we have to listen to people like Edna Warber, who can't carry a tune in a bucket.

Lola nudges me and giggles as Edna makes her way back to the pew following a painful rendition of "How Great Thou Art." Her nylons scritch together with each step as she walks down the aisle. Daddy starts in on his evening sermon. Lightning flashes outside the window, lighting up the stained-glass designs. Lola and I use our fingers to secretly count the seconds between the lightning and thunder to determine how close the eye of the storm is. They say it takes five seconds for the sound of thunder to travel one mile. I never get up to more than one-thousand-ten before the thunder hits, so we're about to get hit with the worst of it any minute.

Lola draws a funny picture of Edna on the back of the church bulletin. I'm trying to stifle a giggle when all of a sudden a huge crackle of thunder breaks loose. It spooks Edna, who leaps out of the pew before crashing back down again. When she lands a *creeeeeeeeeek* sounds from under her. The last thing we see before the electricity goes out is every single person in the same pew with Edna fly out of their seats because the wood split when Edna landed, pinching everyone's behind as the splinter closed. Lola and I can't stop laughing. Thank goodness there's no light or I would be in big trouble for cutting up in church.

With the power out, Daddy dismisses the service early and the ushers lead everybody out with flashlights. When we get back to the house, Lola and I light candles in my room. Chastity is spending the night at one of her friend's house so we have my room to ourselves. We sit on the floor near the window. Lola holds what looks like a yellow Fourth of July sparkler over the flame.

"What's that?"

"Patchouli."

"What's patchouli?"

"It's incense. I stole some from Catherine and John. They burn it all the time."

"What for?"

"Promise you won't tell?"

"Tell what?"

Lola leans forward over the candle, her face lit up like a ghost. "You have to promise first."

"Okay. I won't tell."

"To cover up the smell of dope." She whispers it so low I almost can't hear her.

"You mean marijuana?"

"Yup." She grins. "They get stoned with their friends almost every weekend."

Lola is my idol. She acts as though it's normal to burn incense sticks, wear a bearskin cape, and have a life-size sculpture of a camel in your front yard. I don't even know anyone who drinks beer.

"Aren't you afraid they'll get arrested?"

"Nah, the cops around here are too stupid."

"Cop," I say. "We only have one."

"Exactly."

Lola pokes the burning end of the stick into her mouth. She holds it there for a few seconds before blowing out smoke in rings just like an old pro. It smells a little like sticky buns mixed with burnt tires. When she hands it to me I swirl it around like I do with sparklers before they light off the fireworks over Cherry Lake on the Fourth of July. Lola giggles. Her laugh sounds like blowing bubbles in milk. We open my bedroom window to let the smoke out so Daddy won't smell it. I think about Mama lying in her hospital bed and wish she could know this kind of joy.

23

It's my birthday. Of course it's also Isaac's birthday, but we don't celebrate that. It's always been hard for Mama when my birthday rolls around. At least she doesn't have to suffer through it this time. As if Mama being gone isn't bad enough, my day has already been ruined. Joy came into my room first thing this morning to tell me there's an arrest warrant out for "that creepy hobo who lived in the old school bus." They're charging Lyle with assaulting Rosalie Cutler and molesting another girl. Maybe even for the disappearance of the blind Anderson girl.

Joy is a friend of Rosalie's older sister Virginia, who was there when Rosalie came home after she was attacked. The way Virginia told it, it took their mama three hours of coaxing to get Rosalie to talk and that wasn't until after she got her into the bathtub. What happened was Rosalie was late coming home from school last Friday. When she walked in the door her face was frozen like she'd seen a ghost. Her mama drew a bath to calm her, but Rosalie wouldn't take her underpants off, not even to get into the tub. So her mama just let her get in with them on.

While Rosalie was soaking, her mama noticed a bruise on each of her daughter's wrists and another one on her neck. As soon as her mama mentioned the marks on her body, Rosalie burst out crying. That's when her mama spotted the blood on her underpants and asked Rosalie if she had her period. Rosalie shook her head no, at which point Mrs. Cutler got hysterical and Virginia came running into the bathroom.

"Did someone hurt you?" Mrs. Cutler asked, but Rosalie just cried. Then Mrs. Cutler said, "Rosalie, did that pervert hobo Lyle do this to you?" That's when the room got real quiet, as Virginia told it. She says Rosalie got a faraway look; then she turned to her mama and nodded her head yes.

Rosalie refused to talk to the police, but they got the gist of the story from her mama. They had Rosalie checked by Dr. Tietsma, who said that Rosalie had been messed with down there. I feel real sorry for Rosalie, but I also hurt for Lyle. I know he wouldn't harm her. Lyle couldn't hurt anything or anyone, he's that gentle. I don't understand why she'd say such a horrible thing about him.

Rosalie is back in school today. She's standing all by herself against the outside wall of the gymnasium. Some of the other girls invited her to sit with them at lunch, but Rosalie won't have anything to do with anyone. When I start to walk toward her she gives me a look that says don't come near me. Her brown eyes are as big as quarters backing up her plea, so I move away. When the bell rings, Rosalie is the last one to go inside.

Ronnie Savage sits directly in front of me in science class. He's scratching his crew-cut head with his pen without realizing he's using the wrong end, leaving a bunch of blue ink marks above his ear. I want to take the pen out of his hand and connect the dots. There's a lot Ronnie doesn't know and this is the least of them. I can tell by the way someone looks at me if they're open to knowing what I know. Ronnie isn't asking so it's not right for me to tell him that his mama has cancer. The bracelet he gave her last year for Christmas will end up buried with her by the time next Christmas rolls around. That sounds gruesome and you'd think these visions would scare me when they come, but they don't. The thoughts are just there, real matter-of-fact like, as if I'm seeing with eyes that don't know my emotions.

I used to think the Knowing was a curse, a result of not being born the boy Mama and Daddy wanted. I've come to realize that this thing, this way of knowing things is much bigger than Mama and Daddy's longing. And I've learned to be careful with it. I shouldn't necessarily reveal what I know. But I still don't understand why bad things happen to innocent people. I sometimes wonder what the point is in all these broken hearts. Rosalie may not be the prettiest girl, Ronnie's not the smartest, and Lyle likes to drink a bit, but that doesn't make them bad people. They don't deserve to suffer like this. I'm supposed to trust in God's plans, but sometimes I question them. I really do.

I spend the afternoon in the kitchen, baking myself a chocolate cake with vanilla frosting. I leave the cake on the kitchen table with fourteen candles in the shape of a heart, just in case anybody might have forgotten. I wish I could save a piece for Lyle. The thought of him caged in a cell makes me sick inside. A wanderer like him needs to be free. I hope they're feeding him more than bread and water in that place. He's used to pretty good handouts.

Daddy walks in while I'm making sloppy joes for supper. He glances at the cake, then stops and checks his wristwatch. I can tell by the way he worries the change in his pocket that he didn't remember.

"I've gotta run out for a little bit, Grace. You girls go ahead and eat without me."

"Okay, Daddy," I say. What in the world is he going to find open at six o'clock in Cherry Hill? The only place that's doesn't close up by suppertime is the Dairy Queen.

After we finish our sandwiches, Chastity turns out the lights and then Hope, Joy, and Marilyn join her in singing "Happy Birthday." I stare into the candles and make a wish for Mama to wake up and come home. Just as I'm about to blow them out, Daddy rushes in and drops a package on the table, which puts out two of the candles. I quickly blow out the rest and Marilyn claps her hands.

Chastity made me a leather billfold in Girl Scouts, and Joy bought me a beaded choker. Hope hands me a Bible bookmark made out of melted crayons between waxed paper. I pull the wrapper off Daddy's package and lift out my present: a brand new Holy Bible

341

with a pink leatherette cover and gold-edged pages. When I open it to the first page, a white envelope falls on the floor. Marilyn scrambles under the table to retrieve it. I open the Bible and read the inscription aloud.

" 'Thou art fairer than the children of men: Grace is poured into thy lips; therefore God hath blessed thee forever. Psalm 45:2.' " *With love from Mama and Daddy.*

I run my hands over the words. It's Mama's handwriting.

"She wrote that before she . . ." He pauses to find the right words. "Before she got sick. I found it under our bed. She planned to give it to you for your last birthday."

I hug the Bible to my chest. "Thanks, Daddy."

I look around at my sisters' teary faces. "Thanks, you guys."

Marilyn hands me the envelope and I rip it open. I pull out a gift certificate for $5.00 from Dairy Queen.

"Who wants ice cream with their cake?" I ask.

"I do!" Marilyn jumps up and down.

It's still pretty cold out so we throw on our coats and parade down to the water together, me carrying the cake, just as the sun is starting to set. The color of the western sky is nearly the same as my new Bible. We eat our cake and ice cream at one of the picnic tables outside the Dairy Queen. The top half of a fishing shanty keens in the middle of the lake like a drunken soldier.

Chastity sighs. "I wish Mama was here."

Daddy flinches just a bit. He drapes an arm around Chas. "She's here," he says.

"She's here," he says again, but this time to himself.

24

I look for Lola in the lunch room, but she's not in our regular spot. I finally catch sight of her army jacket at the far end of the cafeteria and race toward her.

"Lola!"

She doesn't turn around, just sits there with her head hanging like a dead flower over the lunch table, an unopened brown bag in front of her. I have to squeeze onto the bench next to her because she won't slide over of her own accord.

"Hey, are you okay?"

She lifts her head and looks at me with watery eyes.

"What is it?"

She starts to mumble something, but it never gets past the lump in her throat and she drops her head back down. I reach over to take her hand, but she pulls it away.

"It's okay," I say. "You can tell me later if you want."

I don't even think about reading her thoughts because it's not my place to. I just stay with her, hoping my shoulder against hers is enough. We sit that way until the bell rings and I get up to go to class. Lola stays put.

"C'mon, Lola. You don't want a tardy slip. One more and you get detention."

"I'll be along. Go ahead." It's the only thing she's said the whole time we've been sitting there.

Lola's seat is empty in history class. As soon as the bell rings I run straight to her locker and wait, but she never comes. After a few minutes the rush of voices and footsteps fade away until it's just me and Vern Johnson, dragging a piece of toilet paper behind his shoe like a surrender flag. He probably got locked in the bathroom by upperclassmen again or maybe they took his pants and threw them in the girls' bathroom and he had to retrieve them. I feel sorry for Vern so I smile at him as he walks by. I can tell by the way he sneers at me that he thinks I'm laughing at him rather than being friendly toward him.

I know where Lola is. It will mean detention for both of us if I skip my next class, but I head for the orchards anyway. It's a

345

warm spring day so I take off my shoes. As soon as my bare feet hit the grass I feel myself sink into it, the snow of last month just a memory. Halfway up the pathway I spot Lola's denim pack leaning up against a tree. I recognize the Earth Shoes dangling from her feet. I move under the tree and look up. At least she's smiling now.

"You came looking for me?"

"Of course I did. I was worried. What's going on, Lola?"

"My parents, that's what." She sits up, swings her bell-bottomed leg over the limb, and drops to the ground. "C'mon. Let's get some sun," she says.

Lola heads over the rise toward our favorite spot. By the time I catch up she's already naked, stretched out on her back in the soft grass as if she grew there. Nudity is a common thing at Lola's house. Even her daddy walks around naked, although he covers his privates with a towel when I'm around, for which I'm grateful.

I pull my shirt over my head. "What about your parents? You have the coolest parents ever, Lola."

"You think so? In that case, it must be cool to get divorced."

I hear myself gasp before I can stop it. "No! Oh, man, I'm so sorry. Why?"

346

She retrieves a beach towel from her backpack and spreads it out on the ground. "Here. You're wasting good rays."

I strip down to my bra and panties, painfully aware of my gangly body next to Lola's voluptuous figure. I lay face down on the towel with my chin propped in my hands. The sun feels as good as anything that's ever touched me besides Mama's backrubs.

"Holy cow, Lola, I can't believe it. Your parents seem so in love."

"My parents are in love with freedom. Turns out that 'free love' has a price."

Lola tugs a blade of grass and spreads it between her thumbs. She brings it to her lips and blows. Lola is the only person I know who can make a good sound come out of two thumbs and a weed. The way she does it reminds me of a melancholy loon. My attempts sound more like a chicken giving birth to a double-yolked egg.

Lola rolls to her side and runs the blade of grass along my back. "I knew this was coming," she says. "I saw my mom with one of her life drawing models. I went out to the studio to get some brushes and I heard them laughing. When I peeked in the window they were naked, painting each other. Not on canvases but actually brushing paint *on* each other."

I don't know what to say so I don't say anything, although I have to admit that painting your body does sound like fun.

"I think John's known about it for a long time. Maybe it was even okay with him. But then he got this job offer in Ann Arbor, so I guess he figures it's a chance for him to start over. I don't blame him. He says he'll visit. I doubt it."

I reach behind me and scratch where Lola is tickling my back with the grass. "He loves you guys. He'll visit. You'll see." I turn my head to face her. She's wearing round sunglasses that make her look like Janis Joplin.

"It's terrible to want what you know you won't ever get," she says. Her eyes fill with tears again.

"I'm so sorry, Lola."

She starts to sob, then scooches next to me and curls up like a little girl. I roll over to my side and put my arm around her as she cries quietly. After a minute Lola picks up her head and looks straight at me. She gently nudges me onto my back and rests her head on my shoulder.

"I love you, Grace," she says.

"I love you too, Lola."

She starts drawing circles with her finger around my belly button.

"Lola . . . ?" I start to say, but she puts a finger first to her own lips and then to mine.

"Shhh," she whispers.

I don't know what to do. It feels weird having Lola touch me like this. I want to tell her to stop, but I don't. She lifts herself up and I know what she's going to do. She's going to kiss me. And she does. Her lips are fuller than mine and could completely cover my mouth, but they don't because Lola barely touches my lips with hers. Like a butterfly, she brushes against my mouth, which I keep closed tight. I feel all funny inside. Lola's big boobs are mushing up against my nearly flat chest. She presses harder on my mouth; then pushes her tongue through my lips.

I jerk my face to the side. "Lola, stop it!"

She pulls back and looks at me, frowning. "Why? Don't you like it?"

"Yes. I mean no."

"Don't you love me?"

"Well, yeah, but not like that."

"Like what?"

"Like . . . well . . . like I would a boy."

Lola giggles. "Of course not, silly. I'm not a boy!"

"I know, but it's not right. God wouldn't —"

"Wouldn't what? Want two of His creations to love each other?"

"But —"

Lola cuts off my sentence with another kiss. She takes my hand and puts it on her breast. It is the softest thing I have ever felt in my life. She lets out a moan. I pull away from her.

"That's enough," I whisper.

"Okay," she whispers back.

Lola rests her head back on my shoulder and we lay like that so long we both fall asleep until the train whistle blows as it moves slowly through town. We're both sunburned, me on the front and Lola on her side. On our way back toward the school I finally break the silence.

"Lola, we can't. I can't be . . ."

"I know. I know, Grace. It's okay."

I struggle with my thoughts before gaining the courage to bring up my question. "Have you done stuff with a girl before? I mean more than what we did?"

"Once. Last summer at a Joan Baez concert that my parents took me to I met this girl a few years older than me. She played the flute and danced like a goddess. She told me I was beautiful." Lola sighs.

"But you are beautiful, Lola."

"Well, not to boys." She laughs. "Thank goodness," she adds.

"You really don't like boys?"

"Oh, I like 'em just fine. I just don't want to kiss them. Girls are so much softer." She reaches out and strokes my cheek with the back of her hand. I flinch just a little, but enough that she feels it and pulls her hand away. "Sorry, Grace."

"It's okay."

Lola stops walking and looks at me. "You've never been kissed before, have you?"

My face gets hot. I don't answer.

"You're so wholesome. You've probably never even masturbated."

"It's a sin," I say softly.

Lola groans. "You have got to get a better god." That laugh again.

I feel my face turning redder.

"Hey, don't worry. I promise I won't come on to you again. I know it's just me. I feel lucky that I got to kiss you. You really are lovely."

Hearing this I'm relieved, and a little sad at the same time.

25

Ms. Pierce always makes us girls line up in the gym for roll call before phys ed so she can check to be sure we're dressed in the dorky one-piece jumpers we have to wear for class. We've been standing around for ten minutes waiting when Jill Baker jumps out of line and grabs a basketball from the equipment box and starts bouncing it. She dribbles it to the same rhythm she's chewing her gum, which we're not supposed to have in gym class. Jill's not the type to play by the rules.

Jill stops and balances the ball on her right hip while she decides which girl to throw it to. She doesn't even look at me. Holding it out in front of her, she bounces the ball as high as she can and Sherrie Mayfield catches it. Sherrie bounces it to Connie Simmons, who does the same thing. Pretty soon everybody is running all over the place bouncing balls and making lots of noise, except for a couple of the unpopular girls who are still standing in line, holding their hands over their ears.

I find a spot on the bleachers and watch as the girls in my class get wilder and wilder. Ms. Pierce has never been late and gives us a hard time when one of us is tardy. I don't join in, partly because I don't like basketball and partly because I like Ms. Pierce. She's younger than most of the other teachers and drives a VW Bug with flowers painted on it. She says "Outa sight!" whenever anyone makes a score in our games. And she wears maxi skirts and peasant blouses, unlike the rest of the lady teachers who dress in skirts or pantsuits.

Nobody notices me get up and walk toward the showers. Ms. Pierce's office is at the end of the hall just before you get to the bathrooms. I peek inside, but the room appears to be empty.

"Ms. Pierce?"

No answer. Photographs line her desk. One of them is of her husband, whose hair is longer than Ms. Pierce's. They have different last names. She told us she kept her own because she doesn't think women should go around giving their names away just because they're married. Probably the same reason she insists on being called Ms.

instead of Mrs.

Ms. Pierce has one of those office chairs
you can twirl in and since nobody's around
I can't resist the temptation to give it a spin.
Except when I turn the seat toward me I
see a dark red blotch on it. It's still wet.
Several little puddles of what I'm sure is
blood dot the chair. I touch the spot, then
bring the scent to my nose to be sure.

I'm sure.

I follow droplets of blood to the bathroom
stall reserved for teachers. Her shoes and
legs are visible because she's sitting on the
floor in there.

"Ms. Pierce?"

"Grace, is that you?"

"Yeah. Are you okay in there, Ms. Pierce?"

"I'll be fine. I don't think I can hold class,
though. I'm not feeling very well."

I lean against the cold door of her stall.
"You got cramps?"

She doesn't answer, just starts crying, and
I can tell by the sounds that she's trying to
stop up the sobs with her hands.

"What's wrong?" I say, but she doesn't
answer. "Can I come in there with you, Ms.
Pierce? Maybe I can help you."

She cries even harder, but she's not trying
to cover it anymore so I take that as an
invitation. Not wanting to trouble her to

stand, I crawl under the door. She's leaning against the toilet, a headband of dried daisies sitting cattywampus in her messy hair. As soon as I get near her a shiver runs through me. I feel a presence, like someone just left but part of them is still hanging around. Ms. Pierce has lost more than just blood.

"Ms. Pierce?" She lets me take her hand. "Did you . . . did you pass a baby in the toilet?"

"We've been trying to have a child for three years," she blurts out without looking at me. "I finally tested positive three months ago. I was so hopeful and now it's gone. It's probably because of drugs I took in college. I don't deserve to be a mother." Ms. Pierce sucks in her bottom lip and chews on it, then turns. "I shouldn't be telling you this. I don't know why I told you that."

"I'm so sorry, Ms. Pierce. You don't have to worry about telling me. Nobody believes half of what I say anyhow." She smiles at me through her tears. I consider leaving it at that but decide to go ahead and say what I know. "She isn't gone. I can tell you that."

Her smile drops away, replaced by her serious teacher look. "Grace," she says, gently touching my arm, "I had a miscarriage. Do you know what that is?"

"Sure I do. You lost a baby. But that girl isn't gone, Ms. Pierce. She's still in this world. In fact, she's still in this room."

Ms. Pierce pulls her hand away from mine. "Grace, what on earth are you talking about?"

"Well, it's kind of hard to explain and I don't blame you if you don't believe me, but —"

"Wait. You said that *girl*. Why did you say it was a girl?"

"Is. She is a girl, leastways this time around. Do you want to know more? I can ask her."

"Grace!" Her mouth drops open, then closes. "You're serious, aren't you?"

I nod. "You want to know more?"

"Yes," she whispers. "Please."

"Okay," I say. "We need to sit real still."

I close my eyes and in my head I ask, *Why'd you leave?* The answer comes in the sweetest voice I've ever heard in my head. Almost like bells. When it's quiet I open my eyes and take Ms. Pierce's hand again.

"She says there was something wrong with how she came to be here. After you and her daddy made a place for her, there was a change of plans so she had to leave."

Ms. Pierce sobs. "I got angry with Marc because he said I needed to stop thinking about having a baby and just be happy. It's my fault she left."

The bell-like tinkle of the little voice grows louder.

"No! She says it's not your fault, just poor timing on her end. She says it happens a lot and you shouldn't blame yourself. She's chosen you and your husband to be her parents because she loves you both and she'll be back."

Ms. Pierce smiles through her tears. "Really?"

"Really. She's super sure about that part."

"I've heard things about you, Grace. That you see and hear things the rest of us can't. I don't believe in gossip so I didn't pay much attention to it but . . . you're for real, aren't you?"

"It's called clairvoyance. Lola looked it up. I call it the Knowing. Folks don't believe me so I don't talk about it. Plus it scares people and it's why I don't have many friends."

"That's too bad for them," she says. "I have a feeling you're a very good friend."

Ms. Pierce looks at me and then inside the toilet. "I believe you." She reaches up to flush the handle and as she does a petal from one of the dried flowers from her hair flutters into the bowl. It twirls around in

357

the bloody water before going down the drain.

"I should get the school nurse," I say. "Don't worry. I won't tell anyone what I know."

"I know you won't, Grace." She leans back against the stall wall. "And I won't tell anyone what you know either."

"Thanks, Ms. Pierce. People already think I'm weird."

She smiles at me through drying tears. "I don't think you're weird, Grace."

I smile back at her and turn to go.

"Oh, and, Grace?"

"Yeah?"

"You can use the door this time."

"Right," I say, and I stand up. Maybe too quickly because a sparkly light plays in front of my eyes, then disappears just as quickly as it came.

The following Sunday I stand in front of the bathroom mirror inspecting my body when Chastity walks in without knocking. I quickly cover myself with a towel because I don't like her looking at me naked. Compared to her I look like a stick. At twelve Chastity already wears bigger bras and fills them out better than I do. Her round body looks just like those ladies in the old paintings in Joy's encyclopedias. I can easily picture Chastity surrounded by little cherubs while she swings on a rope hanging from a tree, her dress made from satin.

"Need a couple of Band-Aids, Grace?"

"Very funny, Chas. You could knock, you know."

"Why?" She grins. "Doesn't appear you have anything to hide."

"C'mon. We're going to be late for church."

We get there late anyway. I don't think Daddy understands how much Mama used to help move us along. Chas and I meet up with Hope in the church foyer. She got a new set of rollers for her seventeenth birthday and slept all night in them. Half of her hair is curly and the other half is flat because some of the rollers fell out while she was sleeping. Hope likes the way the curls bounce when she jumps so she's making a big spectacle of herself. To tell the truth, the way she's grinning almost makes me want to jump up and down with her.

"Settle down, Hope," Daddy says. "This is not a circus."

"Can I go in now?" Hope asks.

"Go ahead. But go quietly."

Hope turns on her heels and almost trips as she bounds up the stairs toward the auditorium. The last thing I see of her is a fuzzy pink roller bobbing up and down on the back of her head. Guess she forgot one.

Today's the day that people go forward to accept baptism. Not to get baptized right there and then, but later this summer in Cherry Lake. You have to be at least twelve to go forward according to our church rules because a child can't understand the symbolism of baptism until then. Also, Daddy has to approve your baptism. The first time he denied me as punishment after catching me in the closet talking to Isaac for the umpteenth time. I went forward again when I was thirteen and Daddy turned me down again, this time on account of my feeding Lyle. "You're still not ready," he said, crushing my hopes once again. I've decided not to even ask this time.

Today's service is short compared to Daddy's usual sermons in order to leave room for the Call to Baptism. Daddy quickly tidies up his preaching and then Loretta plays "Just as I Am," which is the signal. That's when Daddy steps down from the podium and spreads his hands out and says, "Come unto me," just like in the picture of Jesus on the wall behind him. Except that Jesus isn't wearing a polyester suit with a clip-on tie.

Anita VanDyke stands up first thing and walks down the aisle. I already knew she'd go forward because she's been bragging about turning twelve for weeks. She's wearing what Mama would call a "smart" outfit, a lavender jacket and skirt with her purse and shoes dyed to match. I'm wearing one of Joy's old dresses and scuffed-up shoes, so I suppose I've got me a pretty dumb outfit. Mrs. Gardner walks forward next. She moved to Cherry Hill with her four kids after her husband ran off with one of his students at the college where he teaches. She wanted to start over somewhere new. Everyone knows she's looking for a husband. I say good luck since the widowed women outnumber the single men by three to one around here.

By the time the song is almost finished, four volunteers for next month's baptism at Cherry Lake have gathered in front of Daddy, not including Chastity. I can tell he's pleased by the way he pulls his pants up after inflating his chest. Then all of a sudden up pops Hope, who races down the aisle with that curler still floppin' in back of her head. Joy lets out a laugh and more than a few snickers travel around the room. Hope was already baptized several years ago. Daddy explained to her that it only takes once, but she insists on going forward every time.

Daddy smiles at Hope and announces the date for baptism when the lake is warmer. He opens his Bible to read a closing prayer. All of a sudden big old Edna Warber grunts as she stands. The room falls silent. A few gasps sprinkle across the auditorium as Edna moves toward the front of the sanctuary. Daddy's face goes a bit pale. I'm pretty sure the whispers all say the same thing: *How's Pastor Carter going to get Edna back upright once he dunks her?*

After church Daddy announces that we can go with him to the hospital today. He says we don't have to come along if it will upset us. It would upset me more not to be able to see Mama. I'll take what I can get, even if it means visiting Mama in her dreamland. Chastity decides to stay home again and Hope has a Bible class. I get in the car along with Daddy and Joy, who lets Marilyn sit in her lap. Joy has taken her responsibility to Marilyn as seriously as she takes money. And that means always keeping track.

Mama has a new roommate, a bald lady with liver cancer. Joy snooped in the patient bed chart while she was sleeping. The lady's face is the color of Grandpa's cigar ashes, and her eyes have sunk into their sockets. When the old lady pukes it makes Joy gag so she only stops for a minute to glance at Mama before taking Marilyn to the waiting room to read books. Daddy walks up to Mama's bed and stares at her. He doesn't sit down, just stands there like he's going to wait her out.

The other lady keeps staring at me. She looks lonely. I can't take it anymore so I walk over and say hi. She doesn't answer, but the corner of her mouth pulls up a bit. She glances at her water glass and back at me. I hold the straw to her cracked lips and wait while she sucks up a couple swallows, then drops her head back on the pillow. Her collarbones bulge against her papery skin and her breath is foul. Everything about her is foul.

"Can I get you anything else?"

She makes a sound, but I can't understand the word. I take a step closer and turn my ear toward her.

"Help." It comes out scratchy, but I hear it.

"Help how?"

She grabs my arm. The light coming through the window shines directly on her face and suddenly I recognize her. It's Bony Nurse from when Marilyn was born. She pleads with her reddened eyes. She thinks I can help her like I helped my baby sister, but I don't know what I did with Marilyn. It was more like Marilyn did it herself and just needed me to jump-start the process.

"Please . . ." she squeaks.

I want to run away, but I don't. Something tells me the sick old lady in this bed is no longer the same Bony Nurse from that day she yelled at Aunt Pearl and me. It's like she already has one foot in the next world. I look over at Daddy. He must not have heard or else he's just ignoring us. I glance at the name on the clipboard above her bed. Her name is Betty. Betty Hopkins. I rest my hand on her belly. It takes almost all of her strength to put her other hand on top of mine. I close my eyes.

I don't see anything, but I feel it. The mass inside her is thick and ugly. I wait for my hand to start buzzing like it did when Marilyn was sick but instead of heating up it goes cold. I open my eyes and look at Betty. Her dry eyes try to tear but nothing more than a prickling comes of it. Her hand loses its grip and falls away. She gives me a half smile, then closes her eyes and falls asleep.

"You can go sit by Mama if you want to, Grace."

Daddy's voice startles me and I whirl around to look at him.

"What's the matter? Why are you crying?"

"Nothing. Well, actually because of this lady in the other bed."

Daddy looks over my shoulder toward Betty and back to me. "You know her?"

"Sort of." I glance down at my feet. "Daddy? Will you pray for her?"

He smiles, pleased with the sound of that coming from me. "Of course I will, Grace. Now go on and sit with your mama. But no funny stuff, you hear?"

"Yes, sir."

Daddy retrieves his Bible from a chair and heads over to Betty. He holds it close to his chest and bows his head. "Our Dear Lord in Heaven," he says quietly. "We ask that You bless this woman in her time of need. . . ."

I sit next to Mama, take her hand gently in my own and close my eyes. She's still on the porch, but today I can see the whole house, including the front door, two windows, and the wood ceiling that the swing hangs from. Red and yellow Indian paintbrush blanket the meadow on either side of the house. It's warm, like summertime. Mama holds up a glass that sparkles in the sunlight. She waves for me to come sit by her, so I do.

When I slide in next to her on the swing she hands me a glass of lemonade as if she's been expecting me. The ice cubes clink against the glass, the kind like Aunt Pearl has, frosted light blue on the outside. I take a sip, perfectly sour and sweet. I'm surprised at how real everything seems in this world where Mama lives.

Mama smiles and nudges me. "Good, huh?"

I grin. "Real good."

She gives the floor a kick and we start swinging, back and forth, back and forth. The ceiling creaks with each change of direction.

"How long you planning to stay here, Mama?" I can't help but ask it.

"Oh, I don't know. I rather like it here, Grace."

"Yeah, I can see that. You've got it pretty good here. And I know you needed a rest but —"

"Grace." She lays her hand on my arm. "I didn't want to leave you, any of you. It's just that . . ."

Mama puts her feet down heavy enough to stop the swing. She moves a tiny bit away from me and then turns so I can see her face. It glows in the afternoon light.

"It was too hard. That's all I can tell you. Some people can take a lot of hard times, but I'm not cut out that way. When Hope got hurt, I thought I would die from watching her suffer. When Isaac didn't survive it made me so sad I didn't think I could go on. Then Marilyn was sick and suddenly I felt like everything that made me happy had another side to it. Do you know what I mean?"

"Like singing the blues? They're so beautiful, but they're so sad."

"Yes! Like that, Grace. Except that it was more like having to sing happy songs when you felt like singing the blues."

Mama stands and walks across the porch to look out over the meadow. She's barefoot and wearing a sleeveless sundress with tiny yellow flowers on it that I've never seen before. It doesn't have any pockets. All of Mama's clothes have pockets. Most of the time they're full. She turns around and leans back against the railing. Mama looks radiant in spite of the topic of our conversation. I can't remember seeing her this happy. Ever. Which worries me.

"Nobody believes me when I tell them you'll wake up. That divorced lady, Sharon Gardner? She brings a casserole over at least three times a week. I can tell by the way she gets all gussied up and flutters her eyelashes at Daddy she thinks he's up for grabs." I'm trying not to cry. Tears seem like they would spoil a place as beautiful as this. "You're coming back, right? I mean, when you feel rested?"

Mama walks back over and crouches on her knees in front of me. She takes both of my hands in hers. "I can't answer that, Grace. But no matter what happens I want you to know that I love you. I know you think I love you less because you lived and Isaac died, but that's not true. I love you even more knowing that you carry him with you."

"But if he'd been born first, then . . ."

She stands and pulls my head to her belly, kissing the top of my head. "No. No, Grace. It wasn't your fault. You were meant to be born." She leans back and takes my face in her hands. "You're special, don't you think I know that?"

"But Daddy —"

"Your daddy doesn't understand. He loves you, Grace. He really does. He just doesn't understand."

The wind changes direction, sending a chill up my back. Mama clutches herself, looking at me. Everything starts to fade, but her smile never does.

"Time to leave, Grace."

I open my eyes to find Daddy standing over me. I'm afraid of what I might have said out loud, but he doesn't holler at me. Instead he takes his fat thumb and wipes a tear from the corner of my eye.

"Let's go," he says to me. Maybe to Mama, too, as if she will forget all about that silly coma and just follow us out of the room.

As soon as we're back home I run upstairs and sneak into the closet. I push a bunch of Chastity's dresses toward the center of the bar and sit on the board. It's dusty from not being here for a while. That and with Mama gone, Joy doesn't think of all the places that need dusting when she hands out chores. Also, I've grown too tall for this space. My knees are nearly to my elbows.

"I'm scared, Isaac."

Hello, Grace.

The sound of his voice settles me down inside.

"I'm afraid Mama's never coming back home from the hospital. Either she'll just stay in that coma or . . . she'll die."

There. I said it.

I can understand why you must be afraid. And sad.

"I want her to come back home!" I tilt my head back, as if by doing so he will see me better, see my broken heart. I want him to agree that her coma is nonsense.

When he doesn't answer, I start to beg.

"Can't you help, Isaac? Isn't there anything you can do from where you are?"

What I can do is listen to you and do my best to offer comfort.

I kick one of Chastity's stinky shoes across the closet. "It's not fair. Maybe *I* need a rest, too. Maybe I'd just like to quit like Mama."

Grace, please. Listen to yourself.

He doesn't need to tell me. I hear myself and I sound pathetic.

"She's so happy, Isaac. You should see her. She looks twenty years younger over there. And she's so . . . so completely loving. Like I remember from when I was very little. Even before I . . . *we* . . . were born. Do you remember, Isaac?"

Of course I do.

"Do you remember everything? Like dying?"

Yes, I remember dying.

"Were you scared?"

Only for a moment.

"What was it like?"

I was overcome with a sense of calm. I

370

imagine it was kind of like how it was for you being born and then being held for the first time. I felt . . . held.

He says this with a sigh in his voice. I think about that day in the tree and the peaceful feeling I had when Isaac moved through me.

"Isaac?"

Yes?

"Will I ever see you again?"

Yes, Grace. One day we will see each other again. I promise you that.

There's so much more I want to ask him, like whether I'll ever see Mama again. But for now this promise is enough.

26

On the second-to-last day of school a police car pulls up in front of the principal's office. The sheriff wants to interview some of us girls about any possible run-ins with Lyle. Gossip spreads like Velveeta in a town this small and somehow word has gotten around that Lyle and I are friends. I'm tired of all the nasty talk about him and the way people look at me and whisper. He hasn't even had a trial and most people have already decided that he's guilty. The thing I like most about living in a small town is also the thing I least like about it.

I'm watching the back of Luanne Conklin's head through the glazed glass door on Principal Plummer's office. Her blond ponytail dances around like a bobblehead as she talks. Apparently she was one of the girls who caught Lyle peeing near the old abandoned school bus a few years ago. That was when the rumors first started and also about the time Lyle started hiding out in our loft.

When the door opens Luanne glides past me holding her books to her chest. Principal Plummer stands in the doorway and motions for me to go in, but I don't move. Miss Lohman stops typing and peers over her glasses, first toward the principal, then back at me.

"Grace, come on in now," he says. His bald head is shiny and has a weird dent in the top. He's almost as tall as the doorway.

It's all I can do to lift my body off the chair. My blouse is stuck to my skin from sweating. Partly because it's hot and partly because I'm so afraid of saying the wrong thing. I sit in the chair opposite from the principal's desk. Sheriff Conner is leaning against the wall to his right, holding a pad of paper.

"Hello, Grace," he says. "I just have a few questions and then you can go, okay?"

I nod.

"Do you know Lyle Miller?"

I pick at the flower design that Lola embroidered on the knee of my navy blue jeans. Daddy won't let us wear faded denim, so Lola tried to make them look cooler. We washed them about a dozen times, but they still look brand new. Plus they're high-water because Daddy also won't let us wear pants any lower than the tops of our shoes.

"Grace?"

I nod again.

"Has he ever spoken to you?"

"Yes."

"I'm sorry, Grace, but you're going to have to speak up."

"Yes," I say again.

"Has he ever touched you?"

I look up from my jeans and straight at the sheriff. Everybody knows I'm a terrible liar. Even if I wanted to I'm no good at it because my face gives me away. "Yes, but not like how you're thinking."

The two men trade glances, their eyebrows doing a secret dance between them.

"What do you mean by that?"

"I mean it was nothing bad."

"But he touched you."

"In a good way. He put his arm around my shoulder when I was sad."

"Has he touched you anywhere else?"

Ugh. I was hoping he wouldn't ask that. "He's put his hand on mine, on my knee once. He meant to comfort me." As soon as the words are out of my mouth I realize it sounds a lot worse than it was. I can't stop the tears from coming. "Lyle is a good person!" I yell, jumping to my feet.

"Calm down, Miss Carter." Sheriff Conner makes a note, then closes his pad.

The principal points toward the chair. "Sit down, young lady."

I remain standing. "It's not what you think!"

Principal Plummer picks up the phone and mumbles something into it. The door opens and the secretary appears.

"Please escort Miss Carter back to her last class."

Miss Lohman puts her arm behind my back and leads me out of the office. As soon as we're in the hallway I dart in the opposite direction and bolt through the front doors. I run two blocks before stopping at the railroad crossing. I decide to take the back way home so I can be alone with nobody's thoughts but mine. I kick off my shoes and roll up my jeans, stepping from one wooden tie to the next. Fresh grease splotches the rails, along with a severed raccoon. A murder of crows caws at me from their perch in the poplar trees that line the right-of-way. I toss both halves of the raccoon into the woods. The birds fly down all at once and cover it like a black cape, squawking and bickering.

Balancing, I put one foot in front of the other on the warm rails with both arms straight out. I take a couple of steps, teetering side to side as I walk. In my head I pretend to be Olga Korbut on the balance beam.

"Grace! Grace! Grace!" the crowd chants.

"A perfect ten!" yells the announcer.

My fans throw me flowers and kisses. In real life I slip off the rail. To save face from my imaginary fans I make like I meant to dismount. I bow toward the crows, but they're too busy eating lunch to pay me any attention. Behind me I hear clapping. I whirl around to find a youngish guy applauding. Amazingly, he looks almost exactly like Jesus except his beard is downy and scragglier.

"Not bad," he says, smiling.

I'm embarrassed and a little afraid because there's nobody else around. I've never seen this guy before. I turn and start walking as fast as I can toward home.

"Hey," he calls behind me. "I didn't mean to scare you."

I keep walking and don't slow down until I spot a huge spread of Queen Anne's lace at the edge of the woods. I look behind me to make sure I'm alone before skipping down the hill to pick a bouquet for Mama next time we visit. The biggest patches lie near the far edge, so I wander over to grab a few of those.

When I reach the treeline something catches my eye. I walk closer and find a blue quilt with little stars sewn into the corner of each square. Somebody took a lot of trouble to sew each of those stars on there. I know this because Aunt Pearl made all of us girls a quilt and it took her a whole year to finish each one. Mine has pink and yellow squares with ballerina slippers sewn into the very middle. Aunt Pearl knows that I love dancing, even if we aren't allowed.

The quilt is a little dirty, but I think I can clean it up and save it for Lyle, when he gets out of jail. I toss my flowers into the center and pick up a corner to fold it up. As soon as I touch it my whole body spasms and I can barely stay upright. I want to let go, but I can't because somewhere in my head a voice, a young girl's voice, stops me cold. She's screaming, but the moans sound like they're coming out of her nose.

My whole body starts shaking and I'm filled with a dread so terrifying I can hardly bear it. I feel like I'm going to explode. It's as if the girl's hand is over mine and she's making sure I don't let go of that blanket. Usually when I have a vision it's like a movie. This is different. I can't see her because I'm inside her, looking out through her eyes.

Someone's behind us.

Don't you dare make a sound, you hear? The devil will grab you and pull you all the way to hell if you make a sound.

I can feel his sweat dripping on my/her neck and smell his minty breath. He pushes us forward, then shoves us facedown on the quilt. I hear cloth tearing, a belt buckle, a zipper. His big hand covers our mouth. And then searing pain.

God! No, please no! Oh God, it burns! Mama! Mama, please make him stoooooop!

Behind us he grunts, one hand on our neck and one on our wrist. Each thrust pushes our face against the fabric. We scream into his dirty palm as he groans. A train roars by before everything goes quiet except for the sound of his last words over and over in our ears.

You tell it was me and the devil will grab whoever you tell, too.

I open my eyes slowly, surprised to find that I'm still standing. The quilt drops from my hands and I want to run, but I'm frozen in place. I fall to my knees and vomit. As I wipe my face with the hem of my shirt, I hear footsteps.

"Are you okay?"

I raise my head to find the Jesus guy

standing over me. He puts a hand on my shoulder and I let out a scream.

"Whoa," he says. "You having a bad trip or something?"

I stagger to my feet, backing up. "I've gotta go," I say.

I take off running.

"Your shoes!" he yells from behind me.

Daddy will be angry about me losing them, but not even Jesus could stop me from running as fast as I can all the way home.

"What's the matter, Grace, you sick?"

Daddy raises his fuzzy eyebrows at me and I try to smile, but I can't. He's made liver and onions specially for me because I got all my Bible verses memorized for the third week in a row. I'm one of the few kids I know who likes liver and onions. Tonight he might as well be serving mud patties. I have no appetite. He gets up from his chair at the head of the table and stands next to me. His hand on my forehead feels so good. I live for the moments he comes on soft.

"You're clammy but no fever," he says, and goes back to his chair.

No, I want to tell him, *keep your hand there and don't let go. Don't ever let go.* But instead I say, "I don't feel so good. May I be excused?"

Daddy nods and tells Chastity to take care of the dishes for me tonight.

"But, Daddy!" she protests. He gives her The Look. She passes it on to me, but it doesn't even faze me compared to how awful I already feel. I have met the devil and I know his name.

27

Sheriff Conner's office sits above the post office, but he has a separate telephone in his house for police business. Usually he just rides around town in his cruiser real slow, most likely because he can cover the whole town including the rural areas in about three hours. He stops to talk to people, adults mostly, but sometimes kids, too. In the evenings he double-checks the doors of the grocery, the hardware, the café, and the Dairy Queen. He counts the paddle-boats and canoes near the dock in front of the rental place to make sure none are missing. Then he walks through the cemetery and ejects teenagers making out in their cars.

When he's not patrolling he's either at home or having a cup of coffee at the Cherry Hill Café. Mostly he's home, ever since his son, Scott, was reported missing in Vietnam. His wife took the news real hard.

Mrs. Conner doesn't much come out of the house anymore. Daddy doesn't call on her because she's Catholic. He read about it in the Oceana *Chronicle* but everybody knows everybody else's business in Cherry Hill long before it's published in the paper. Daddy says she's probably rubbed her fingertips raw on that rosary, wasting her prayers on Mary instead of going straight to God. I feel sorry for the Conners. Just like Daddy, the sheriff lost a son and then lost what used to be a loving wife.

Sheriff Conner is in his yard trimming the edge of the lawn the first time I ride by on my bike. I'm too nervous to stop. What if I'm wrong? But I'm not. I know in my heart what I have to do. I ride by a second time. This time I wave and he waves back. Well, this is just stupid. I can't keep riding my bike around the block past his house. Next time. Next time I'll stop. I'll go right on up and tell him everything.

I take a wider tour around Cherry Hill to collect my thoughts. I have to wait for the train to pass before I can cross Fourth Street. When the last car chugs past me, I spy the sheriff in the distance, sitting on the top step of his stoop. It's now or never. I walk my bike over the bumpy tracks before jumping back on. The front wheel turns up his driveway as though someone else is steering.

"Hello, Grace," he says, wiping the sweat off his tan forehead with a red bandanna.

"Hi," I say.

He swallows the last of his water and sets the empty glass by his feet. "Something I can do for you?"

I start to panic and think about making up an excuse for being here, maybe offer to help with some yard work, but nothing comes out of my mouth except "Um . . ."

"What is it, Grace?" He leans forward, all concerned-like. He should be. I'm about to dump the biggest news he's ever had dropped in his official lap, next to a drowning or a car wreck the past several years. I set my bike down in the grass since it doesn't have a kickstand.

"I need to t-t-ell you something."

He pats the cement next to him and scooches over to make room and I sit down.

"It's a shame what happened to Rosalie," I blurt out.

He puts his big hand on my shoulder. "You know I can't talk about that. Is that why you came here?"

"No, sir. I mean yes, sir. I came to tell you that Lyle didn't hurt Rosalie."

Sheriff Conner's rugged face softens.

"Now, Grace, I realize Lyle is a friend of yours." He pauses, then starts up again. "You can't help him and you shouldn't let his business trouble you. You're much too young to worry about things like this. I promise you he will get a fair trial."

"But, Sheriff, I *know* Lyle didn't do it!"

He lets out a deep sigh. "How could you possibly know such a thing, Grace?"

"I just do."

He grabs the empty water glass and stands up. I think he's had it with me. He reaches for the handle on their front door.

"I know who hurt Rosalie," I say.

He sits back down. "Did Rosalie tell you something?"

"No, sir. She won't talk to anyone. And I know why. Because our church janitor, Harold Weaver, told her she'd go to hell if she did. He told her that whoever she told would go to hell, too."

I swallow hard and wait for the sheriff to dismiss me.

"Harold Weaver?" he asks out loud, but not to me.

Sheriff Conner wipes a chunk of mud off the toe of his shoe with the red bandanna, then wads it up and shoves it inside the empty glass, like he's stalling before he tells me that liars go to hell, too. "Grace," he

384

finally says. "Do you realize how serious it is to make an accusation like that?"

"Yes, sir. I do."

"Then why on God's earth would you say such a thing?"

"Because it's true." I know better than to tell him *how* I know, so I say, "There's a blue quilt with stars on it down by the railroad tracks just past the feed mill, where it happened."

When his glass hits the sidewalk and shatters I jump, but I don't stop.

"You locate his wife and I think you'll find she recognizes that quilt."

He grabs both my shoulders, narrowing his graying eyebrows. "How do you know about that quilt? And what makes you think it belongs to Harold Weaver?"

"You won't believe me if I tell you."

He lets go of me and starts picking up the biggest pieces of glass. "You know this is a small town, Grace," he says. "There aren't many secrets in Cherry Hill." He opens his bandanna and lays the biggest chunks of glass on it. "Are you telling me this is one of your premonitions?"

"No, sir. A premonition is knowing something before it happens. This is just knowing."

"Hello, young lady."

Sheriff Conner and I both look up, startled by Mrs. Conner's voice.

"Why don't you come inside and have a glass of lemonade and some cookies?" she says.

Sheriff Conner's eyebrows go from furrowed to a question mark. He seems puzzled at his wife's invitation but nods at me like it's okay, so I stand up. Before I turn around he puts his finger to his lips to let me know I shouldn't say anything to Mrs. Conner about our conversation. I wouldn't anyway, but I dip my chin so he knows I got the message.

"I'll be in after I clean up this mess," he says.

I've never been inside the Conners' house before. It's a ranch style, newer than most houses in Cherry Hill, and real modern. Gold shag carpeting, wall to wall, and a bumpy ceiling with little sparkles in it. Mrs. Conner leads me to the living room. She motions toward the velveteen sofa. "Have a seat, Grace. I'll be right back."

She returns with an authentic Coca-Cola glass full of ice-cold lemonade and a small plate of chocolate chip cookies. When she sees me looking toward the photographs on the fireplace mantel she sets the plate on the coffee table.

"That's Brian," she says, pointing to the picture on the right. "And next to him is our other son, Bobby."

Both brothers have shaved heads and look like they could be twins.

"They're at the police academy. Bobby will graduate this year."

"I'll bet you're real proud of your boys, ma'am," I say.

Mrs. Conner takes down a two-sided frame with a picture of a long-haired hippie on the left side and a soldier in full uniform on the right. "And this here is Scotty. He's missing in Vietnam." She fondles the edges of the frame. Dark circles ring her blue eyes like half-moons. "Ah, but you probably know that from the newspapers."

"Yes, I heard that. I'm real sorry, Mrs. Conner."

She hands me the double frame. I know what she's going to say next.

"I realize it's probably just rumored nonsense, but they say you can tell things and I heard you just now talking to my —"

"It's okay," I say. "I'll do it. But I can't promise anything. And you can't tell my daddy because he doesn't like it."

"Of course not, Grace."

I hold the pictures against my chest and close my eyes. I feel light and fluffy, as

387

though my feet are floating and my head is full of cotton. A terrible case of the giggles comes over me. The part of me standing in the Conners' living room holding the photos worries that Mrs. Conner will think I am being disrespectful. But the part of me sitting in a smoky room in Vietnam doesn't care.

"Just one more toke for the road," I say, but it's not me saying it. I double over, laughing. It tickles. Everything tickles.

"Barbara!"

Sheriff Conner marches across the room. I almost drop the photo frame, but Mrs. Conner catches it. He snatches it away from her and places it back on the mantel. "What in God's name are you doing?"

"I'm sorry, Sam. I know it was stupid. I was desperate. Thought it couldn't hurt to ask her."

"Grace can't help us, Barbara. She's just a young girl with a wild imagination."

I open my eyes. I've recovered from the giggles, but I really want one of those cookies. I slide closer to the coffee table. "Excuse me," I say, reaching for a cookie.

Sheriff Conner clears his throat. "Grace, you better go on home now."

His voice is like Daddy's when he means business. At this point I figure I don't have anything to lose, but they certainly do, so I spill a few beans.

"I know about Scotty," I say.

That shuts 'em up right away. They step closer together and reach to touch each other's hands.

"He's alive. He was captured a couple years ago but recently escaped and found his way to a town. He plans to get ahold of his platoon after he has a little fun first. He's got real bad memories and smoking the grass helps."

They're both staring at me. I can't tell if it's because they believe me or because they don't know how to tell me they think I'm crazy.

"Can I have another one of those cookies, please?" I ask as politely as I can. Suddenly I'm starving.

The Conners look at each other, then back at me. Mrs. Conner hands me the plate and watches as I eat the last two cookies.

"Could I have one more, please?"

Mrs. Conner practically runs to the kitchen to fetch more cookies. The sheriff puts his hand on my shoulder. "Are you feeling okay?"

"Oh, yeah. I'm fine. In fact, I feel really

good." I can't stop grinning. "Really, really good."

Sheriff Conner shifts his balance from one foot to the other, fondling his leather holster. He looks down at the floor, then back at me. "Grace, did you really see Scotty?"

"Yes, sir, I sure did. He's in a smoky place, a bar or something, and he's okay. I think you'll be hearing from him real soon. Oh, and I didn't want to tell Mrs. Conner this part because she might be worried, but he got shot in the foot. Not by them, by himself. Shot himself accidentally when he was, you know, high. Before he was captured."

Sheriff Conner breaks into a big grin. "Wounded, huh?"

"Yup, guess they'll have to send him home."

"Guess so."

Another pause.

"Good Lord, Grace, you wouldn't be funnin' with me, would you? I mean, it would kill Mrs. Conner to get her hopes up like that."

"I don't lie, Sheriff. I didn't lie about what happened to Rosalie, either."

He looks at me with the sad face of a dog that wants what you're eating. Mrs. Conner returns with the plate piled high. I nestle a cookie between my teeth and shove one in each of my two pockets.

"Thank you, Mrs. Conner," I say through my teeth. "These are the best cookies I've ever had."

"Thank *you,* Grace," she says, and already I can see the lump coming up her throat.

I can see the lump coming up her throat.

28

Daddy's busy working on notes in his
church office for this afternoon's baptism
ceremony at Camp Blessing. I hate inter-
rupting him. The church office is off-limits,
but I need to tell him about the quilt and
what happened. I'm afraid he won't believe
me. Harold Weaver has been the custodian
ever since Daddy brought him to the Lord
in a jail cell. But if Daddy finds out what I
told Sheriff Conner before I tell him myself
I'm likely to be in more trouble than I've
ever been in before.

"Daddy?" I walk up to his desk and finger
the back of the metal chair in front of it.
"Can I talk to you?"

He doesn't even look up when he answers.
"Grace. I've already told you that you're
not ready for baptism. I'll let you know
when I think you are."

"But, Daddy, that's not what —"

"No buts. Now go help Joy with household

chores. I need to get ready for today's service."

He turns his back to me and grabs a book from the shelf behind him. He opens it on his desk to a place marked with a torn church bulletin and runs his finger over yellow highlighted words. I stand there for an extra minute before finally giving up. Maybe I'll tell him after the baptism service. He's sure to be in a good mood then.

Something about the day when all these people gather at the water makes me feel warm inside. Like I'm part of a bigger family, what Daddy calls the Family of God. I picture folks all over the country standing at their own bodies of water, holding hands and singing "Shall We Gather at the River" just like we do at Cherry Lake. It's the best day of the year. Even if it's Chastity getting baptized instead of me today.

When we arrive at Camp Blessing the beach is already full of people waiting around for the service to start. Daddy let me bring Lola, maybe as a consolation prize for not getting my turn today. She begged to come when I told her Edna Warber was getting baptized. I made her promise to be on her best behavior. We run down to the beach and stand close to the front so she has a good view of the action. The people getting baptized are lined up to the right of the dock, near the water's edge. Daddy's got half a dozen volunteers to dunk today, including Edna.

I was surprised Edna had never had her baptism. I suspect it has something to do with a fear of sinking. I suspect Daddy might also be having the same reservations, but the screen door on the camp lodge slams closed and here he comes down the hill. He likes to walk down separately after everybody else. This is a day he looks forward to more than any other. I can see it in the way he looks over his flock as he approaches, his hands held out as if he's holding an invisible staff. In my imagination I half expect them to start bleating, but they all just say, "Praise Jesus!"

With his head bowed and his Bible pressed to his chest he makes his way to the sandy beach. When he gets within earshot we hear him praying to himself as he walks. He joins Mr. Franks and Burt Lohman, who stand beside him with their backs to the lake. Daddy sets his Bible on a post and slowly raises his head to meet the eyes of his congregation. He looks from face to face, nodding just enough to acknowledge each person. One of the important parts of the

baptism is that those of us not being baptized have a role as witnesses. It's a ritual
that pleases both Daddy and his congre-
gants, every individual knowing they've
been seen. And Daddy knowing that they
hunger for his nod.

He takes the hand of each of the men
standing on either side of him. The men
extend their arms to the side and grab the
hands of the first two people to their right
and left. Everyone else does the same until
we're all holding two people's hands. I'm
holding Esther Swanson's hand on one side
and Lola's on the other. Daddy starts singing "Shall We Gather at the River" in a voice
that's better suited for "Onward, Christian
Soldiers." It used to be Mama's job to start
the singing and it was a lot better. I want to
stay angry about not getting my baptism
today, but as the song carries through the
crowd I'm filled with gratitude. Listening to
the voices fill the beach with the familiar
song feels a little like waking up in your bed
after you've been away for a time and suddenly realizing you're home again.

When the song ends Daddy lets go of the
men's hands and everyone else does the
same except for Lola and me. She yanks on
my hand, pulling me closer to the water's
edge so we can see better. Six people are in

the baptism queue, three adults and three children. Earl Felt, Mrs. Gardner, and Edna Warber will go after the kids, Chastity, Anita VanDyke, and LaVonne Davidson. Daddy takes off his suit coat and hands it to Burt. He walks backward into the lake and stops when the water reaches the waist of his black pants.

" 'Suffer the little children to come unto me,' " he says.

Chastity takes that as her cue. She slips out of her shoes and tiptoes out to Daddy, who is beaming like a brand-new lightbulb. Lola squeezes my palm so hard I have to pry her fingers off my hand. I think she's even more excited about the whole baptism thing than Chastity.

"Easy, Lola," I whisper. "You're hurting my hand."

"Sorry," she says, and lightens her grip, but only a little.

Chastity has chosen a white peasant dress with puffy sleeves and a big bow in the back for her baptism. Joy promised her it wouldn't be ruined in the lake but as soon as the water reaches the edge of Chastity's dress she freezes and looks at Joy. Joy nods for her to go on. It takes half a minute for Chas to get up the nerve to take another step. Finally she turns back toward Daddy, who moves forward to take her hand. He pulls her to him until the water is just below her chest.

Daddy smiles at his daughter as she hands him the white lace hankie she borrowed from Mama's dresser drawer.

"Chastity Ruth Carter, do you love the Lord?"

"Yes." I see her mouth move to form the word, but I can't actually hear her.

I hear Daddy just fine. "Do you understand that to be baptized is to be washed in the blood of the Holy Lamb of Christ?"

Chastity nods. Daddy lays the handkerchief over her face and holds her nose as he places his other hand behind her back and prepares to dip her.

"Then as a servant of our Lord I baptize thee in the name of the Father" — he dunks her once — "the Son" — under she goes again — "and the Holy Ghost." One last dunk and then he stands Chastity back on her feet. "Amen."

When she turns toward the beach her face says everything. Carefully curled hair lays flat to her head and the bow on her dress droops like wilted leaves. A ribbon of green slime clings to the front of her dress. She looks down at herself and then back up at the crowd. For a moment I think she'll burst into tears, but when the people start to cheer "Praise the Lord!" her expression changes from disgust to delight. Suddenly it's as if Chastity is onstage facing a throng of admiring fans. She smiles, hiding the agony of each disgustingly squishy step as she emerges from Cherry Lake.

Mrs. Franks drapes a towel over Chastity's shoulders and points her in the direction of the lodge, where a couple of church ladies are waiting to help her out of her wet things. She gently steps away from the crowd. As soon as they turn back toward Daddy, Chastity runs willy-nilly up the hill to get out of those soggy clothes.

Anita VanDyke and LaVonne Davidson go next, then Sharon Gardner, who cries all the way through her baptism. She hugs Daddy a little too long, pressing herself against him in a wet dress that is now nearly see-through. Daddy motions for Mr. Franks to come get her. Mr. Franks wades out and just about has to pry Mrs. Gardner off Daddy.

Lola nudges me with her shoulder. "Whoa. Did you see that?"

"Hard to miss," I say.

Earl Felt rolls up his pant leg and drops his wooden leg on the bank. I've never seen his stump before, the result of a tractor accident way back when he was a teenager. He hops to Daddy on one leg but manages pretty well both out and back.

And then all that's left is Edna Warber. The crowd falls nearly silent. This is the biggest gathering Daddy has had since he became pastor of The Church of the Word. It's no secret that most of them are here to see big Edna sink or float. A giggle escapes from Lola, but I give her a look. I don't want to get in trouble and also I feel a little sorry for Edna.

Edna waddles her way slowly toward Daddy, her left fist tightly closed around a plain white hankie held high above her head. She's draped in a multicolored muu-muu that looks like a bedspread with head and arm holes. When she finally reaches Daddy he goes through the usual list of questions. Then he gathers up all his faith and gently tilts Edna, who surrenders to his arms.

"In the name of the Father . . ." Daddy's voice trembles.

In the moments that follow it feels as though we are all under the water with Edna. Lola holds her breath and puffs out her cheeks like Louis Armstrong preparing to play his trumpet. Some of the ladies have their hands over their mouths.

". . . and of the Son and of the Holy Ghost!" he blurts out all at once, with a desperate look toward Burt and Mr. Franks. The deacons rush into the water, shoes and all, to help rescue Edna from drowning and Daddy from a hernia. The three of them reach down and pull Edna to her feet. She sputters and coughs as everyone lets out a breath together. The men stand beside her like proud doctors who have just delivered their first baby. They glance at each other, not wanting to embarrass Edna but not knowing what to do next.

It's Edna who breaks the tension. She lets out a laugh and splashes Burt. Burt smiles as he reaches down and splashes Edna back. When Mr. Franks laughs she splashes first him, then Daddy. Mr. Franks turns around and splashes Burt. Lola lets go of my hand and races into the water, kicking and splashing. The next thing I know the whole crowd of onlookers are in the water having a splash fight. Everyone except Daddy, who quietly walks around the edge of his crazed congregation and up the hill to the lodge, his white feet flashing like deer tails in the dune grass.

Daddy never said a word about it on the way home. I think part of him wanted to splash along with the rest of us, but the preacher part wouldn't let him. The thing that struck me most about what happened today was that he didn't try to stop us. It was one of the most generous things I've ever seen him do for his parishioners and as far as I know, the best baptism service Cherry Lake has ever known.

I know Daddy only said yes to me spending the night here at Lola's because she came to the baptism service with me today. Maybe he's convinced I can bring her to the Lord, or better yet, convert her whole family. I have no intention of trying to convince anyone here to become a Christian. I've seen the Purdys' rituals, how they celebrate the winter solstice and worship God's creation of nature every single day. Watching Catherine plant a tree and say a blessing over it last year seemed about as sacred a thing as any Scripture I've ever read. And that tree is thriving, so maybe God hears all the prayers, even the ones from heathens.

Lola and I sit with our feet dangling in the shallow end of their pond. John dumped a bunch of baby turtles in the water, but the raccoons and possums got all but one. Now it's just lily pads, cattails, and a solitary shy turtle.

Lola points to the edge of the pond.

"There it is!"

I squint, trying to see what she sees. "That's not a turtle, it's a leaf." I toss a small stone in the direction she pointed to prove it. The leaf tilts to one side before flipping upside down.

"Dang it. I thought that was him."

"Are you sure the critters haven't gotten to it?"

"Maybe. I hope not."

We watch a group of water spiders scoot across the surface of the pond, leaving little ripples behind them. The sun has made its way to the far end of the sky. Crickets start singing their heads off at the edge of the woods, and a whip-poor-will practices its evening song. Demeter and Persephone whinny back as if in conversation. Lola slaps a mosquito on her arm, smearing a tiny splotch of blood. She stands and wipes her hands on the seat of her cutoff shorts.

"The sun's almost down. Wanna go inside?"

I tilt my head back to look up at her. "Would you mind if I hang around here for a while?"

"Of course not. Do you want me to stay?"

"No, I'll be in later."

"Okay. Be careful not to trip on any bricks near the back door when you come in.

John's building a kiln for us." She laughs and adds, "Someday."

"I'll be careful," I say.

Lola leads the horses to the barn, then runs into the house. I sit until the moon rises above the pond, casting a ball of light on the surface. The air is humid and a dank smell radiates from the water hole. I glance around to make sure nobody is watching before slipping into the dark water. I'm still wearing my Sunday dress from earlier today and it billows around me. The bottom of the pond is pure muck and feels slimy under my feet, but I keep going. I stop when I'm chest-deep.

Drawing in a big breath, I close my eyes and dip under. The warm water rushes into my ears, drowning out everything except my thoughts. As I come up for air I say the words out loud. "In the name of the Father" — dipping again — "the Son" — one more dip — "and the Holy Ghost." I push the wet hair off my face and turn, coming face-to-face with the turtle. He blinks slowly, little moons reflected in his watery eyes, before he dunks and swims away.

"Amen," I say.

When I get to the bank a hand reaches for mine and pulls me onto the grass. Catherine drapes a colorful blanket around my shoulders and grasps my arms. She looks into my face and smiles. "Amen," she whispers, before pulling me to her chest and wrapping her arms around me. I sob into her collarbone, soaking her blouse with pond water and a lifetime's worth of tears.

29

Summer is almost over and still Mama lies half in this world, half out. I'm the only one who rides along with Daddy to visit her anymore. Not even Hope. Now that she been accepted to become a missionary in Africa next spring, she has taken to praying for herself more than she does others. Chastity spends most days showing off her tan down at the beach. What she misses in attention from Mama she gets from the boys — most who would never guess she's barely thirteen. Joy started taking summer classes in order to graduate a year early. So it's just Daddy and me who will visit Mama today, each of us with our own private reasons for wanting her to get better.

"Hurry up, Grace," he says as I tie my shoes.

A knock on the door startles us. We both turn to see Sheriff Conner standing on the other side of the screen door.

"Reverend Carter?"

Daddy opens the door, but the sheriff stays put on the stoop.

"What can I do for you, Sheriff?"

"I was wondering if I could have a word with Grace."

"We're about to leave for the hospital. Can it wait until later?"

I take a few steps backward, trying to make myself invisible behind Daddy.

"It's about the Anderson girl."

"The blind girl? I thought the family left town."

"The grandmother did. But the girl . . . she's still missing." He takes off his hat and wipes his head before putting it back on. "It will only take a moment, Reverend."

"I'm sorry to hear that, Sheriff. We'll add them to our prayer list." Daddy narrows his eyes at me, then turns back toward the door. "Does this have anything to do with that Lyle Miller?"

"I can't say, sir."

Daddy frowns. "Grace is a juvenile. Anything you need to ask her you can ask in front of me."

I feel the blood go out of my face despite my heart pounding a mile a minute. If he tells Daddy about my vision with the quilt, Daddy will be furious. I step out from behind Daddy and plead with my eyes for him to keep our secret.

"Hello, Grace." He turns back to Daddy. "I understand, Reverend. I'll come back when you have more time."

He tips his hat and walks down the front steps. I let out my breath in relief.

As Daddy and I walk toward the VW bus I notice the sheriff accidentally drop his handkerchief.

"You dropped something," I say.

He turns and watches as I stoop to pick up the white cloth. It's not a hankie, it's a sock. A girl's anklet with lace trim. As soon as I touch it my body goes stiff and cold. Sheriff Conner nods ever so slightly at me. I ball the sock up in my fist, trembling, then drop it back on the ground. I know where the blind girl is.

Sheriff Conner bends over to retrieve the sock.

"Cherry Lake," I whisper before running to the bus on wobbly legs that feel like rubber.

"Anything you need to tell me, young lady?" Daddy asks when we pull out on the highway.

"No, sir."

Neither of us say a word the whole rest of the way to the hospital. I don't want to think about that poor defenseless blind girl. I try to shake the thoughts from my mind. I understand why Mama blocked the Knowing. I don't want to know what happened to her or how she ended up in the lake. I just want to sit with Mama on her swing in her special place and forget about everything else. Being with Mama calms me. I wish I could stay there with her forever.

When we get to Mama's room, Daddy stands with me by her bed for a while, part of the time praying silently and part of the time just staring at her. I get tired of standing and sit in the padded chair next to Daddy. Eventually he leaves me alone with her so he can call on other patients.

"No funny stuff," he says. "I mean it."

I nod and wait for him to leave.

Something is different today. I'm not sure if it's the light or the place, but as soon as I cross over I know something is definitely out of the ordinary. We're not alone, Mama and me.

"Mama?"

"Grace. It's you."

Her voice is like candy.

"Yes, Mama. Where are you?"

"We're over here. In the grass."

We? I turn my head to follow her voice and there she is. There *they* are. She smiles, the sweetest, fullest smile to ever fill her face.

"Who's that with you, Mama?"

His back is to me, blond hair so light it looks like a halo around his head. An angel? I feel myself moving, not walking, more like a movie camera zooming toward the center of this place, the center of my mind and Mama's world.

"Welcome, Grace. We've been waiting for you."

As soon as he speaks I feel every cell in my body unfold.

"Isaac?"

He turns his head to face me. Tears tickle at the back of my eyes, then flood my face. He's beautiful. Blond, like Mama and my sisters, but the same height as me.

"Isaac!"

It's been nearly fifteen years since I've touched my brother, since we were curled up against each other in Mama's belly. I fall into his arms, filled with the memory of the most familiar thing I've ever known.

"Isaac! Isaac, it's really you."

He holds me tighter. "It's me," he says.

Panic surges through me like a quickened pulse. "Wait? Why are you here? You're not taking her . . ."

"I was just talking with Mama."

I glance at our mother. She's beaming.

"But why? How? Does this mean she's going away?"

"No, Grace," he says, holding my hand. Mama takes my other hand so we're standing in a circle. "I'm not dead and I'm not dying," he says.

"Then why . . . ?"

"She called for me. The same way you do sometimes. I've just shared with her how much she's needed. How much *you* need her."

I look into my brother's clear blue eyes, wanting more than everything to believe him. He tilts his head and smiles, the sun highlighting the heart-shaped birthmark on his neck.

"Mama? Are you going to wake up? Are you going to come back to us?"

Before she can answer, a loud voice bellows behind me. I feel my hands slipping out of Isaac's and Mama's grasp. The three of us look around for the source of the intrusion. I feel myself being pulled backward through a dark tunnel. I can barely see Mama and Isaac, who now look like tiny lights at the end of a hollow tube.

"Mama! Isaac!" My voice echoes in the tunnel.

A searing pain in my shoulder brings me

back to the hospital room. Daddy has jerked me up out of Mama's bedside chair, his eyes wild with anger.

"We're going! Now!" he yells, spit flying from his mouth.

"But, Daddy! I have to talk to her! I have to tell her to come home!"

He yanks again on my arm and I yelp. I look back at Mama as he drags me out of the room, pleading with my thoughts, but her expression is flat.

We drive home with me holding my arm, sobbing, and Daddy mumbling under his breath. It's the longest half hour of my life. Finally, we pull into the driveway. I grab the door handle, but he reaches across me and locks the door.

"What?" I glare at him. As much as I love my daddy, he has really hurt me. Not just my arm, but the fact that he yanked me out of Mama's and Isaac's reach before we were finished. He's ruined everything.

"I want to talk to you." He says it firmly, in his preacher voice.

I don't say anything.

"We're going to hold a special prayer meeting next Wednesday."

I turn to face him. "It's my turn to watch Marilyn on Wednesday."

"You're coming to the meeting. In fact,

the meeting will be especially for you."

"For me? Why?"

His thin lips tighten into a straight line. "Because I said so, that's why. We're going to pray for you."

"But I don't need praying for, Daddy. Mama does."

"Right now you need the Lord even more than your mama. There's something dangerously peculiar going on with you and I believe it may be the work of the devil."

"I am not peculiar!" I blurt, surprising even myself.

"Scotty Conner came home from Vietnam this week. He's telling people you told his parents stories about him that only he could have known. How'd you know those things about their son? You tell me that right now."

"You won't believe me. You've never believed me." I grip my right shoulder with my left hand and massage it.

"I can't promise I'll believe you, but I will listen. I can promise you that."

I want to tell him. I want with all my heart to tell him about the Knowing and where it comes from. I know I'll just be setting myself up for another disappointment, but I'm so tired of it. I'm so tired of always having to defend myself.

"Okay. I'll tell you. But you can't interrupt and you can't get mad."

"Go ahead then. I'm all ears." Daddy turns and leans against the car door. He drapes one arm over the back of his seat and rests the other on the dashboard. The steering wheel makes a dent in his belly.

"Whenever you're ready," he says.

I let out a big breath.

"Ever since I was born I have known things. Like how people feel or what they want, where they've been and where they're going. Sometimes what they've done and what they're gonna do. Well, sort of. More like what they plan to do, because sometimes it changes."

Daddy's breathing speeds up a little, his belly rising and falling. He's looking at me with a bunch of words on the end of his tongue bursting to get out. I keep talking before he breaks his promise to listen.

"People are afraid of me when they find out I have this gift. I call it the Knowing. Isaac . . ."

Daddy grunts, giving himself away. I close my mouth and glare at him. When he settles down I go on.

"Isaac told me that everyone is born with this ability. It's like we all have these little cords strung from our hearts straight to God, but most people are frightened of the

413

gift, so they unplug. They don't want to know any more than they have to. Especially hard things, like when Mama knew Hope was going to get hit by the ice-cream truck."

Daddy flinches, but he stays quiet.

"For some reason I didn't close off the connection. In fact, it's gotten stronger over the years. I used to have to be in my closet to speak with Isaac, but now I can visit him in my mind anywhere, anytime. And when I visit Mama I can see her in the place where she is, where she lives inside her sleep."

Daddy leans forward, impatient.

"Go ahead," I say to him. "Ask what you want."

"So what you mean is that you can read people's minds."

"Sometimes. Some people's minds are always open and easy to read. Other people have to invite me. And some have minds that are sewed up really tight. I doubt I could read them even if they asked."

"Are you saying you actually communicate with your mama when you visit her in the hospital?"

"Yes, Daddy. That's what I've been trying to tell you! I've wanted to convince her that we need her. That she needs to wake up. And today Isaac was there."

"There? Where?"

414

He's broken the interruption rule, but I don't care. At least he isn't getting mad.

"The place she's created for herself. It's beautiful, Daddy. She sits on a porch swing in front of a white house with lilac bushes and there are butterflies all over and —"

"You can see her? You're saying you can see your mama in, in some other world? That she's okay, that she's not brain damaged?"

"Yes, I can see her. She's fine, Daddy. She's happy. And today Isaac came and she was, well, glowing."

Tears well up in his eyes. I've never seen Daddy cry, ever, not even when we got the news that his own mama had died back in Mississippi. He reaches toward me and I fall into his big chest and sob for Daddy and Mama and our whole family. He strokes my hair.

"I'm so sorry, Grace. Whatever it is that's happened to you, we'll fix it, I promise you. I know you miss your mama and I know I've been too busy to be there for you girls, but —"

I catch my breath and pull my head away from his chest. "You don't believe me, do you? It's the truth, I swear it. I'd have to be crazy to make all this up!"

"I don't think you're crazy, Grace. I just

415

think you need some help, that's all. I'm going to get you some help. I'm going to pray about it. I'm going to do my duty as your father and as God's disciple to make you well again."

I unlock the car door. Daddy tries to grab me, but I wrestle away. I run toward the beach, wishing like everything there was a way to step out of this hurtful world and into Mama's perfect one.

When I get to the lake I see the patrol car first, then the boat. Sheriff Conner stands on the far bank as two divers rise to the surface, shake their heads, then drop down again. The sheriff waves when he sees me sitting on the bench. I don't wave back. I want to disappear inside myself. Every time I tell the truth I end up getting in trouble. Why should I help him? Or anyone for that matter?

The divers surface again. Sheriff Conner scans the lake while the divers climb back into their boat. He rubs the back of his head, then looks at me. I turn away. I'm tired of people only liking me when they need my help. And I'm tired of being the oddball. I stare at the canoes lined up on the shore and try to shut off my brain. The harder I try, the louder I hear Isaac's words.

Truth frightens people. You're one of the

brave ones.

I look back toward Sheriff Conner and point toward the left, where Cherry Creek joins the lake. He nods and motions for the divers to change direction. I turn and walk toward home.

30

Chastity flips through the S&H Green Stamps catalog and stops on a page with hair brushes and mirrors. "We almost have enough to get a set of hot rollers!"

I close the refrigerator door and snatch the catalog away from her. "You know Mama's saving up for the silverware set with stars on the handles. We only need to fill eight more books."

"Mama's not coming home, and she certainly doesn't care about some dumb old silverware anymore."

"She is coming home!" I sit on the catalog so she can't get it back. "Why do you have to be so selfish?"

Chastity licks a stamp and sticks it to her forehead. "Hey look, Grace, maybe you can cover me in Green Stamps and trade me for another sister."

When I don't answer her, she pushes away from the kitchen table and flops in front of the fan in the living room. I stash the Green Stamps books on top of the refrigerator. It's way too hot to cook dinner so we have cold macaroni salad and some watermelon, but nobody eats at the same time. Everyone just comes and goes when they please now except for on Sundays when we have dinner together at the table after church. I hope the heat breaks before tomorrow. I can't imagine turning the oven on if it's still this hot.

It's not just the heat. I can't remember it ever being this humid before without actually raining. No matter how slowly I move, my skin breaks out in a sweat with each step. I wander out to the backyard and sit in Mama's old lawn chair waiting for an evening breeze to cool me down. In the field next to the house the fireflies are playing tag, like kids in a game of Marco Polo at the lake. Blink, here I am, blink, here I am, blink, now I'm over here. When I was seven I caught a whole bunch of them and put them in a jar by my bed. It was kind of like a living nightlight. In the morning they were all dead at the bottom of the jar, even though I'd put grass in there and punched holes in the lid. I felt terrible. There are some lights that you shouldn't try to hold on to.

The sky tonight is like a mirror of blue waves glowing above the fireflies. After a while the bugs get tired and their lights fade out, except for the occasional flicker. But the sky, it just keeps glowing prettier. I've never seen anything like it.

The screen door slams at the back of the house. "Grace, is that you?" Daddy asks.

I was worried about what Daddy might have planned for me, but he seems to have forgotten about the whole prayer meeting thing. We haven't spoken of it since the hospital visit last Saturday. I know he won't invite me to go with him to visit Mama anymore. I'm not about to ask. I plan to hitch a ride myself from now on. Lola hitchhikes all the time and she does just fine.

"Over here," I say.

"What are you doing out here in the dark?"

"It's not dark, Daddy. First there were fireflies and now the sky is glowing."

He tilts his head back. The sky is bright enough that I can see his face lit up in the pinkish blue light. His look changes from curious to worried, brows up, brows down. All of a sudden he runs back to the house and yells into the screen.

"Everybody get out here! Right now!"

I jump up from my chair and stand next

to him. He's shaking.

"It's beautiful, isn't it?"

Chastity and Joy wander out of the house, each holding a bottle of ginger ale. Hope is right behind them, all three in their cotton nightgowns with Marilyn resting on Joy's hip.

"What is it, Daddy?" Chastity asks.

"Look up! All of you!" he says. His face looks a little crazed, eyes darting this way and that, like he's just remembered something really important. We all stare in amazement at the marvelous show the sky is putting on.

Marilyn wriggles out of Joy's arms and toddles over to me. I scoop her up and point to the sky. "Look, Marilyn," I say.

She tilts her head back against my cheek.

"Prit-tee," she sings.

Joy starts to climb the trellis on the side of the house.

"Joy, get back here!"

She ignores Daddy and pulls herself onto the roof. Daddy walks backward until he can see her. She's stretched out across the shingles with her hands behind her head.

"This is not a game." Daddy's voice cracks. "The heavens are opening!"

Now I'm getting nervous. All these years hearing talk about the second coming, is this it? I never thought the end would be this beautiful.

"It's not the rapture. It's the aurora borealis," Joy says, sitting up. "The northern lights."

I can tell by the way Daddy massages his forehead that he's thinking hard. He looks around at all of us and back up at the sky. He turns and walks quietly into the house. The rest of us stay in the yard watching the light play across the stars. Nobody says a word about Daddy's freak-out. Pride may be a sin, but we owe him the generosity of a dignified exit.

One by one my sisters head back inside. I stay put. The lights are so beautiful, all pink and green and purple, like a wall of colored glaciers hanging from the night sky. I don't want to miss a minute of it.

"Mighty pretty," says a voice from behind me.

I turn around slowly, not believing my own ears. "Lyle! Oh my gosh, it's you!" I leap out of my chair and wrap my arms around him, squealing. "They let you out!"

"Shhhh," he says. "Can't let nobody hear you, girl."

He pats my back, waiting for me to quiet down. I take his hand and lead him behind the barn. We sit with our backs against it, watching the sky. I lean on his shoulder. He smells cleaner, but his familiar scent lingers beneath the soap.

"You saved my life, little lady. I'd have died in that cage, you know." He says it softly, into the night air.

"I just told the truth. They had no business blaming you in the first place. People are so dumb. They think because you don't have a house you don't have a heart? It isn't fair."

"Life isn't fair, is it, Grace?"

I sigh. "At least the truth came out on your side."

"They got their man. The girl spilled her guts about what he did to her. And the other girl — the blind one they found in the lake — he confessed to that as well. Made me sick to hear it. Sheriff Conner let me watch through the two-way window. I think he felt badly for arresting the wrong person. He's a good man, that one. Made a mistake is all."

Lyle picks up a rotting walnut, rolls it around in his fingers, and tosses it in the air. It catches the colored light on its way down.

"I'm leaving town, Grace."

"No! You can't go. You just got back. Especially now that they've let you out and your name has been cleared."

"Legally, yes. But there are those who will always believe the first version of that girl's story. I've got to move on."

I open my mouth to protest but decide against any more pleading. I'm beginning to learn that people know what's best for them.

"Wait here," I say. "I'll be right back."

I run into the barn and retrieve the green quilt I asked Aunt Pearl to make for Lyle. I'd hidden it in the loft right after she sent it to me.

"Here," I say. "This is for you."

He unfolds the quilt and clicks his tongue approvingly. "It's a beauty, Grace. You shouldn't have."

"Aunt Pearl made it. It's a way for you to always keep me with you."

He runs his ragged hands over the quilt, smoothing out the lines, then hugs it to his chest. "Thank you, Grace. It's the best gift I've ever received, next to gettin' out of that stinkin' cell."

I hand him the locket. "I found this in the loft."

He kisses it. "I thought I'd lost it down by the creek."

"I had a terrible vision. A woman. A cabin near a lake and . . ."

"My wife," he says. "Annie."

424

"I know. I'm so sorry."

He takes my hand and squeezes it. "Shh-hhh. Doesn't matter now."

31

Prayer meeting is held at 6:00 on Wednesdays. The youth groups gather in the church
basement while the adults do their thing
upstairs in the auditorium. Chastity got
lucky. Daddy let her stay home with Marilyn, who has a sore throat. Normally Joy
would watch Marilyn, but she's driving the
church bus tonight. I no more want to be
here than in a math class, but it's not like I
have a choice. Nobody has ever given us
kids an option whether or not we want to
go to church and nobody ever will. It's
understood that if something is happening
at The Church of the Word all of us will be
there.

We're singing "I Have Decided to Follow
Jesus" when Esther Swanson peeks her head
in the youth-room door. She calls to me
from the doorway with the crook of her
shaky finger. Esther has something called
palsy. Her right hand shakes a bit and she

occasionally spills th
on communion Sund
me help in the nurser
me out of the service,
me. I sing in my head, *I*
low Esther, as I follow her
Esther's usually nice to
she seems a bit crabby. W
front of the nursery, she mot me to
follow her into the main auditorium. As she
reaches for the doorknob, her hand is shaking a mile a minute. The second the doors
open I immediately know something's off.
I've never seen our congregation quite like
this before. The pews are empty. The whole
lot of them have gathered up front with
Daddy, as though everyone joined the choir
and left no one to listen. Daddy's standing
two stair-steps up from the rest of the
people with his Bible open in his left hand.
He waves for me to come forward. I feel a
twinge in my stomach.

"Come here, Grace." He says it in his
preacher voice, not his Daddy voice.

I walk slowly up the aisle. A hot wind from
the window fan blows my hair back from
my face. I feel as if I'm in one of those
dreams where I forgot to put clothes on and
everyone is staring at me. When I reach the
front of the room the crowd parts and then

. Something in Daddy's ⸻aces, makes me want to run, ⸻. I'm blocked in. I turn in circles ⸻g for a break in the ring of bodies. ⸻sing my impulse to bolt, they close in tighter. I'm terrified.

"Isaac . . ." I call to him in my head, but it comes out my mouth.

Esther inhales sharply, startling Daddy and he drops his Bible. Everyone gasps because it's a sacrilege to let the Word of God touch the floor, even worse than the American flag. When Daddy leans over to pick up his Bible, ink pens and tracts fall out of his shirt pocket, making even more of a mess. Several of the ladies stoop down to help him, like a flock of teacher's pets clamoring for an A+. His face reddens from embarrassment or anger, I'm not sure which. Probably both.

Daddy narrows his eyes at me. "Who were you just talking to, Grace?"

"Nobody," I say. "I wasn't talking to anyone."

He looks down around the circled congregation. "My dear sisters and brothers in Christ, Grace claims to speak with her mother, who is in a coma; she predicts the future, she knows the past, and she communicates with the dead. This Child of

God, my beloved daughter, is constrained by the arms of Satan. I ask you to join me tonight in demanding that Beelzebub leave this girl and that the Lord God Almighty fill her with the spirit of His everlasting love."

"Amen! Praise Jesus! Hallelujah!" They all chime in with the right words, but I can tell by the pauses that they're just as nervous as I am.

"Daddy," I plead quietly. "I *am* filled with the love of God. I always have been."

Daddy nods to Mr. Franks and Mr. Tuttle, who quickly grab hold of my arms and legs. I panic and kick at Mr. Tuttle, but he just grips harder. They stretch me like a hammock between two trees and lower me to the floor. With the deacons' hands still clutching my wrists and ankles, I search the murmuring heads hovering over me for a single sign of comfort. My eyes dart from face to familiar face, but they all look as afraid of themselves as I am of them.

I can't keep my head up. When I let it drop, it clunks onto the threadbare red carpet where Daddy sometimes paces when he preaches. Daddy moves down the stairs toward me, holding his Bible above his head. He places his right shoe firmly on my belly. He clears his throat and gathers up his voice.

"Release this child from the greedy grasp of Satan!" he shouts.

"Amen!" they answer.

It's as if he's turned into a tent-revival preacher overnight. Something has taken over his eyes. They look past me, past everyone, and I start to wonder if maybe the devil has got *him.* I half expect him to start speaking in tongues.

"Anoint this child with the blessed Blood of the Lamb!"

I close my eyes. This can't be happening. *Isaac!* I shout his name, this time in my head. But my brother is silent. I haven't spoken with him since the day we visited with Mama. Maybe when Daddy wrenched me away from them he scared Isaac away for good. Is he still there with Mama in her special place? Are they waiting for me to come back? My head hurts. My heart feels like it will explode at the thought of losing both Mama and Isaac. Tears burn my face. Everything feels hot. A fire blazes in front of my eyes. It's so real I start to believe maybe I've gone to hell. Maybe Daddy's right, I *am* evil. Maybe it's the devil come to take me home.

I can't breathe. Flames lick at my toes. Chastity is screaming.

Chastity?

The heat and smoke blast my face until I choke. I open my eyes. "Fire!" I yell.

"Yes!" Daddy answers. "God has put the fire of the Holy Spirit upon you!"

"Amen, Brother!" they all chime.

"No!" I say, trying to sit up.

Daddy presses harder with his shoe. Someone hands him a white bucket.

"In the name of our Lord and Savior Jesus Christ, I cleanse you of the devil's filth!" He dumps the entire bucket filled with cold water over me.

"Daddy, stop!"

His face is a million miles away, caught up in the drama of the moment. It takes every ounce of my strength to roll out from under his shoe. I jump to my feet, wheeling around to face him. The crowd backs up as my soggy hair whips across their surprised faces.

All except Daddy. He reaches toward my head. "Release this child from the evil grip of —"

"Be quiet, Daddy!" I scream.

The room falls silent, leaving only my words echoing off the organ pipes. Even Daddy is stunned into silence.

"Our house is on fire!"

Water pours off me into a puddle on the

carpet. Esther's palsy has grown from a trembling hand to a full-on flapping. I feel sorry for her. I feel sorry for all of them. I shove Burt out of my way. The rest of them part like the Red Sea as I charge toward the heavy doors at the back of the church.

Smoke plumes billow above our house. I race across the street, reaching the yard just as Chastity crawls out the front door, coughing. "Where's Marilyn?" Chastity goes into a hacking fit and I can't understand a word. She points to the upstairs window of Marilyn's bedroom, then drops to her knees and dry heaves in the grass. Behind me the entire congregation stampedes up the long driveway with Daddy leading the herd. Panting, he bends over Chastity. He steadies her shoulders with his hands.

"What happened?"

When she tries to speak the coughing starts up again.

I point to the house. "Daddy, Marilyn's still in there!"

His face goes all pale and dead-like. He runs to the front door, but the flames throw him back. I close my eyes and concentrate. I feel Daddy and the rest of them staring at me, but I don't care anymore. In my mind I see Marilyn. She's not in her bedroom. She's tried to make it out of the house. The thick smoke has tangled her way.

I dash to the backyard. My hair and clothes are still soaking wet. I pray that it's enough to keep me from being burned up as I carefully walk through the back door and into the thick wall of smoke. I use my memory instead of my sight to guide myself to the kitchen. I find Marilyn with my left foot, just inside the doorway. She's unconscious. I feel around for her arms and legs, but she's wrapped in a quilt. When I try to scoop up the bundle I realize something or someone is wrapped around her. I pull harder until she's free. As I crawl backward, I nearly trip over another pair of legs. I find his face with my hands and instantly recognize the scruffy chin.

"Lyle!"

He doesn't move.

"Get up, Lyle!"

A rush of scorching heat sears against my face and hands. Marilyn jerks in my arms. "I'm coming right back for you, Lyle! I'll be right back!"

I lift Marilyn and turn for the back door. Outside I hear Joy screaming. The smoke is like pepper in my lungs and throat. I trip and fall. I can hardly breathe and I'm all turned around. Then another smell reaches my nostrils, a faint trail of White Shoulders

433

perfume. Hugging Marilyn tightly, I scramble to my feet and follow Mama's scent to the back door.

I cough my way to the outside with Marilyn hanging like a rag doll in my arms. The yard is filled with children and adults from the church. Sirens yowl in the distance, coming closer. The crowd is a blur, voices around me like noisy katydids scratching at the edges of my eardrums. The fierce heat of the fire pushes at my back and I keep walking until I reach our big tree. Daddy and Joy race up to where I stand holding my little sister like a burnt offering. *Here,* I think. *Here's your sacrificial lamb.*

Daddy weeps as he gathers Marilyn out of my arms. The charred green quilt falls to the ground. "No, no, no," he says, holding her cheek to his.

A fireman gently straps an oxygen mask over her little face. Joy and Chastity run up and throw their arms around Daddy, crying. I turn back toward the house, but Sheriff Conner grabs my arm, holding me back.

"Lyle's in there! I've got to go help him."

"You can't, Grace. Let the firemen do their job."

"But I promised!" I scream, trying to pull away from him.

He holds on tight, motioning to a couple of firemen with a hand signal.

"He's just inside the kitchen door! Please save him! Hurry!"

Two yellow suits disappear up the back steps and into the back porch but instantly reappear, rearing backward from the heat. They look toward the fire chief and shake their heads.

"No!" I scream. "I promised!"

Sheriff Conner grabs me and holds me to his chest. "It's too late, honey," he says. "I'm sorry."

The crowd hovers around us, speaking in hushed voices. I hear my name slide off their tongues. *Saved her. A miracle. An angel of the Lord.* I bury my face in Sheriff Conner's shirt. *Did you hear them, Daddy? An angel of the Lord* . . .

"Grace?" It's Daddy's voice. "Grace, I know you're angry with me."

I peel myself from Sheriff Conner's shirt to look at Daddy. He holds his gaze on me for what feels like a millennium.

"Did you start that fire? With your . . . with your mind?"

"Daddy, no! I didn't start it, I just saw it. How can you even think that?"

I look at Joy, blue eyes wide in disbelief. I turn my gaze toward Chastity, who moves

435

closer to Daddy.

She tugs at his sleeve, her face blackened with soot and guilt. "Daddy, I . . ." Chastity starts to speak, then coughs.

I give her a look, shake my head only the slightest bit to let her know not to say it. I know it was her curling iron. It doesn't matter that she left it on. It doesn't matter how this happened. As far as Daddy's concerned the fire started the day I was born alive and Isaac dead, the day I robbed him of a son and the happy wife he'd married.

Joy jogs over to where two attendants are loading Marilyn into an ambulance. "I'm going with her," she says, not asking, just stating what is a fact. She grabs on to the ambulance attendant's shoulder and climbs inside. He slams the doors shut and they pull away with the sirens wailing. Daddy follows behind in our bus. Groups of people file into the yard and watch as the firemen slake the thirsty blaze with fire hoses. One of our neighbors takes Chastity by the hand and leads her back toward the church. Nobody sees me slip away from the crowd like a leaping-off flame, leaving them to whisper in hushed voices.

When I reach the end of the street I turn and watch the black cloud billow upward. I stand for a long time holding myself, shivering, thinking about my wonderful friend Lyle and what he did to save Marilyn. I turn and start walking toward Highway 31. As the fire crackles behind me I feel every hope that Daddy would finally understand me go up in smoke along with our crumbling home. Tomorrow, stories will pass through telephone wires and grocery lines until the truth has faded into an exaggerated remnant of what really happened.

When I reach the highway I stick out my thumb. I feel like I have nothing left to lose. The first car to come along, a rusted Chevy van, pulls over and waits for me. I run up to it and open the passenger door. Sitting in the driver's seat is the bearded guy with long, wavy hair and sandals who appeared at the railroad tracks the day I found the quilt.

"Where you going, sis?" he asks.

"Anywhere," I say.

He says that's where he's headed, too, so I hop in.

I'm a mess, but he doesn't mention anything about the ashes on my face or my dirty clothes. In fact, he doesn't say anything at all except to tell me his name is Robin. Maybe because of the silence or maybe because he likes it, he turns the radio on. After a bit he leaves the highway and drives slowly along the back county roads. I stay quiet until Bill Withers starts singing "Lean on Me" and I burst into tears. Robin downshifts to pick his way over washboard ridges in the road. We pass a cornfield with stalks half again as high as me. He pulls over and shuts off the engine.

"You wanna talk about it?"

Something about the tenderness in his voice opens an inner window I've kept closed for most of my life. I tell him about Mama and Isaac and Lyle. I tell him about the Knowing. I talk and talk and talk until I'm exhausted and my words give way to tears again.

"It's not your job to make your father understand you," Robin finally says. "That's something he has to figure out for himself. All you have to do is be exactly who you are and eventually he'll realize that when he looks into your eyes he's looking into the eyes of God. Anybody can see that."

"Not my daddy."

"Stop trying so hard to please him. Let him see with his own eyes what it means to have someone as beautiful as you for a daughter."

"I'm not beautiful."

He lifts a curtain of smoky hair from in front of my face. "Yes, you are. Inside and out. I've only known you for a few hours and that much I can say for sure."

I feel myself blush but hopefully the ashes on my face cover for me.

He starts the engine. "Where to?"

"Can you take me to The Church of the Word in Cherry Hill?"

I guide Robin back toward our neighborhood. He pulls into the church lot across the street from what's left of our home.

"Take your time, Grace," he says. "I'll wait right here."

I climb out of his van and walk as discreetly as possible toward the church, away from what's left of our house. I've lost track of time. The sun has just set so it must be going on ten. A couple of firemen continue spraying everything down even though the flames are out. Most of the gawkers have left, but Sheriff Conner's police car is still parked in the driveway. He stands in the front yard writing on a pad of paper. He looks up when he sees me pass under the streetlight. I wait for him to call me over, but he just nods his head slightly and watches as I walk back into the church.

I head to the restroom and splash water over my face, my neck, and my hands. A trail of blackened water swirls around the rust-stained basin before running down the drain. When I reach the front door I turn back toward the auditorium. I take a deep breath before pushing through the big doors into the empty sanctuary. The soft lights along the walls are still on. Slowly and deliberately I walk up the aisle like a bride whose groom has left her at the altar. When I reach the pulpit steps I freeze. Small puddles still dot the carpet next to the overturned bucket. My head fills with voices — men, women, Daddy — all speaking at once. I cover my ears and kneel on the bottom step, but the voices continue. Jesus looks down at me from the picture behind the dais, his hands outstretched.

I stand and climb the three steps until I reach Daddy's place on the platform. Turning to face the empty pews, I rest my hands on the podium. I see what he sees, feel the power and the blessing all at once. I feel the ache of each person waiting for truth and hope. I feel him, his heart, so full of desire to save each one of them. And I hear his words, the ones he starts every single service with. I open my mouth and they tumble out.

"This is the day the Lord hath made. Let us be glad and rejoice in it!"

My words echo off the organ pipes, the walls, the stained-glass windows. I race down the aisle and out the door to where

Robin is waiting. He's holding a charred book of S&H Green Stamps in his hand.

"I found it on the sidewalk." He blows on the front cover, sending ashes onto the dashboard.

I flip through the tattered pages, smiling through tears.

"Are you okay?" he asks.

"I am," I say, tossing the book in the back of the van. "For the first time in a long time, I'm okay."

We pull up in front of the hospital and Robin sets the brake. He reaches behind the seat and hands me the shoes I left at the railroad tracks that day. I kick off my dirty patent leathers and put them on. They're tight, but I can still squeeze into them.

"You take care of yourself, sis," he says.

I grab the door handle. "Thanks for everything."

He smiles. "I should be the one thanking you." He tilts my chin with his hand and kisses me lightly on the forehead.

I climb out and look at him through the open window. "Will I see you again?"

"I hope so," he says. "I really hope so."

The hospital is quieter than during the daytime. I slip past an empty nurse's station

441

and almost make it, but an aide stops me.

"Whoa, visiting hours are over," he says.

Before I can open my mouth a female voice comes over the wall speakers. "Code Blue, ICU! Code Blue, ICU!"

The voice is familiar, but I can't quite place it. The aide wags his finger at me, then spins on his heels toward the elevator. As soon as he's out of sight I take the stairway to Mama's floor and tiptoe into her room. The bed closest to the door is empty, neatly made up with clean linens. I touch the cold edge of the footboard where Bony Nurse once lay and a shiver runs through me. I know whose voice that was on the loud-speaker. I stroke the folded blanket at the foot of the bed. "Thank you," I whisper.

I move to the other side of the room, where Mama's face glows in the moonlight, her pillow a blue-white cloud beneath her blond hair. I slide the chair closer and take her hand. Instantly I'm there, wherever there is, standing next to a lake.

"Hello, Grace," she says.

"Mama!" I wrap my arms around her and cry into her chest.

"Shhhh, there now," she whispers.

"Mama, one of my best friends in the whole world died and it's my fault!"

"Oh, honey, don't believe that."

"But it is my fault! I was mean to Lyle."

"The man you were feeding in the loft."

I pull away from her chest. "You knew about Lyle?"

"Yes, I knew. I used to leave him food, too."

"You weren't afraid of him like other people?"

"He was a good man, a piano teacher. He used to drive an ice-cream truck in the place we lived before we moved to Cherry Hill until . . ."

"Wait. Lyle is the person who ran over Hope?"

"It was an accident, Grace. She ran behind the truck when it was backing up. No way for him to have seen her there."

"He was so nice to me. People accused him of being creepy, but he listened to me and he didn't judge. And now he's gone!"

Mama shifts her gaze toward the lake and I follow it to the silhouette of a man gently rowing away from shore. His paddle plays in the water, light reflecting off the droplets with each rhythmic stroke. I look up at Mama's face.

"Is that . . . ?"

She nods, smiling. "Look toward the other side."

I strain my eyes until the small form of a

woman comes into view. She's standing on the end of a dock, her arms waving.

"But how can that be if they're dead and you're not? How can we all be in the same place?"

"I don't know, Grace. There's a lot I don't understand. But does it really matter?"

I sigh. "I wish I lived here."

Mama wraps her arm around me as the sun sets on the far side of the lake. "It will take time to put our lives back together. You might not believe this, but your daddy needs you. Your sisters need you. And I need you to be there for them, Grace. You're stronger than any one of them."

"Wait, you said *our* lives."

"Young lady, you need to leave."

My eyes bolt open and I drop Mama's hand. The aide has returned with backup. A young nurse holds out her hand. "Come on, honey," she says. "You can come back during visiting hours."

I let her lead me out the door and down the hallway, turning once to catch a glimpse of Mama sleeping.

32

Today is Lyle's funeral. I asked Daddy if I could say a few words about Lyle and he said no, that it wouldn't be necessary since most people don't know him.

"But that's why I want to speak for him," I said. "So people will know that he was a good person."

Daddy won't budge. Says if I keep bugging him I'll have to stay home.

Our family has been staying at Cherry Lake Lodge. Church members and neighbors donated money to pay our rent. Bags of clothes, canned goods, and toiletries line the porch, where people drop off things they think we might need. Daddy's wearing the only suit that survived the fire, the one he keeps in his office at the church for emergencies. The waist of the pants are too small, so he has to wear them under his belly. And he can no longer button the middle button of the jacket. Considering what happened I don't think anyone is too worried about how he's dressed.

I sit with my sisters in the front pew. I want to be here, but Daddy made the rest of them come, probably to keep an eye on me. The casket is closed because of how Lyle died. They had to roll it to the front of the church on a cart since he had no pall bearers. When I look at it I start sobbing. I can't stand the thought of him gone. I do my best to erase the image of his ashes and replace it with the shadow of his figure on the lake and the happy reunion with his wife. A smile breaks out across my face when I think of them. But then I take it back real quick before somebody notices and thinks I've gone completely crazy.

When Loretta stops playing the organ music, Daddy opens with a prayer, the same one he says at all funerals. He nods at Edna Warber, who walks up and sings "In Times Like These" and for once, does a pretty good job. Daddy approaches the podium and looks out at the smattering of people dotting the pews. The church is nearly empty except for Sheriff Conner, half a dozen church members, and a few people who are mostly just curious. Daddy calls them funeral-crashers. He says some people feel more alive when they are around death

446

for some reason.

Daddy pulls a pair of reading glasses from his suit pocket and perches them on the end of his nose. He opens his Bible and begins to read the same verse he always reads at funerals.

" 'Fear not, for I have redeemed thee. I have called thee by thy name and thou art mine. When thou passest through the waters . . .' " Daddy pauses and looks at me. He seems flustered, like he's lost his place. " 'I will be with thee.' "

He stops reading and gazes toward the window. He knows these verses by heart. He's said them a thousand times. Something's wrong. Maybe everything has finally taken its toll: Mama, the crazy exorcism thing, the fire, and now Lyle. I stop feeling sorry for myself and start feeling sorry for him. *Come on,* I think, *you've got this.*

He clears his throat. " 'And when thou walkest through the fire, thou shalt not be burned; neither shall the flame kindle upon thee . . .' "

His voice cracks. He takes a drink from a glass of water hidden under the dais. He looks down at the casket and frowns. People start fidgeting nervously in their seats, wondering if Pastor Carter is about to have a nervous breakdown. My sisters exchange worried glances, eyebrows furrowed in worry. Daddy squeezes his temples in the way he does when he has a headache. Mr. Franks starts to walk toward Daddy but he waves him away.

Daddy closes his Bible without finishing the Scripture passage and blurts out, "I hated this man," pointing to the casket. "I hated him for running over my eldest daughter and then I hated him even more for something horrible I believed he did. And when I had evil thoughts I prayed to the Lord for Lyle Miller's swift punishment rather than Our Father's merciful forgiveness." Daddy drops his head and wipes his eyes with a handkerchief. "I'm the one who needs forgiving. Lyle Miller was no saint, but neither am I. He was the victim of gossip and false rumors. I strive every day to be Christ-like in my desire to spread the gospel. But the Lord pays more attention to our actions than our words."

Daddy steps down from the pulpit and grabs hold of a handle on the side of Lyle's casket. "This man died trying to carry my baby girl out of a burning house. The least I can do is carry him out of the Lord's house."

Sheriff Conner stands and moves to the other side of the casket and grabs a handle.

Then the deacons, Mr. Franks and Burt, walk up and join them. Joy tries to stop me, but I run up and grab a handle along with a handful of other men and, finally, a weeping Edna. We slide Lyle's simple casket off the rolling platform and walk quietly past my sisters. We walk past Mrs. Franks, Burt's wife, and three women I don't recognize. No music. No prayers. Just Lyle and us. Just the way I think he would have preferred.

We carry Lyle past the hearse to the tiny cemetery behind the church, where the gravediggers have already made a hole. My sisters and the rest of them catch up to us just as we set the coffin on the ground next to a pile of dirt. Daddy looks around at our faces. He starts in on "The Lord's Prayer." " 'Our Father, who art in heaven, blessed be Thy name.' "

Everyone joins in, eyes closed, reverently praying over Lyle. My eyes are open. I want to remember this. I look up at the sky, imagining Lyle floating toward heaven. I look at the dirt, the hole, the wooden box. Then I look over at the flowers lining the edge of the cemetery. With the last "amen" I dash over and pull up a handful of Queen Anne's lace. I run back and lay one on the casket.

"Goodbye, Lyle," I say.

I hold out my handful of flowers for the others. Daddy takes one and places it next to mine. One by one, everyone takes a flower and lays it over the others.

People trickle back into the church basement for refreshments. I skip the food and sit on the front steps holding the last flower. Tears flood my face. I will miss him so much.

Someone hands me a hankie. I turn to find Robin standing over me.

"What are you doing here?"

"I came to see if you needed a friend."

I nod my head. He sits next to me and reaches for my hand. My sisters spill out of the church and walk in a wide circle around us. They stand at the bottom of the steps whispering to each other. A pink Cadillac screeches to a stop in front of the church. Aunt Arlene jumps out looking more disheveled than I've ever seen her. Reddened eyes blink back a mixture of tears and mascara that streaks down both sides of her cheeks. She glances toward our burned-down house across the street, then moves toward us, her long arms outstretched. She gathers Joy and Chas and Hope close, squeezing them together like a bouquet in a too-small vase.

She motions for me to join them, but I stay put.

Daddy appears in the front door of the church holding a plate of chocolate cake. "Arlene, what are you doing here?"

She lets loose of my sisters and races up the steps to hug Daddy.

"The funeral is already over, Aunt Arlene," Chastity says.

Aunt Arlene turns toward her. "I couldn't get through on the phone so I rushed here to tell you the good news. I was sitting there next to her bed when she came to." Her blotchy face goes bright as she grabs Daddy's hands in hers. "She's awake, Henry. Isabelle is awake!"

Daddy's eyes flash. He glances toward us girls, then pulls away from Aunt Arlene and races to her car, dropping the cake on the sidewalk. The Cadillac spins out, spitting gravel as it shimmies out of the lot onto the road.

"He took my car!" Aunt Arlene stands with her arms hanging at her sides like broken wings.

My sisters start jumping up and down. "Mama's awake! Mama's awake!"

Robin squeezes my hand. "Don't you want to join them?"

I watch my sisters as they dance around

in a circle, their smiles suddenly brighter than I can ever remember.

"Nah," I say. "Let them have their moment. I'll just ruin it for them."

"Go on," he says, nudging me with his shoulder.

I stand and walk toward my sisters. The closer I get the more they tighten their circle. I move past them and walk on up the sidewalk toward the lake. Robin catches up to me about a block away.

"You want to go see her?"

I stop in my tracks.

"More than anything."

When I reach Mama's room, she's sleeping. Two doctors stand at the foot of her bed. One of them says, "I'm sorry, young lady, but Mrs. Carter can't have any visitors yet, only her husband. He's down in the cafeteria if you want to talk to him." They both turn their backs to me, as if I'll say, "No problem. It's only my mama who's been in a coma for over a year. I'll just come back later."

I walk closer. "Mama?"

One of the doctors, the tall one, reaches for me but stops when a sound comes from the bed.

"Grace . . ."

It's only a whisper, but that one breathy syllable is all I need to know that Mama is back here with us. With me.

I rush to the side of her bed. "Mama!"

Her face is pale, but there's a light in her eyes that was missing before she left us. She raises her hand slightly before it drops weakly at her side.

"Oh, Mama," I say. I touch her face, feel her hair, and finally, her soft hand. "You're back." I lift her hand to my lips and kiss it.

Mama's fingers crawl awkwardly across my cheek in the way that a baby tries to make her hand do its bidding. She fondles a lock of my hair that, even after shampooing twice, still smells like smoke. Her hand drops and her eyes flutter.

"Mama!" I say, dropping my head to her chest. "Don't go back!"

The shorter doctor puts his hand on my shoulder. "Don't worry, sweetheart," he says. "She's not going anywhere. She's just exhausted. Your mother visited with Reverend Carter for quite a while. We need to let her rest so she can get her strength back."

He tugs gently at my shoulder and I back away from the bed. Mama appears to be sleeping peacefully, each breath drawing more life into her body.

"You can come back in the morning," a

nurse says, pulling me aside. "Go find your father. Just follow the floor arrows to the cafeteria."

Fluorescent lights buzz above me as I walk the long hospital hallway. I'm suddenly so tired that my feet feel like chunks of cement. With my head down, I count the squares on the waxed floor to keep me from collapsing from sheer joy and relief. Sensible white shoes shuffle past me in both directions. A creaky cart with metal wheels rolls by. The hallway is a blur of whispering nurses, silent janitors, a bloody-gowned doctor. I don't look up at any of them. I follow the arrows until a pair of familiar black shoes comes into view. I slowly raise my head.

He's standing a few feet away from me, his shirt untucked, eyes red from fatigue or crying or both. My head spins dizzily. I freeze, not knowing what to expect.

"Grace," Daddy says, moving toward me.

When I flinch he stops.

"Your mama says it was you who convinced her to come back, all those times you sat by her bed." His chin quivers and a tear runs down his unshaven cheek. "She told me about how she was just like you until . . ."

I don't move.

"I'm sorry, Grace. I'm so, so sorry." He

454

takes another step toward me. "Honey, please . . ."

I stumble forward and fall into his big arms, sobbing.

33

Fall 1974

Mama has come back changed. She may
have told Daddy it was because of me, but I
know she wouldn't have awakened unless
she'd decided to be here by her own choice.
She's stubborn like me. Joy says Mama's
back to the way she was before Isaac died. I
still have a faint memory of how that was,
the lilting way she carried us before the
weight of the world crushed her heart.
Maybe after seeing Isaac she finally understood that a person doesn't have to be next
to you to be with you. Whatever it is, she's
come out of that sleepy other place more
awake than she ever was before.

We had to tear down what was left of our
old house and build a new one. Mr. Franks
owns the Farmers Agency in Cherry Hill so
the parsonage had good insurance. Mama
insisted on a front porch with a swing. She
says she doesn't remember anything from

the time we found her in the barn until the day she woke up from her coma. She spent some time in rehab relearning to walk after being in bed for so long. Other than that she's pretty much back to normal. Better than normal.

Mama's not the only person who's changed. Daddy's shoulders have rounded, his foot falls less heavily, and day by day I see a softening inside him where it used to be hard. He gave Joy enough to pay for college tuition from money left over in the donation collections after the house burned down. Sometimes she calls and I can tell by the way he laughs he's really proud of her. Hope moved to Africa, where she teaches Bible School in the jungle. Her letters come to us smelling like a whole different world. I was afraid Mama wouldn't let her go, seeing's how she'd missed out on nearly two years of her life already. But Mama's not as afraid of things anymore. She's not afraid of herself anymore.

And she's started singing again. We finally figured out what gift Marilyn got from Mama. One day when Grandpa was visiting, Marilyn was sitting on his lap and out of the blue she started singing "In the Garden" in the most angelic voice ever. We all stopped what we were doing and listened until the last note; then Mama scooped Marilyn up and swung her in a full circle. She kissed her on the forehead and said, "We're going to sing duets!" Marilyn grinned like a drunken jack-o'-lantern.

Robin and I are going steady. I wish I had a picture of everybody's face when he first walked into our yard. I know Daddy wanted to tell him to get his long-haired hippie self off the property, but Robin was too quick. He pulled on a nail apron, climbed up the ladder, and started pounding nails into the roofing shingles before Daddy could object. By the end of the day Daddy saw what a good worker he was so he didn't bother him. But he never took his sights off Robin the whole time.

Lola approves of my boyfriend. She calls him JC, for Jesus Christ. They get along because Robin is an artist like her and most of her family. He lives in an A-frame studio over in Little Dune that he rents from his uncle. He blows glass into all sorts of beautiful creatures, but his specialty is birds. People buy them as fast as he can make them. My favorites are the owls.

Mama and Daddy are sitting on the porch swing holding hands when I get home from school. Chastity bounds out the front door, headed for the beach.

"I'll be back by supper," she calls out behind her.

Chas has all the boys chasing her now that she's in high school. Daddy keeps a pretty close eye on her. She joined the drama club and won the role of Dorothy in this year's production of *The Wizard of Oz*. I suppose she'll move to Hollywood someday, although I think she'd do better to stay where there's not so much competition.

"You all right, honey?" Mama asks when I climb the porch stairs.

Today hasn't been an easy day. Lola broke it to me that she's moving to Berkeley, California, with her friend Stephanie at the end of the year. Stephanie has been accepted at the University of California. Stephanie is like Lola. Not an artist but in the way she prefers girls over boys. Lola says there's more opportunity for artists out west. I expect there's also a lot more room for free love, which Lola has plenty of.

"I'm all right, Mama," I say.

Mama squeezes Daddy's hand. "There's someone here to see you, Grace," he says.

I look around for Robin's van, but I don't see it. Maybe it's broken down again and he had to hitchhike.

"Is he out back?" I ask.

They both giggle like a couple of little kids. Behind them, from inside the house, a figure appears at the screen door. My heart bends in half when she pushes it open.

"There's my SweePea," she says as she waddles toward me.

My knees almost buckle.

"Well, what you waitin' for, girl? Come here and give your Aunt Pearl a hug before she dies of missin' you."

I throw my arms around her. I have to bend down because I'm a good foot taller than her now. She smells as wonderful as ever and her hug would like to melt me into a puddle of sweet cream.

"Lord have mercy, you've grown," she says, when we finally let go.

So have you, I think, but I don't say it. Aunt Pearl has gotten fatter since I last saw her. And her hair is nearly all gray.

Mama and Daddy walk quietly into the house and I swear Daddy winks at me. I swear it.

Aunt Pearl and I sit on the swing until suppertime, filling in the gaps in our lives. After supper we come back to the porch with iced tea and continue our talk well past dark. I tell her how much I've missed her. I tell her about Robin and Lola. I tell her about Lyle and how deeply it hurt to lose him.

"Sorrow is the good Lord's toll for love," she says, shaking her head. I know by the way she says it that Aunt Pearl has paid a great debt for the generosity of her big heart.

After we've tired of current and not-so-current events, she changes the subject to the Knowing. "How do you plan to use this gift God gave you?" she asks, pulling her sweater around her shoulders.

I sit silently for a minute, then get up and walk across the porch. Leaning against the white railing, I turn to face her. I know there's no wrong answer to her question, but I so want her to understand.

"I think that the Knowing uses me, not the other way around. I think I'm just supposed to stay open and let the Knowing be a way to show other people how to listen for the truth rather than hide from it."

Aunt Pearl smiles. Her approval slips out with a pleasant sigh. I look down at her slippered feet and grin. They barely reach the floor. She takes a sip of her tea and pats the empty spot next to her on the swing. I stretch out beside her with my head in her lap. There are some things you grow more into than out of.

EPILOGUE

Summer 1977

Robin and I live in a cabin we built together. Aunt Pearl lives on our land in a trailer that she bought. After my high school graduation, Robin and I took a trip to visit Aunt Pearl. We never came back. When we saw the sign HEAVEN, MISSISSIPPI, POPULATION 147 we just grinned at each other, pulled off the highway, and started looking for our own piece of paradise. We've been here a year now. Although a part of my heart remains in Cherry Hill, Michigan, Mississippi has always owned me. I love sending Mama letters from Heaven.

I'm hanging wash on the line when my water breaks. It's August, hotter than all get-out and humid, too. Robin is out in the shop firing some pieces for an art fair that's coming up. I don't call him or Aunt Pearl right away because I figure I have some time. But it turns out this baby is ready to be born. By the time I reach the house it feels like somebody is standing on my stomach, pushing everything toward my bottom.

I knew the moment I became pregnant. I felt a quickening in my heart of hearts. Not the one that beats inside my chest, but the one that feeds my soul. A few hours after Robin and I had made love in our water bed last November I awakened from a deep sleep. I sensed a reunion of body and spirit that was only a millisecond in time but infinite in its lasting effect on me.

Aunt Pearl warned me about the pains, but my labor is about as gentle as any woman could ask for, which is exactly what I did. Isaac used to say God isn't a wishing well, but when I was feeling worn-out by the seventh month I asked Him right out to go easy on me. My prayers must've been heard because it isn't an hour after I yank on the porch bell and Aunt Pearl and Robin come running that our son eases himself out into the world. Robin snips the cord like we learned from Aunt Pearl. She wraps our baby in a warm towel and hands him to me. I put him to my breast and weep as he suckles, running my fingers over the heart-shaped birthmark on his neck. When he whimpers in his sleep, I curl myself around him, tucking his familiar body against my belly, and nuzzle his delicate ear.

I'm right behind you. I'm right behind you. I'm right behind you. . . .

464

ABOUT THE AUTHOR

Eldonna Edwards is the subject of the award-winning documentary *Perfect Strangers* and author of the memoir *Lost in Transplantation,* both of which follow her choice to donate a kidney to an anonymous person in need. Her debut novel, *This I Know,* won the Lillian Dean Award for fiction based on its opening chapters. Also a veteran massage therapist and former journaling instructor, Eldonna is a born storyteller who "cut her teeth" on the back of Southern Baptist pews in her provincial Midwest hometown where her father was a preacher. The voice in this novel comes straight from the heart. Eldonna currently lives on the central California coast with her long-time partner.

The employees of Thorndike Press hope you have enjoyed this Large Print book. All our Thorndike, Wheeler, and Kennebec Large Print titles are designed for easy reading, and all our books are made to last. Other Thorndike Press Large Print books are available at your library, through selected bookstores, or directly from us.

For information about titles, please call:
(800) 223-1244

or visit our website at:
gale.com/thorndike

To share your comments, please write:
Publisher
Thorndike Press
10 Water St., Suite 310
Waterville, ME 04901